THE KAMIN'S DAUGHTER

Nithya Sashi

THE KAMIN'S DAUGHTER

1st Edition published in India by Vishwakarma Publications in March 2023

ISBN - 978-93-93757-24-1

Disclaimer

This is a work of fiction. Names, characters, places and incidents are either the product of the author's imagination or are used fictitiously and any resemblance to any actual person, living or dead, events or locales is entirely coincidental.

Published by:
Vishwakarma Publications
34A/1, Suyog Center, 7th Floor, Gultekadi Marketyard Road,
Giridhar Bhavan Chowk, Pune: 411037, Maharashtra, India.

Mob.: 9168682200
Email: info@vpindia.co.in
Website: www.vishwakarmapublications.com

Cover: **The Book Bakers**

Typeset and Layout: **Vishwakarma Publications**

Printed at: **Deepak Multi Offset, Pune**

Author's Note

THE KAMIN'S DAUGHTER came to life in my mind, several years ago when I started toying with the idea of a story about female coal mine workers. A labour of love, the book finally took shape in 2018 when I realized that it had a life of its own. I was simply a messenger with a clear mandate–to present this story to my beloved readers.

This book is dedicated to Amma and Appa.

My father worked hard to give us a beautiful life. Despite being surrounded by the blackest of coal, our lives were always lit with the joy of togetherness, knowledge and love. My parents, both very unconventional people, ingrained a deep love for books in me from childhood. I grew up admiring the classics, and it was just a matter of time before I made the transition from an avid reader to a writer. No matter what, Amma and Appa always had my back, supporting all my fancies and idiosyncrasies. Amma read each and every line I wrote with the glee of an ardent admirer and shared her comments like an unforgiving critic. When I first narrated the summary of my book to Appa, he immediately agreed to share inputs about his life as a young mining engineer. Some incidents in the book are fictional. Most incidents are a fictionalized take on real-life incidents that I witnessed.

This book would not have been possible without the support from:

First and foremost, I thank Suhail Mathur, the rockstar Literary Agent of The Book Bakers, who worked hard to get the best publisher for my book. Suhail's eye for detail and creativity helped us nail the perfect-looking book cover. Thank you Suhail and Team TBB!

I am eternally thankful to Team Viswakarma for accepting my book and loving it as much. Without you all, this book would not be possible.

A huge shoutout to Dhivya Balaji for her time, effort, and patience in helping me polish my script.

Last but not the least, I would not have completed this book without the guidance from my Guru, Sai Ram.

Prologue

MAY 8, 2000

Chirimiri Coal Mines
5:00 a.m.

REGULARITY IS A curse. It dulls your senses and makes you blind to anything untoward that comes hurtling your way.

It was supposed to be a regular day for the underground coal mine workers—as regular days can get. The workers–a small, motley group of first-timers and veterans–spent major parts of most sun-kissed days several feet under the earth, romancing the black gold, heaving up tons of coal every hour for consumption by fat capitalists and middle-class consumers alike.

As was their usual, they had had their morning meal: raw onions, green chillies and a few rotis. Now they were ready for a long, onerous day of work—digging up coal. They were lined up at the mouth of the mine, waiting for the go-ahead from their supervisor, a young over-enthusiastic chip of a man called Nirmal. Nirmal Mahato.

A typical shift lasted for several hours, where the workers dug up coal and loaded it onto multiple feeder lines that ran through the mine to the pit-head, wherein the coal got loaded onto the waiting cars. From there, the coal was either sent to a storage facility or the railway sidings for unloading onto railway wagons. A flurry of trucks transported this to waiting goods trains, which then chugged away to far off plants, where the plant owners squeezed the last ounce of energy from the coal and produced electricity. Chirimiri mines were considered top-notch due to the quality and quantity of coal produced.

It was another matter altogether that this electricity blew life only into exorbitantly- priced chandeliers in obscenely huge mansions and swanky upmarket condos, but never knocked at the workers' doors. The workers and their families usually adjusted with a kerosene lamp; or if kerosene became dearer, they used mud *diyas*. Most often, they just co-existed with darkness, both inside and outside.

Children of that generation were yet to see an electricity-lit home, though their aspiration levels were high. They studied in the small government-run school, which had no electricity either. On cloudy days, they made do with an odd lamp or two. Or better still, skipped school. Rains were always welcomed with glee. Rains meant no school. Rains also meant an occasional puff on the stealthily pocketed *beeri*, or a chance to run across slippery, green, moth-covered fields, a hurried scramble up the small hillocks, and feisty waves at the passenger trains chugging past their small, sleepy town.

The workers shuffled their feet in impatience andy waited for the lift that would descend into the earth's belly. On that particularly balmy morning, Nirmal stood with a notepad, marking entries. His head was bowed, his large eyes focused on the task ahead. He carefully marked each worker's attendance on the notepad he was holding. Satisfied, he nodded at his Manager standing beside him. They were ready for the next shift.

After slogging to complete a diploma course in Mining Engineering from Calcutta, Nirmal had started working as a supervisor in the Chirimiri Coal Mines. Over the years, he had gained a lot of respect due to his knowledge about the mines.

There were constant, fierce whispers about his elite background. Some people said he came from an affluent family. He had seen good times and money sat well on him, they said. In comparison to the unlettered *junta*, he was well-educated, wore clean clothes, and was always well-groomed; almost like a *saheb*. He even spoke impeccable English like the *Babus*. Some workers called him *Babu*–though, at times, it was intended to be delivered like an expletive. But mostly, it was obsequious.

Senior Managers often sought his opinion about the safety aspects of the mines. His acute observation skills, coupled with his in-depth knowledge, made him a formidable asset.

Earlier that week, Nirmal had accompanied a technical quality team that had been called to fix a suspected methane leak in their mine. Since it was a non-gassy mine, they had not followed the usual procedure of carrying canary birds or air lanterns to detect the presence of methane. The team's head had given a clean chit, which meant that workers could recommence the mining activity. After obtaining clearance from all the concerned teams, the manager had okayed this shift. However, from experience, a sneaky suspicion crept up Nirmal's spine that remnants of the deadly gas might still be floating around–waiting to claim any orifices left open in invitation. He had warned his superiors that they had to check it out. They had quashed it, insisting that the quality team had okayed it, and they could not stop production.

The suspicion in Nirmal's mind refused to perish. Frightening, fleeting glimpses of what could happen kept floating in his mind's eye.

Breaking his reverie, the capsule lift came up, groaning with the effort of rising several feet to the surface from the belly of the black earth. The workers piled in, and the lift inched down, groaning audibly, creaking and heaving like an old woman snapping at unruly kids.

Nirmal spoke softly to his mates, 'Be careful, do not make sudden movements when you step out. And please do not switch on your cap lights after you step out. Do it now.' It was the standard operating procedure. Nirmal was merely repeating the instructions, knowing very well that everyone knew them by heart. Veterans nodded. Akash, a new recruit, stared blankly at Nirmal.

The crazed look disturbed Nirmal, and he tried to grasp what his intuition was telling him. He tapped Akash's shoulder and raised his eyebrow, asking for affirmation. Akash shrugged and shook his head, immediately looking away while his fingers curved tighter around a small liquid-filled capsule in his trousers' pocket. The lift stopped after a few brief grunts. When they opened the gate, Nirmal looked down when he noticed Akash's sudden movement out of the corner of his eye. His eyes grew wide with horror as his mind registered the object in Akash's hand.

'No… no!' Nirmal lunged to grab the object from Akash, who stepped out of the lift swiftly. The other workers stared–some curiously, some with utter boredom dotting their brows. Akash smiled and ran his thumb over the small dial on top of the capsule's lid. Nirmal lunged again, trying to grab Akash's hand, but it was too late. The odourless gas had filled the small space, and when Akash pressed the button, the flame caught on, permeating every inch of the area and an inferno raged.

Within seconds, it had turned into a fiery bright orange ball, burning everything in its path.

Nirmal's last conscious memory was of a smirk on Akash's face.

■

The Journalist

MAY 1, 2000

Bhubaneswar | Ashiana Apartments,
Block 49, Flat 10A
6:45 a.m.

POETS HAVE SELDOM been bashful about chronicling the pristine beauty of early mornings. To anyone with a poetic temperament, even slobbered mornings would seem intensely romantic, invoking a passionate juxtaposition of words with intense emotions.

Oft, one witnesses the *jugalbandi* of these repeated elements, the interplay of the soft not-yet-warm sunlight with the cool morning breeze, the floating scents of the woods, the romanticized scent of thick foliage, and the raw, cerebral appeal of near-perfect silence, owing solely due to the slumbering realities of the human population make it a perfect time to slacken one's mental scampering. Such was the case on this particular day.

The sunlight played hide-and-seek with the early morning dewdrops that perched daintily on the leaves of the Parijata tree. A bunch of squirrels scurried about, noisily declaring their presence to the human inhabitants, at times pausing to oversee the surroundings, looking for better prospects. A Koel couple sat daintily on the lower branches of the tree and sang a song heralding the dawn in their mellifluous tones. The tree's branches just about brushed across one of the balconies of the Ashiana Apartments complex, which housed several hundred families from the nouveau rich specimens of humanity. The newly rich were generally scoffed at. Old money venerated. As if the money even bothered.

The balcony jutted out from a chocolate-coloured wall and had huge delicately carved balustrades painted a shocking white with coral-coloured globules, which gave it a look of huge chocolate balls hanging in the middle of a white sky. If one were to look up, this is what would meet their gaze.

The balcony's closed door had attracted a gentle film of moisture that gave it a frosty appearance; the curtains inside, gently billowing. From the outside, it resembled any of the hundreds of balconies at this hour. Silent. Unmoving.

It led to the minimally furnished, square-shaped master bedroom of the house. Facing east, the flat got a lot of sunlight in the morning.

In the middle of the room, slightly angled towards the balcony, stood a king-sized bed with delicately carved headstands. A bedcover in soft mauve covered the huge bed, its corners neatly tucked in, giving proof of its occupant's perfectionist nature.

A lone woman slept on the bed, a soft velvety lavender-coloured quilt partially covering her slim bare legs, half hanging from one of the sides. Her hair lay loose around her head. A small, almost-bare bedside table contained a lone table lamp with a designer watch for company. Though left bare to the level of being considered frugal, the bedroom included a lavishly painted extravaganza–a piece of modern art that had caught the owner's eye and found its way there taking up the entire wall.

As the sun sighed and started its day, a faint sliver of golden light sneaked in through the gaps between the heavy curtains and fell on the woman's face, waking her. She moaned softly, turned, hugged another pillow, and continued to sleep. The air-conditioner hummed softly, throwing cool air on her.

The shrill ring of her mobile phone woke her. Mobile phones were still a fancy item. Groaning, she stirred, fumbled until she located the source of the sound, focused blearily on the phone, and took the call.

'Koena! Please come over as quickly as you can!' A man–distraught, high strung–spoke in an urgent tone.

'Who is this?' Koena mumbled, her head fuzzy with sleep and the voice was muffled enough to be unrecognizable. She brought the phone to her eye level and checked the screen. The name registered somewhere in the depths of her brain, and irritation bubbled up like bile.

'Sagar! What do you want now? I came home just a few hours ago! Call me later… I need to sleep.' Anguish and alcohol-induced drowsiness made Koena burst out. She tried to rub the sleep out of her heavy, tired eyes, which felt as if someone had rubbed sandpaper on them. Her head was pounding–the hangover would kill her. The dimples on her cheeks deepened as she frowned.

'Please, please… Don't cut the call. I'm sorry. I know you want to rest. But this is an emergency.' Sagar supplicated. Almost pushing twenty-eight, he worshipped the ground Koena walked on.

Red lines had creased on her cheeks where the folds in the pillow casing had pressed against her ivory cream skin, making her look like a warrior. She rubbed the area absent-mindedly, and her face reddened further. A gentle flick of her head helped arrange her straight dark hair neatly. She tucked a few strands behind her ear and settled in a comfortable position on the bed, eyes still closed.

'Sagar… I'm exhausted, I just can't do it. I'll call you later.' Koena complained, and almost pressed the 'end call' button.

'No, no. Hold on. I know, I know, I'm so sorry, but you have to come to the office immediately. Okay, as soon as possible…It's very urgent–breaking news!' Sagar pleaded, his voice almost a whine now.

Taking pity on the boy–her protégé at work–Koena reluctantly agreed. 'Alright! Will start as early as possible!'

Groaning, she sat up on the bed. Her mind had registered Sagar's tone. Emergency! It always meant high priority.

Emergency? What could have happened? Wait. I don't do breaking news. Why is Sagar calling me?

She dialled Sagar back.

'What is the emergency? Are you already at work? By the way we don't do breaking news! Call Dubey! Where is Tim?' Koena hissed into the phone.

'I know. Tim asked me to come early. This is something else, Koena. Tim needs somebody… no no, he needs us… to cover something. Just come, please.'

'Fine!'

The disconnected call weighed heavily on her mind. She wanted to crawl back into her cosy bed and drift off. But she rubbed her eyes and sat for some time on the bed, trying to clear her head. A few gentle stretches usually did the trick, but today her body refused to wake up.

She called out to her cook for a cup of coffee and went to the washroom to freshen up.

The party last night had been fun. Expensive liquor and sumptuous food matched the beat of great jazz music. For the hard-working executives of the network, the monthly party at the Taj meant a lot of things–a time to chill at the network's expense, build relations, lick the boss' ass clean, and if lucky, get laid.

Most others, those at the lower rungs, looked forward to these parties for two reasons alone: the free booze and upper-class food.

Koena was not 'most people'. She was not a habitual drinker, but she could hold her booze well. But the damn alcohol had housed itself in her head this time, thumping away like an African drum.

I must go easy on the booze hereafter. Ouch, my head hurts.

A subtle knock sounded, and the cook came in with a tray carrying a mug of steaming black coffee–just the way she liked it. Sipping it, Koena wondered about the emergency call.

Eons ago, when she was a trainee, she had once attended a mandated, very uppity-looking promotional event where cocktails were being consumed as if they were going out of fashion. That was when the realization sunk in that many business deals got sealed, and the news got made in between gulps and not on the streets or offices. Over the next few years, apart from shedding the tag of a newbie, Koena also picked up the slang and the swag of a true-blue journalist. And soon after, to embed cozily into the fabric of her occupation, she taught herself to discern between wines and whiskies. The use of blue cheese vis-à-vis the various ways one could incorporate goat cheese in a professional conversation while casually throwing in a word about the expensive getaway she had planned to Amsterdam. Once the wide-eyed babe in the woods, Koena quickly became an intrinsic block of the corporate party circuit and a darling of the media masters she was indebted to serve.

Still fuzzy with all the alcohol sloshing around in her cells, she tried to make sense of the train of events. Not that it was very important right now. She just wanted to clear her head.

When had the party ended? Was it last night or this morning? Did those idiots mix something stronger in the booze? I have never had such a bad hangover.

'Ouch!' Koena massaged her head with her index fingers, wincing in pain.

The coffee was certainly helping her attain much-needed clarity. Next, she needed some food in her tummy to chase her hangover away.

That was when she noticed the cool unslept side of the bed. She frowned at the pristine bedsheet, caressing the fine fabric, her mind mulling over a million possibilities. She wondered aloud, 'Where is this man?'

Rubbing her throbbing temples, she muttered! 'Aah! How forgetful of me.'

Did he say Kolkata or Pune? I think it was Kolkata.

Pouting, Koena returned to her coffee. Shom's absence suddenly felt heavy. He had mentioned that he would be back in a day after his cookery show shoot. The absence of familiar sounds from the washroom and smells associated with her husband sent a stab of loneliness through her, making Koena cringe. She hated to be alone. The emptiness and the stillness of the house suddenly started scaring her. Should she switch on the TV for some background noise or just try to call Shom? Maybe the TV was a better idea. Or would a generic chat with her only offspring give peace to her restless mind?

Koena wondered forlornly, looking at her phone. Her 16-year old son, Kit, would also be busy with his morning routine, getting ready for school. Koena decided against disturbing him.

Eighteen long years together, and Shom still made her go weak in the knees.

Shrugging, she decided to get ready.

Let me get my ass to the office.

The bedside clock showed 7 a.m. Koena usually left for work by 9 a.m. Today, she would have to leave early.

I can always return early and catch up on my sleep. Shom would also be back by then.

Nothing like a hot shower to refresh your brain...someone had once told Koena. She agreed with the person and the sentiment, but could not, for the love of God, recollect who it was. Not that it mattered anyway.

After the shower, she took her time to choose her attire for the day. While dressing, her mind went back to Sagar's pleading voice.

He sounded quite distressed. I just hope it is something lame... not something earth-shattering as he had described. He is certainly an unrelenting cribber. But, weren't most men like him? Contstant cribbers?

Sipping her second coffee, she browsed through all the news channels quickly. The cook, a woman in her late forties, who had mastered the art of going about her work surreptitiously, brought Koena her breakfast: a bowl of Poha and curd with a hint of jeera powder, you know, just to accentuate the taste. Koena thanked her and continued to watch TV while she chewed her breakfast. The headache had decided to ebb, finally. A tablet won't be required, Koena decided.

By 7:30, Koena was ready to leave. She grabbed her bag and car keys and left instructions for dinner with the cook before rushing through the door, locking it behind her. A fabulous cook and an adept housekeeper to manage the household were the two prime asks Koena had when they had moved into this four-bedroom fourteen hundred square foot apartment, 18 years ago. Shom had immediately agreed, which freed up a lot of time for the couple to indulge and finetune their artistic sensibilities and dabble in social climbing. They had rapidly moved up the social ladder and got entrenched in the well-heeled circuits of Bhubaneswar. In any case, Koena could not cook to save her ass.

Koena slowly drove out of her building, onto the main road, and towards Rabi Talkies Square, a few blocks away from her apartment complex. There was very less traffic at this hour, she noted, as her mind turned over the little information Sagar had given.

The office building loomed ahead, and Koena switched to active brain mode. She drove to the entrance gate and honked lightly. The security guy recognized her car and wished her a good morning.

After the perfunctory checks, he lifted the bar to let her in. Koena waved at him and drove in.

Her routine was set in stone. 'A creature of habit' was how she loved to describe herself.

She made her way to her office, mentally organizing her day. She entered the elevator and pressed the button for the fourth floor. The offices of the TV Nineteen Network (TNN) were located on the third and fourth floors of the multi-storeyed Shyamantaka Complex, a posh office space in an upmarket locality. Their stylish receptionist Laila came in only by 9 a.m. The office was practically empty at this hour. The walls looked grim and morose without the babble of voices vaulting off them.

Koena briskly walked to her desk, locked her bag inside the drawer before looking around to spot Sagar, who noticed her arrival and rushed towards her. He plonked down noisily on a chair, sighing loudly. She always visualized him as a bull, making all sorts of noises through his nose.

Closer observation revealed a light stubble and dark circles under the light brown eyes. The wavy black hair looked equally dishevelled. His dusky skin had broken out in several places. Sagar also looked perpetually sad, with a hangdog expression. It was obvious to Koena that he had not gone home after the party. He was still dressed in the silk party shirt he had worn last evening. *Gosh!*

Koena clucked her tongue sympathetically, 'Oh ho, what have you done to yourself? You look as if a two-ton truck ran over you. Did you go home? Boy, you look wasted. Do you need coffee?'

Sagar nodded eagerly at the mention of coffee. Together they walked towards the pantry. Their L-shaped office had a sunny spot where a small pantry had been set up. With glass walls, the pantry was the most cheerful place where all the juiciest gossip got exchanged.

'Do you think the pantry guy would have come in?' Koena elbowed Sagar while walking.

Sagar shrugged, 'I have never come this early… no clue…'

Koena perked up when she noticed the cheerful pantry guy at the stove, making fresh coffee for anybody who had decided to work late or come in early. He also offered cookies and pastries for those looking for a sugary treat. Koena grabbed both. The poha in her tummy adjusted and welcomed the newcomers.

Small mercies run this world.

They got their coffees and returned to their desks. Koena munched noisily at her cookies and pastry. She looked at Sagar who was quietly sipping his coffee. Koena sometimes got worried about the hours Sagar pulled. She decided to talk to him about it.

■

MAY 1, 2000

Delhi: AB-17 | Mathura Road
3:30 a.m.

BOOM!

The explosion happened when the city was still in slumber–some *daaru*-induced, some owing to the ruminations of marijuana and the acids in the stomach. And the rest, thanks to the deep entrenchment of the butter-soaked aloo parathas in the guts of those who had consumed them.

A suicide bomber sneaked into AB-17, a bungalow set in the ultra-posh locality, and pressed a switch attached to her jacket. The harm was minimal, as the bungalow's occupants had gone on an impromptu vacation. Only an elderly security guard and his family remained behind. The bomber who took her life would never know this. She let out a guttural cry, '*lal salaam*' before sealing her fate, as instructed. As rehearsed.

The feeble echo of that cry would linger for days in the minds of the sleepy security guards of the adjacent bungalows. Some would be unsure of its origin. Some would be unsure if they actually heard it.

The luxurious expanse of the building became nondescript rubble in no time, blown to smithereens. The explosion sent shock waves around; a few literal.

First, the neighbours rushed out–rudely awoken, dazed and zombie-like.

Then the paperboys came. Mouths agape, the hands holding their paper bundles shaking with fear and foreboding. The security guards of the nearby bungalows rushed out after, to see the dramatic black smoke coiling, unfolding, gurgling upwards like a sea monster. They had never seen anything like this. Jaws dropped to the grounds.

The acrid smoke travelled upwards, filling the area with a stench so powerful that pinching the nostrils did nothing to block it. It settled in every pore of the body, like an ugly reminder of this humiliation. The onlookers eventually scattered, holding clothes over their noses and muttering dark unenviable obscenities at the person who had done this. Some bright fellow eventually called the police. The sleepy policemen of

Delhi lumbered in as soon as they were summoned. The mind-numbing audacity of this act in itself was a shocker to many. The toll of heads that would roll was becoming interesting speculation and statistics for the people gathered there.

Indians love gossip and melodrama at whatever the price is. They just gorge on it like they would on a samosa swimming in layers of chutney.

When the initial inspecting team saw the extent of damage and realized whose house had been targeted, their tired brains kickstarted, and adrenaline surged through their bodies to call for backup. This was national security stuff. A committee would be formed in no time, and they had to cover their ample asses from future trouble.

Quickly, a team cordoned off the area, and senior officers were informed. The buck had started rolling. In no time, the area was teeming with black cat commandos, and the sleepy officers of Delhi Police were dragged out from the warm beds of their mistresses or wives. After a couple of hours, bulging police uniforms were jostling for space with men from all cadres strutting around with no actual knowledge of the incident.

There were dead bodies to account for. Four, to be precise. The security guy, a man probably in his late fifties, his wife, a woman of indeterminate age, and two teenage boys.

The Police Chief confirmed that the CM was not present at the time of the blast, but the security guy and his family had perished in the blast. By then, some busybody had called up a news channel, and the media hounds came sniffing. Pushing their mikes towards anyone who cared, they rattled out their questions.

Rat-a-tat. Rat-a-tat.

Pointed, random, inane questions.

Are the CM and his family dead?

What will happen to the State?

What was the attacker wearing?

Why do you think they blew up his house?

Do you think this is a burglary?

Do you think this is a terrorist attack?

Do you think Pakistani ISI was involved?

Do you think there is another angle to this explosion?

Do you think there is a foreign conspiracy?

It took a few hours for the police to control the situation.

■

MAY 1, 2000

Maldives, Seashore Resort
6:30 a.m.

SEASHORE RESORT, A quaint faraway resort in Maldives often welcomed guests who surreptitiously occupied their rooms. Currently, the titled occupant of AB-17–the current CM of Delhi–scowled hard when his phone rang incessantly, forcing him to cut short his session with the Chinese prostitute. After wrapping a towel around his ample waist and dismissing the prostitute with a brush of his hand, he growled into the phone. The caller had a short message to deliver.

The CM heard it carefully and barked, 'What the fuck is happening? Who dared to blow up my bungalow?' His voice boomed in the oak-panelled plush hotel room. Holding the phone close to his ear, he paced across the room. His fists were clenching and unclenching in anger. His ample belly jiggled as he walked. The prostitute slithered away without making any noise, waiting to be summoned again for her services. She stood silently outside the room, caressing her long shiny black hair.

Inside the room, after listening to the full report, the CM relaxed and smiled. He let out his breath in a whoosh. His brows untwined themselves. Rubbing his ample belly with his right hand, and still holding the phone in his left, he pondered some more. Arriving at a decision, he nodded.

Fine.

Things were not as bad as they seemed, he decided, disconnecting the call. He knew what was expected of him when he landed in New Delhi. He then opened his room's door and beckoned the petite woman.

He would have to work on his erection again. *Damn!* He thought, pushing the woman down on himself.

In a few hours, he attended a video press conference and confirmed that he was alive and kicking. He also pulled his portly wife and two sons into the camera's frame showing proof that they were all safe. He congratulated the police for their fantastic work and promised to get to the core of the issue. He was not taking any chances with national security, he assured.

After the press conference aired as breaking news, more people started clamouring to witness the free melodrama. Some came in their fancy cars and took pictures. Some came from as far as Gurgaon so that they would be captured by the many TV cameras positioned there. Not every day did one get to witness such a glaring attack on the vestigial remnants of the honour of the security agencies. And to the *dilliwalahs*, a mere rumour was enough to stoke their almost perpetual carnal desire to witness the unusual and forbidden.

All the government-allocated sturdy Nokia phones were constantly ringing. Photos were being clicked at an astonishing rate. This was the greatest show ever. The *dilliwalahs* were lapping it all up. The Delhi Police was sitting on a veritable law and order problem, a hissing volcano ready to burst open like a gurgling worm-infested sore.

The incident had ripped apart and laid bare the ugly underbelly of the system, and every policeman was running for cover. The heat had turned up brutally, enough to singe even the pubic hair of the khaki-clad.

The police swept the entire area multiple times but could not find any suspicious movement or traces of any explosives. The bomb squad was working overtime. The CoP was visibly fuming at this security breach, which was a black mark on his otherwise illustrious career record. Lutyens' Delhi was a no-no, and the terrorists had intentionally stirred a hornet's nest. Every officer worth his salt was pulled into duty, and the media was hounding anyone they could lay their hands on, be it a maid or a paper *wallah*. They did not even spare the dude with green-coloured hair who had come in a Hummer from Haryana just to take a selfie with the carnage.

Delhi was now a fortress with the police crawling over every crevice known to man. The media was having a field day, as usual.

■

MAY 1, 2000
TNN Office
Bhubaneswar
8:15 a.m.

WHEN SAGAR CONCISELY reported the sequence of events without leaving anything out, Koena sat transfixed, shocked at the sheer audacity of the macabre act. Having led an almost cloistered and upper-class luxurious life for several years, she had been lulled into a whimsical state of euphoria, in dissonance with reality.

Detached mentally from the ground realities of people, who romanced the dust and braved the winds, Koena had limited herself to idly wondering about the lives they led-the people who travelled like human masses in trains and buses, people who lived at the mercy of the elements, and people who were less fortunate than her, in terms of money and security. Often, she pondered about life, staring out from her balcony, delicately balancing a fine glass of Cabernet or Merlot.

But Koena also realized that certain incidents had a devastating effect on her. While internalizing the effect of the calamity, she confronted her innermost frailties and her constant ruminations on things that threatened to undo her core.

Tim dropped over just then. Koena shook herself out of her reverie.

'Aah, there you are! Koena, Sagar... Guys, get ready; I need you both to cover this Delhi incident. I have a contact who will help you out in Delhi. Get a few sound-bytes, cover the incident, and come back pronto. Same day return.'

Koena and Sagar did a double-take.

'Tim, where is Choubey? Isn't he the one who usually covers all this? I mean, I have no problem going, but Sagar and I have rarely done any real-time coverage.' Koena tried to argue with her boss, the Editor-in-Chief of TNN, Tigmanshu Sanyal–who preferred going just by Tim.

'Choubey and his assistant have gone to cover another important assignment. No one else is available. I urgently need someone to do this–it is time-sensitive. You guys get going; I have arranged for tickets. It is a day trip. You can touch base with Laila for the tickets and any advance you need. Give me a call once you reach. I'm texting you the number and address of my contact in Delhi–my nephew, Anand. He will take you to the spot and arrange everything.' Tim said and walked away without waiting for a response. Koena looked at the receding figure in frustration.

'What the…' She muttered but controlled her rising irritation. In their line of work, this was normal. She had been in a few emergencies earlier.

Looking forlornly at Tim moving away, Sagar clucked his tongue and managed, 'Tough cookie, he is, no?' He was petrified of Tim and barely managed to say anything in front of the man. This was universal knowledge, and other colleagues teased Sagar for this.

Koena shrugged. She didn't care what Sagar thought of Tim, 'Ok, let us get to work then. I have a few essentials in my backpack, which I will use. What about you? Do you want to get something for the trip? You figure out what you want to do while I check what Laila has for us. Meet you at the reception in a ten.'

She got busy checking her backpack.

They met at the front desk as planned, and after collecting the tickets and money from Laila, left for the airport. The flight was at 10:50, and they had to rush. Laila had booked a taxi and they managed to board the flight on time.

■

MAY 1, 2000
Delhi
12:15 p.m.

BY THE TIME their flight landed, it was afternoon. Sagar looked around, his saucer-shaped eyes ready to bulge at the gorgeousness of the Delhi airport. The colleagues rushed to the exit as they didn't have any checked-in luggage.

'Can we grab a quick bite, Koena?' Sagar implored, eyeing a café hungrily.

After munching on the ridiculously expensive and almost cold sandwiches, they made their way out of the airport. Stepping out in super humid Delhi, they looked around for Anand, their contact. Koena called Anand from her mobile phone. He answered on the first ring. Anand was a well-connected man and promised to get things done very quickly. Koena had met him once at a party back in Bhubaneswar, and he had seemed pleasant, *a jugaadu.*

When he arrived, Koena introduced Sagar to him. Anand ushered them to his car. Since they were returning the same day, they had very little time left, and urged Anand to help them out as quickly as possible.

'So, did you guys get any *khana*? When Kaka called me, I was about to doze off. I had just returned from the site. It is a mess. You will see it soon.' Anand smiled at them while navigating the thick Delhi traffic. 'Here, have some *ghar ka khana*...Mom insisted...' Anand said and handed over a tiffin box, which emanated a divine smell. Koena and Sagar dug into the delicious aloo parathas made by Anand's Mom and asked him to thank her. Satiated, Koena's mind turned to the task at hand.

'Do you have any clue about the bomber? When did this happen? And most importantly, why?' Koena had been dying to ask these questions.

'Hmm, good questions. Why? I don't know...I guess that the Maoists are involved. You know the rumour about the bomber shouting 'lal salaam' and all that. But it could be anybody–certainly some group with deep pockets and hatred for the CM.' Anand concluded, his brows creased in deep thought. He turned to look at Sagar sitting beside him and at Koena via the rear-view mirror while expertly manoeuvring the car in Delhi traffic. Koena nodded, her mind in a thought spiral of its own.

'Hmm. Never heard of such a blatant violation of a security system. It is like some group desperately wants to grab attention.' Koena voiced her opinion.

At that moment, Anand nodded, meeting her eye in the mirror.

'Precisely.'

'Hmm. Let us see.' Koena muttered. She spent the next hour soaking in the sights and sounds of Delhi. This was her first visit to the city. Sagar had been to Delhi before and so was busy reading the newspaper to catch up.

Anand switched on the radio, and the trio rode in silence, listening to the news, lost in their own worlds. When they reached Civil Lines, they could see colourful police tapes with the words *Police Line Do Not Cross* written on them in bold letters, tied around trees and buildings. All roads were barricaded.

The entire North Civil Lines area had been cordoned off. No media people were allowed inside. Only residents were being let in, that too, after careful inspection.

'Looks crowded. Has the entire city descended here?' Koena asked, craning her neck to catch a glimpse of the source of the billowing smoke.

Anand nodded, assuring that he would do something. He drove around and parked in a shaded area. Asking them to wait in the car, he went out. Koena and Sagar got ready with their notepads and pens. Sagar had brought a camera, courtesy-Tim. They alighted and looked around.

A huge crowd had already gathered near the enclosure – tugging and pulling – mostly curious onlookers out on a joy ride to take pictures of the tragedy, and to add to the repertoire of experiences they could boast about.

A distraught senior police officer was barking orders to his team. The heat was unbearable. Sticky, smelly sweat dripped down brown and wheatish skins, pooling around ankles and armpits. Koena tried unsuccessfully to arrest the perspiration with her feel-fresh tissues; It was of no use. After what seemed like half an hour, a heavily perspiring Anand rushed back, locked his car, and beckoned the duo towards a narrow alley.

'We have to take this back alley to reach the spot. Come on. Hurry, we have only ten minutes.' Koena felt a sudden dip in temperature when they entered the tree-studded avenue. *Anand knows his routes well,* she noted, hurrying to keep up with the lithe men.

Man of many virtues.

'You grew up here?' Koena enquired, slightly short of breath, marvelling at his ability to discover routes.

'Yep. My parents shifted to Delhi when I was little. Mainly because of Baba. He had a government job. Ma was a teacher in DPS.' Anand smiled, revealing perfectly white teeth.

'Hmm, interesting. You seem to know your geography well. I'm amazed.' Koena nodded appreciatively. She had begun to sweat profusely again. She dabbed unproductively at the pouring sweat, and abandoned the effort after a while, realizing the futility of using a dainty handkerchief to stem the tsunami of perspiration.

'Thanks. I'm more like a wanderer. I have this insane urge to keep discovering. New things. New places. New historical sites. New people,' Anand said. Soon, they reached the venue. The stench hit them first. Anand handed out masks, which Koena and Sagar gladly plastered on their faces. Within minutes, however, they realised the inefficacy of the semi-transparent material and stowed the masks away. Mentally switching off the response to the olfactory function was the only way out. They tried their best to do that.

Striding along, they made their way to the temporary police booth. After asking the duo to wait, Anand strode ahead to speak to the DGP, who was obviously not ready to say anything to the media. Tight-lipped and meticulous was how people described him.

Miraculously, Anand had the necessary clout to make any doors open for him. Koena marvelled at the speed and efficacy at which Anand manoeuvred the ranks. *Jugaad.* The essence of this short word hit Koena. She smiled.

She looked at Sagar to see if he had noticed this too, but he was lost in thought.

'Do you like her?' Koena asked, waving her hand in front of Sagar's face to get his attention.

'What? Who?' Sagar sputtered, coming back to the Earth.

'Nothing, just kidding. Why are you so quiet?' Koena asked, searching for her sunglasses in her backpack. Thrusting them on her face gave her the much-needed respite from the tremendous heat. Feeling better, she repeated her question.

'I'm thirsty actually.' Sagar confessed, taking out a water bottle and finishing it in a swig.

Koena checked her watch-a beautiful Longines collector's piece, a gift from Shom. She lovingly ran a hand over the dial. It was 2:30 p.m.

'Tch, tch… boy. Slowly. Be kind to your throat.' Koena smiled indulgently. *This boy.*

Anand was speaking with the DGP in a low tone. The officer looked over at Koena and Sagar. After a quick word with one of his subordinates, he waved them in and asked an inspector to help them with their queries.

'Ask whatever you want. No problem. They have heard it all, and by now, they have even considered an alien attack.' Anand leaned over and winked. Koena unsuccessfully tried to stifle an amused chuckle.

Anand shook hands with the inspector, Ram Singh, and introduced Koena and Sagar. Koena got down to work. Sagar prepped his camera while the inspector stood ram-rod still, only his eyes moving, carefully noting each movement.

They wrapped up their work with speed. Anand helped them with the script, and Koena was sure they had not left out any loose ends. When Anand went to thank the DGP, Koena checked out the extent of damage done to the building. Three fire engines stood near the back gate. A few firefighters were sitting and chatting, sipping tea in plastic teacups. They had done what they could.

Koena stood staring at the rubble, amazed at the aspirations of the group that had sent a bomber to Delhi.

Who did this?

In India–in *jugaadu* India–you don't just drop a bomb on Lutyens! It was like flipping the middle finger at the political biggies in their bedroom.

She walked a few feet away from the men, observing, mentally noting down nuances. Beyond the enclosure, she could see huge TV vans and reporters talking to anybody they could push their mikes at-security guys, newspaper guys… anyone who had a remote chance of knowing anything about the incident. She stood transfixed as each channel tried to outdo others and itself by getting sound bites from the *bai*, the *paperwallah* and any passer-by who seemed eager to share some sketchy details of the attack. Looking at Anand, she realized how privileged they were to be able to pull the correct strings and get allowed inside.

Surely, the guys jostling for a foothold outside the enclosure would give anything to be let in. Thanks, Tim!

After mentally acknowledging Tim's connections, she turned her attention to the rubble. The truth was that nobody had actually seen the bomber get inside. No one knew how she had bypassed the massive security cordon near the CM's house. Oh, but all of them knew it was a 'she'. And someone somewhere had heard her shout *'lal salaam'*.

Koena walked back to where Anand, Sagar and Ram Singh were standing, speaking in soft tones. As she approached, Ram Singh gave her a polite nod. She asked him if they had a picture or if anyone had seen any stranger walking around. She asked about the CCTV footage. Ram Singh shook his head in the negative to every question.

'No, ma'am! We do not have anything solid to proceed with.'

A well-planned execution with absolutely no clue about the bomber: it looked as if she had been airdropped. However, the police chief seemed unsure if the bomber was a woman. Koena, though, was sure of one more thing. She was sure the group would target the CM again.

Poor man. It was so tough to be a politician.

Koena thought lazily and wondered at the callous handling of such an incident.

Where were the duty officers who would have been stationed to man the stretch? Someone wondered aloud–loud enough to be heard by the DGP–to create a ripple of guffaws among the lingering crowd.

Koena and Sagar hung around for some more time. Anand had to talk to someone about something. One of those discussions was *jugaadu* types, which gave Delhi its moniker. *Jugaadu Dilli.*

Koena and Sagar perched on a car's bonnet and waited for Anand. They had gathered whatever they could, and Tim had also called to say that the Delhi team was ready to take over. Finally, Anand emerged from the khaki crowd and beckoned. Silently, they made their way to the car.

'So, hopefully, you have got everything you needed? I spoke to Tim Kaka and he seemed quite pleased.' Anand looked at them questioningly, his thick bushy eyebrows lost in his hairline.

'I guess so. I can't thank you enough for helping us, Anand. I'm sure we'd be totally lost without you.' Koena expressed her gratefulness.

Anand simply smiled.

Their return was uneventful.

■

MAY 1, 2000

Biju Patnaik Airport, Terminal 2, Bhubaneswar
10:30 p.m.

WHEN THEY LANDED in Bhubaneswar, it was very late. Tim had arranged a cab to pick them up. Sagar got off enroute and promised to come in early the next day.

■

MAY 2, 2000

Ashiana Apartments
12:15 a.m.

KOENA REACHED HOME and sent the report to Tim before crashing on her bed without even changing.

Tomorrow is a new day.

I will…

■

MAY 2, 2000

Ashiana Apartments
5:45 a.m.

THE MORNING SUN rays seemed brighter. Or was it the May heat? One could not discern.

The air conditioner was still purring softly, blasting cold air on Koena. The room was relatively cold compared to the slowly increasing humid heat outside. The midday sun in May roasted the skins of people to a fine brown, the colour of mustard.

Knock, Knock!

Knock, Knock!

A shrill female voice followed the persistent knocks.

'Didi!' The voice sounded again, this time more persistently–more loudly–and managed to permeate the layers of fog that had invaded Koena's tired mind.

She stirred but did not wake up fully. A corner of her brain activated a signal and reminded her that it was a normal workday, a glorious Saturday, but Koena's body refused to budge. She kept sleeping, her breath falling in rhythm. The events of the previous day were too much for her to process. The perpetual lack of restful REM sleep made her feel tired and weak. Her eyes felt heavy, she felt almost drugged.

'Go away. I need more sleep,' Koena murmured, loud enough to make the cook stop knocking. The ever-punctual cook came to work sharply at 5 a.m.

The cook knocked again after about an hour, and this time, Koena got up.

After drinking two cups of black coffee, she coaxed her brain into functioning.

She stretched languorously, actively blocking any thoughts of attempting her usual Yoga routine. Struggling against her body's strike, Koena completed her stretches and sat down in padmasana. Closing her tired eyes, she forced her mind to shut out all noise and clutter. Deep calm soon pervaded her restless mind.

She opened her eyes and stretched her limbs. Her arms felt tired. Usually, she felt energetic and pumped up at the end of a yoga session, but today it was not to be. When your usual routine fails to provide the much-required succour your brain craves for, then you just exist, zombie-like. Today was one of those days.

Booting her cranky computer, Koena first checked her emails. There was one from Tim. He had responded to her draft report submission email and asked her to make some changes. She replied with a simple, 'Yes, boss.'

She closed her inbox and started browsing the news-media websites, which were still a new trend. The news channels were going crazy, covering the horrendous explosion in Delhi. Her phone vibrated just then.

The text message notification broke Koena's reverie.

When are you coming in today?

Koena read the message from Sagar and smiled.

Soon, she typed and sighed, knowing that Sagar hated such incomprehensible vague answers.

'Don't I just love to irritate people?' Koena giggled aloud, visualizing Sagar scowling at her reply.

Her love for irritating people was like a persistent itch; the one you scratch and feel nearly orgasmic. Well. Almost.

Another long day had dawned. TNN functioned on Saturdays also. Much to Koena's irritation.

Koena wanted to focus on her incomplete assignment–a report on the life of sexual–abuse victims. It was a subject close to her heart, and she wanted to spend some quiet time doing her research. Some of it would come from her own experiences, and she had realized that she might not be mentally prepared to face her own demons.

She dressed in deliberate, leisurely movements, idly watching the news anchor repeating the same bit multiple times. Then she switched off the TV and attacked her breakfast–super soft white idlis and freshly ground coconut chutney with just a mention of tadka. It melted in her mouth. She called out to her cook.

'Bina!'

'*Ji,* didi...'

The cook appeared at her door almost immediately.

'The idlis are amazing! Never knew you were a superwoman in South Indian cuisine as well,' Koena managed to stutter, her mouth full of idlis mixed evenly with the thick chutney.

Hearing Koena's praise, Bina's face lit up, 'Thanks, didi.'

After chatting with her for a few minutes, Koena handed her empty plate to the cook and got ready.

■

MAY 2, 2000

En route to Work

8:00 a.m.

AS KOENA WAS driving out of her apartment, her phone came to life and a familiar ring tone played. Koena smiled.

Aah, there he is, the man himself.

Shom was calling to check on her. They had not spoken for more than a day.

'Shom, I was just thinking of you,' Koena cooed, her smile growing wider. A warmth was spreading through her limbs. Shom always had that effect on her.

'I know, sweety. I missed you too. By the way, I'm returning by noon, and I hope you will be back home sooner today.' The last part was more of a statement than a question.

Koena felt a sudden desire to hug her partner.

'Oh Shom, baby! Why do you go on these trips? I hate it when you leave me and go.' Koena said, adjusting her earpiece, feeling her heart grow heavy. She furiously honked at a car slowing in front of her, getting angry glares from the driver. She let the other car–an old-model Honda–pass by, and tried to pull up on the left side of the road. Several cars raced ahead, happy to get the leeway to rush ahead towards an unending traffic jam signalling the beginning of the rush hour.

'Calm down, babe... First, you pull up to a side,' Shom cooed to his wife, 'Have you?'

He knew her so well. Koena was still navigating the traffic, trying to nose into a spot.

'Yeah, yeah! I did,' she said, pulling the hand brake and muttering an angry expletive.

When Koena became emotional, she was prone to spewing choicest expletives and getting into trouble. Shom didn't want that to happen when he was away.

After switching on the hazard lights, Koena adjusted her buttocks on her seat and leaned back, relaxing. Talking to Shom always made her feel better. His smooth-as-honey voice had that kind of effect on her.

He calms me. He is my anchor, my dopamine.

With the AC cooling her warm skin, Koena closed her eyes, letting his voice wash over her.

'Do you know who visited the shoot today, shona? Arav Kumar!'

'Oh my! How does he look in real life?' Koena squealed. *Arav Kumar is cute!*

'He looks better in-person, shona. It seems he is a great fan of my shows. I was like 'wow, we can start a mutual admiration society'. I got an autographed picture for you.' Shom whispered in a conspiratorial tone.

'Yaay!' Koena's glee knew no bounds.

'He also congratulated me on my shows and said I was doing a great job.'

Koena's heart swelled with pride when she heard this.

'Tell me, will you return early today?' Shom asked, his voice dropping to a huskier whisper.

Koena imagined Shom whispering sweet nothings, his mouth pressed against her hair, his voice tickling her skin, his teeth nibbling her ear lobe, sending shivers down her spine, giving her goosebumps all over.

'Yep, I will be back soon, sweety.' She whispered back, her mood soaring, desires stoked, her breath heavy.

'I will look forward to it, wifey. Love you, baby.' Shom whispered, his voice tingling her senses again. 'Shona, by the way, don't forget to get my Tux ready for Guptaji's party in the evening.' He reminded her.

'Is it today? I totally forgot!' Koena asked, her mind in a tizzy, thinking about the amount of preparation that would be required.

What will I wear? Shit. Should I just bunk office and go shopping?

Shom replied in the affirmative. After promising to be home early, Koena disconnected.

I think I will wear the black dress I bought in London. Hmm, that should be fine.

The long day at the office suddenly seemed uninteresting. Koena just wanted the workday to end so that she could get ready to receive Shom. And dress up for the party.

Sigh.

It could not be, though. She had to endure the long, arduous day. There were days when she wondered why she had become a journalist. Aah, yes, that degree she had picked up from that prestigious, expensive college. Thanks to a persistent Shom.

Sigh. I could have been a teacher instead. A computer teacher. Or a Math teacher.

She started the car and made her way towards Rabi Talkies Square. Taking her usual turn, she kept driving…lost in her thoughts…

Bang!

A sickening thump–loud enough to put a neat dent on the smooth metal of the car—made her jump.

'Oi! Hey!' Loud shots interrupted her frenzied train of thoughts.

The screech of metal tearing amidst the loud shouts made her jittery. Reacting instinctively, Koena pushed her foot down on the brake pedal.

Screech!

Her car stopped with a vehement protest. Heart hammering in her ears, she rolled down the window and looked out. Nothing. Puzzled, she craned her neck and caught sight of a woman lying unconscious on the road.

Koena panicked. She had never hit anyone in her life.

Shit. There is a lovely dent I need to take care of…Sigh! Let me see if the woman is ok.

She hurriedly got out of her car, subconsciously remembering to lock it.

A crowd had slowly begun to gather. Koena looked around frantically, looking for a friendly or helpful face. Silent, cold stares met her frightened eyes. Murmurs went around; the loudest was about how women should find their way back to the kitchen and stay there.

The woman who had fainted due to shock lay on the dusty road, looking pale. Her bicycle lay nearby. Koena squatted carefully near the woman, taking care not to soil her dress. A soft touch on the woman's shoulder reassured Koena that the woman was breathing evenly. She asked the people gathered there for help. No one bothered or stirred. They kept staring at Koena. Unblinking. Silent.

People were eager to watch the free drama about the rich woman in a car who had hit a poor woman on a bicycle. Never did they wonder if the poor woman was at fault.

Trying to raise the woman gently, Koena pleaded for help. 'Some water, please.'

Stony, silent stares gave way to soft murmurs. Someone in the crowd recognized her as 'the woman from TV', and the murmurs grew louder. Koena became more panicky.

What if the woman dies due to some internal injury?

She checked the prone woman's pulse. It was slow but steady.

Just then, a woman in the crowd handed Koena a bottle of water. Thanking her, Koena took a few drops and splashed them on the unconscious woman's face. As the water hit the woman's face, her eyes fluttered open.

She tried to sit up. Koena helped her drink some water.

'Didi!'

'Uhh, are you alright? I am sorry… I did not hit you.' Koena managed to say. Her recollection was jumbled.

Did I hit the woman, or had she come on the wrong side?

'You did not hit me. I came from the wrong side. Sorry.'

Upon hearing this confession, the crowd started dispersing. The drama was over.

Paisa vasool!

Koena helped the woman sit up after checking for injuries. There were none. She had presumably fainted because of the shock. Koena requested two women who had stayed back to help her. They obliged, lifting the other woman and helping her into Koena's car.

One of them quickly picked up the woman's bicycle, placed it on the carrier of Koena's car and fastened it with a rope.

Koena realised with a sinking feeling that she would have to take the woman to a nearby hospital.

Let me take her to Dr. Partho's clinic.

Koena drove around the square and took the right exit to reach the clinic.

Partho Clinic boasted of being open 24/7. Koena parked her car on the practically empty road outside the clinic. She got down and ran around to help the woman out who was looking pale and hadn't spoken a word during the short drive. Seemingly lost in thoughts, she had spent the time staring outside. On closer observation, Koena noticed that the woman wore no visible symbols of matrimony. No sindoor that ran the length of her neatly parted hair. No chain. No shakha pola. Nothing.

She is probably from the villages. And single. Or a widow. Or a divorcee.

The woman had long jet-black hair with no evidence of grey, neatly combed and tucked into a bun at the nape of her neck without the aid of any metal clips or ornamental accessories. Clean. Her nails looked neat and well-cut. Koena took all this in at a glance. Her feet were ensconced in clean Hawai slippers. Her saree was draped neatly around her svelte figure. Not an extra inch of body fat. Glowing skin that stretched evenly over a fit form. Koena held the woman's hand when she stepped out of the car. There were no visible signs of injury.

Koena sighed inwardly, staring lovingly at the woman's hair.

What hair. Wow.

'Do you want to call someone? Here, take my phone.' Koena thrust her phone into the woman's hands, urging her to call someone. Maybe a brother. Or a husband. Or even a lover.

The woman mutely shook her head and returned Koena's phone.

'I don't know anyone in this city, Didi. I want to go now. I am okay.'

'First, let us see the doctor, come.' Koena urged and tugged at the woman's elbow gently. The woman brushed Koena's hand away, insisting, 'Didi, I am alright. I must go.'

The woman hurriedly turned, untied and removed her bicycle from the carrier, mounted it, and made her way towards Rabi Talkies Square before Koena could react. Not once did she turn or thank Koena for her kindness.

Koena stood gaping.

'Hey, Koena! What a surprise.' A man's deep baritone made Koena jump out of her skin.

'Doctor Partho!' Koena swirled around and stuttered, her heart thudding loudly. But this time, it was for entirely different reasons. The man had a divine voice, she noted for the umpteenth time. His face belied his age. Despite pushing fifty, his smooth and wrinkle-free skin always made Koena feel jealous. She folded her hands in a greeting. The doctor did the same, put his hand on her elbow and gently guided her inside. Once they were seated, he asked if she would like some tea. Koena nodded eagerly, her eyes glittering at the memory of sipping the divine concoction during her earlier visits. The tea shop next to Dr. Partho's Clinic was very famous.

'So, what brings you here, my lady? Hope that boy of yours is fine.' Dr. Partho asked.

'Which boy, Doctor?' Koena asked, guffawing.

'Oh my, you are a wicked one. I meant the younger one, certainly.' The Doctor joined her laughter. Chuckling, they entered the clinic, which as always, was bustling with patients.

'How do you function amidst this chaos?' Koena looked around at the files piled up haphazardly. There were records everywhere. In the remaining space, there were medicine boxes stacked precariously one on top of another. His patients found space to rest their bums and waited patiently for their turn.

The doctor laughed aloud, making Koena smile. She liked him.

'Oh, ma, I know. This place is quite something. In fact, after we got a new nurse, it is better. She is a wizard at organizing. See, we have a new file room.' Doctor Partho pointed at an antechamber.

'Oh, that should be really helpful.' Koena nodded, agreeing with the doctor's solution.

After chatting for a while about mundane things, Koena told him the reason for her visit. He heard her out patiently and clucked his tongue.

'Some people, you know, are slightly kooky up there.' He said, rotating his finger near his temples.

Koena nodded; her brows knit in concentration. True. Some people did have some loose wiring up there. *Like me.*

'I don't think you must worry your pretty head. That woman was probably under stress or something. And in our country, anything can happen, you know. Aah, tea has come. Come on, have tea with this old man. Very rarely do I get the company of beautiful women like you.'

Koena blushed and took the cup from the tea boy. The delicious, sweet brew laced with just a dash of masala made her sigh. She felt her muscles relax, and the stress of almost bursting a nerve back on the road reduced. Her neck muscles were all bunched up like a group of teenage girls discussing a heartthrob. The tremendous stress response had triggered an intense pressure on her skull. She knew that she would have to pop a pill soon to halt a gleefully-waiting-on-the-horizon migraine.

After tea, when Koena was about to excuse herself, Dr. Partho stopped her. He handed her a brown packet saying, 'Hold on a minute, my dear! Give this packet to your husband… He left it behind.'

'Shom? When did he come here?' Koena demanded, taken by complete surprise. She took the packet and put it in her voluminous bag. It was a normal brown paper envelope, sealed on all sides with tape. Koena could easily recognize Shom's way of packing.

The perfect way. Sealed and double sealed.

'Yeah, he had come to see me the other day. Now… let me recollect. When was that? Oh yes, it was just yesterday. He came with an injured boy. Come to think of it… it was very similar to how we met today. We did minor first aid for the boy, and Shom left immediately. And in a hurry, he forgot this packet on my table.'

Nodding with the recollection, the doctor smiled at her and turned his attention to his duties.

Koena walked out of the cabin after mumbling a quick thanks and goodbye. The last few words were left almost unsaid.

How is that possible? Shom has gone for a shoot. That too to Kolkata, several hundred kilometres away. Maybe Doctor Partho is mixing things up.

At the door, she turned and asked, 'Doctor, are you sure you met Shom yesterday? Or was it the day before?'

It had to be a mistake. How is this possible?

'No, ma. It was yesterday. We had just a couple of people walking in. I remember very clearly. We had tea...chatted a bit about Kit, you, and that latest shoot of his, which he had wrapped up within a few hours. About that actor, Arav Kumar... I remember very clearly.' The doctor confirmed, and again got busy with his work, his head bent over the file. A tuft of white hair over his forehead danced gently in the light breeze.

Arav Kumar!

Koena willed herself to move, but her hands and feet were cold and clammy. The room was rotating slowly. Or was it just her head. Her heart had moved up to her mouth and she could hear her breath slowing down.

What is happening? Did Shom lie to me? What is he hiding? Has he lied to me about the shoot, too? Maybe his shoot did get over earlier? Then why didn't he come home? And who had he brought to the clinic? Why did he never mention anything to me? I need to sit down...

Instead she forced a smile and said, 'Thank you, doctor. I will take your leave now.'

'*Bhalo theko* ma, bye.' Doctor Partho bid goodbye.

Koena slowly walked back to her car. The morning sun was quite warm, and the car had heated up considerably. With her mind clogged up with thoughts of her errant husband's impromptu trip back home, she started the car and let the engine run for a while. *Calm down. Maybe there is a perfect explanation. Yes! I will ask Shom.*

She reversed in a small clearing near the clinic and kept the windows rolled down a bit for the heat to dissipate. She slowly made her way to her office, her mind churning the information she had received.

When she reached the parking area, she noticed that her usual slot was occupied.

Choicest expletives reached her tongue, and she threw them at nobody. She looked for an alternate slot, found one in a sunny corner, grudgingly parked her car and got out.

■

MAY 2, 2000
TNN Office
9:30 a.m.

HER DAY WAS on to a very bumpy ride. She had planned to reach an hour early, but it was already 9:30. Still lost in thoughts about Shom, she reached her floor. Just to be sure, she decided to call Shom as soon as she could. She had to wrap up a few things first.

Koena put it down in the to-do list in her little notebook and went for some coffee. While Koena was getting the coffee, Sagar walked in, holding his mickey-mouse print coffee mug. He was looking shabby and unshaven. Sagar was heavily into comics and was usually ribbed for his choice of stationery. Mickey Mouse mugs. Phantom pens. Mowgli T-shirts.

'Hey, buddy. Good morning, what happened? Did you manage to catch any sleep?' Koena clucked her tongue, taking in the bloodshot eyes and the dishevelled hair.

'Hey! I feel like a zombie…' Sagar mumbled. He gulped his coffee in one shot and reached out to refill the cup.

'Easy, buddy! Go easy; your throat will thank you later…' Koena warned, shocked at the way Sagar had gulped the steaming drink.

'I didn't get to go home. Tim is baying for my blood, man. I hate him.' Sagar cribbed. His breath almost caught in his throat, choking him. Red-faced with the emotion and exertion, he stared at Koena unblinkingly.

'Oh, again? What did you do now?' Koena asked sympathetically.

He is always getting into trouble with Tim.

'Don't ask. I have no idea why,' Sagar shrugged, his head lolling.

'We've got to work on the Seva Niketan assignment. Will you be able to spend some time on it today? I am thinking of wrapping it up ASAP!' Koena said, looking at Sagar quizzically.

He looked ready to sleep on his feet.

'Miss Koena, I am always ready to work with you. For you, I am never tired. If Tim asks, say I died and went to heaven.' Sagar joked, making a funny face. He refilled his cup with coffee and splashed some cold water from the tap on his face. He didn't bother to wipe off the excess water. It dripped down and wet his shirt. Koena looked at the boy with amusement and smiled.

He always refers to me as Miss. This boy! As if he doesn't want to acknowledge the existence of my husband and a teenage son.

Laughing at his antics and silencing her mind voice, Koena made her way to her desk after extracting a promise from Sagar to meet her around noon. She felt a bit better after the mundane exchange.

God! I needed this distraction.

She spent the first half of the day completing the questionnaire for her assignment and wrote down a skeletal framework for the way she had visualized the program. When she checked her watch again, it was already 11:30. She had not realized the passage of time, having been so engrossed in her work. She looked around for Sagar, who was nowhere to be seen. Locking her laptop, Koena made her way to his desk.

Sagar and Koena were a team. Earlier, Koena was part of a larger team led by a man called Subroto. But later, Tim had moved her out and assigned plum projects to Koena. After a year or so, he had allowed her to hire an underling. That was when Sagar was hired.

When she reached there, she held on to the cubicle wall to steady herself as a strong giggle rose. She covered her mouth with her fist, and her eyes welled over with the effort of holding back the laughter. Sagar's cubicle mate was absent, and Koena plonked on the vacant chair, staring incredulously at the snoring figure. Sagar was resting his feet on the table, his head lolling on the chair's headrest. He was fast asleep with mild snores, drooling on his shirt.

Sagar worked very hard and had earned quite a name for himself in the network. Koena was extremely proud of her protégé.

Koena gently shook him, though her heart was not in it. Sagar got up with a jerk at her touch.

'Sorry, sorry, I don't know when I fell asleep,' Sagar apologized profusely, checking the time.

'Tell you what, let's go and grab some lunch! Then we'll work on this assignment.' Koena suggested, her heart going out to the tired young man. His bloodshot, sleep-deprived eyes almost glittered at the mention of food. Sagar loved to eat; eat well, and eat leisurely. Koena had learned it the hard way.

'Great idea. I'm famished. Since I didn't go home, I didn't get my dabba today. I need to buy food. I hope the canteen *wallah* has some nice grub today.' Sagar lived close by in a shared accommodation and had a maid for cooking and cleaning.

Koena chuckled inwardly, catching the gleam in Sagar's eyes. She knew he always perked up at the mention of food.

Sagar excused himself to freshen up before lunch. Koena rushed to her desk to grab her lunch bag. When he returned looking like his usual cheerful self, they made their way to the canteen, chatting about office stuff, rubbishing the new HR policy about the allowance for outstation trips. Sagar had not yet received any mail on his claim, and he was pissed. Even Koena had not heard from HR about her claim for the Delhi trip but she wasn't bothered and she said so. Sagar shrugged.

In the canteen, Sagar ordered a meal of chicken biriyani and Goan fish curry. Koena tucked into her lunch of paneer curry and radish roti. For a while, they focused on the food, letting their minds wander to their respective unknown depths. Koena's mind went into a flashback mode to rewind the morning's incident. She had forgotten to call Shom. *Shit!*

Wiping her fingers on a paper napkin, she took out her mobile phone and checked for messages. There was one from Shom. Received ten minutes ago.

'Hi Baby, I am boarding the flight in half an hour. Love you.'

Koena replied immediately, urging her fingers to type faster, her heart skipping a beat, hesitating just a bit before typing out the last sentence.

Hi, sweety pie. Come back soon. Mmuah. By the way, what is your flight number?

Her hunger was gone; Koena stared at her phone, willing it to come alive. Nothing. The message remained unsent.

She closed her lunch box with a thud and put her head on the table.

Shit. I'm suspecting my husband. What's wrong with me?

The steel table felt nice and cold on her warm head. Other staff sitting at the adjacent tables looked at Koena curiously, ears perked up for a juicy piece of gossip. Aware of the prying eyes and sharp ears, Sagar placed a finger on Koena's arm. A gentle prod didn't evoke any reaction. The prod became stronger.

'What happened? Are you feeling alright?' Sagar finally asked, his voice filled with concern.

'I'm ok. Just tired. I think I'm growing old!' Koena sat up and tried a joke.

'Come on, I know you better than that! Something happened just now. What was it? Whose message was it? Tell me, Koena?' Sagar urged, his eyes growing bigger. He had stopped eating, too. He reached out and placed a finger on Koena's warm hand. She jumped reflexively at the touch. The finger was ice cold. Sagar had this habit of placing his index finger on people to encourage or reassure them. Where people normally would place their palms, Sagar made do with one finger. Initially, Koena had found this weird. But as time went by, she had got used to it.

'Yeah, yeah… Nothing. Just something at home. It was Shom's message.' Koena let out a whoosh and sulked, her face reflecting her state of mind.

She then looked at his plate and the uneaten food and felt sorry for him. Sagar was still looking at her, his ice cold finger lingering on her hand.

To reassure him, she continued, 'Nothing, dear. I just had a tiff with my husband. I am thinking of apologizing. That's all. Happy?'

She smiled stiffly to give credence to her statement.

Looking at her forced smile, Sagar nodded and silently finished his meal. Koena got up, too, her lunch left uneaten. She decided to polish it off later, knowing that her cook hated it when she took half-finished boxes back home.

'Shall we leave?' Sagar asked.

Silently, they made their way to their respective desks and deposited their lunch bags. Koena slumped on her chair and put her head down on the table. The shrill ring of her mobile phone made her jump. She checked the screen and immediately grabbed the phone.

Shom!

'Hi, baby!' His soft voice immediately calmed her jumpy nerves.

'Hey, sweety! Where are you? Why didn't you reply? I got so worried,' Koena cribbed.

'Shh, listen to me, shona… listen. I was getting the security screening done, and I could not reply to your message immediately. Now, I am waiting in the lounge. Since there is some time before the departure, I decided to call you. Why did you ask for my flight number? We spoke in the morning, na? Ok, never mind… note it down.' Shom said, his voice soft and reassuring.

Koena half-heartedly picked up a pen and noted his flight number. Air India. It was always Air India for Shom. He loved their service and the air-hostesses, he had once confessed. He would land in the evening and take a cab, he reassured her.

I want to hold him tight. I miss him.

She urged him to reconsider her offer of picking him up at the airport.

'No, baby, no. I have booked a cab, and you know my thoughts about wasting one's time. We live in the same house, remember? I will go home, rest, and make you a nice meal. How does that sound?' Shom crooned.

Koena imagined Shom working up a storm in their pristine kitchen and smiled automatically. It was such an endearing visual.

With some more deliberation, Koena grudgingly agreed. He did have a point. She had a lot of work. She had to submit her report as soon as possible. After exchanging virtual kisses, she disconnected. Massaging her temples, Koena lay her head on the table. The migraine that had been looming at a distance was now hovering around her, threatening to knock down her weary brain cells.

She decided to take a tablet, just in case. The tablet went down with a small mouthful of water. She needed to calm her mind.

Breathe in.

Breathe out.

Sagar came by just then to check if they could discuss the assignment. Seeing Koena's pale face, he placed a finger on her shoulder and asked, 'That damn migraine?'

Koena nodded. 'Yeah, it's on its way; I can hear it roaring. I have taken a tablet and I just need to close my eyes for a bit. Why don't you pull up a chair and sit down? Just go through the notes I made this morning and see what you can come up with.' She pushed a set of papers towards Sagar and laid her head on her folded hands above the table, closing her eyes against a dull throb.

The medicine kicked in a bit later, and her blood vessels calmed down, allowing a stream of fresh blood through her veins and soothing her aching brain. She breathed in deeply, feeling the fresh oxygen coming in. Her eyes felt heavy. Ten minutes later, the ache receded, ominously promising to visit later. The dull throb remained like a receipt for the pain. *Sigh!*

Gently massaging her temples, Koena sat up. Her eyes were bloodshot.

'Oh my, you look bad. Do you want some coffee?' Sagar asked, clucking his tongue sympathetically, his eyebrows were huddled on his forehead gossiping among themselves.

Koena nodded, taking care not to move her tender head too much in case the ache returned with a vengeance.

'Yes, I could do with a cup. Will get one. Do you want some?' Koena asked and got up to go. Sagar held her back. She felt his cold finger on her arm and recoiled slightly.

This boy is like a reptile. His hands are always cold.

'Wait, sit down. Anyway, I was about to get myself a cup. I will get you one too. Do you want some cookies to go with it?' Sagar asked, his cold finger steady on her arm. Usually, Koena would feel extremely uncomfortable asking anyone to run errands for her, but in the present condition, she didn't mind some help. She nodded and thanked him profusely. Sagar clucked his tongue and was on his way before she could register his absence.

He returned quickly, holding two mugs of steaming hot coffee and balancing a small plate of cookies on top of the mugs, doing a crazy dance. Koena laughed out loud, despite the aftermath of the migraine.

At times, the boy can be funny.

'Let me help you with that.' Koena rushed to take the cookie tray from him.

After dunking the last of the cookies into her coffee cup, Koena thanked Him for giving a reliable colleague like Sagar.

Sagar had begun working on his laptop while Koena was sipping her coffee. Koena drained her cup and focused on her child abuse assignment. They spent the next few hours working efficiently and silently.

Her voice now steadier and louder, Koena asked, 'So, what do we have here? Did you use my notes?'

'Yep. I went through them… And here… this is what I've done,' Sagar said, turning his laptop towards Koena.

One look at it, and she knew they had a winner on their hands.

Sagar had meticulously worked on the raw data she had dumped on him and created a beautiful report. She felt her heart swell with pride. But, with age came experience. She scowled, squinting just enough to enhance the look, knowing well that Sagar would notice it and feel queasy.

Her facial expressions had the desired effect. Sagar squirmed in his seat so much that the chair squeaked.

'Hmm… So, did you use all the notes I gave you, Sagar?' Koena asked, a coolness descending into her voice, looking at him over her spectacles. Her look accentuated her less than warm tone.

Sagar gulped some air before replying, a hint of nervousness dotting his voice. 'Yep, I did. Have I missed anything, Koena? I did go through it as you taught me to...' The last part was almost a mumble.

Koena knew Sagar was getting fidgety. When he mopped the perspiration with a handkerchief that materialized from a side pocket, she gave in. Laughing out loud, she said, 'Sagar, my boy, it is perrrrfffect! I was just playing with you. Am so sorry.'

She drawled out the word to express her joy at seeing something that demanded attention and eventual praise. Sagar let out a loud sigh of relief. Koena looked at the young face and realized how much her words affected him.

'Thank you so much, Koena. I have sent it to you.' He managed.

'Come on! Let's get this show on the road. I'll go, pitch it to Tim. Meanwhile, you chill for a bit.' Koena said, picking up her laptop. Sagar nodded and got up to return to his desk.

'Stay. I'll be back soon.' Koena said, gently pushing him back into his chair.

'Okay!'

On her way to Tim's cubicle, Koena wondered about her strategy for pitching the show.

If I have to wage a small battle, I will. Anything to make Tim understand the importance of this show. Sigh! I will do it.

When she reached Tim's cubicle, he was talking over the phone. Seeing her, he waved his hand, requesting her to wait. When he disconnected, he looked happy. Koena raised an inquiring eyebrow. She seldom saw him happy. Tim was always either angry or tensed. Happiness was a rarity. He leaned over and whispered, his voice conspiratorial, 'Guess what?'

Koena shrugged. She had no idea what would have set Tim going like this. Not many things actually did that. This had to be special.

'Well, we have got a new financier, and my dream project can finally see the light of the day.' Tim's announcement surprised Koena. He had been working on this dream project for a while now–he wanted to start a new channel for kids. She was one of the few people who knew about it. Koena knew this was big news, and she also uncannily knew that this was the perfect time to pitch her report.

What luck!

'Wow, I am so happy for you, Tim. Finally! When are you going to start?' Koena asked. Adding an extra dose of joy in her voice, she grinned widely.

'Soon, very soon. I am so happy. Oh, did you have anything for me?' Tim asked, eyeing her laptop questioningly.

'Oh, yes! I forgot why I came here. Tim, I'm so happy; this is finally going to happen.' Koena gushed, her voice dripping with extra-large doses of organic honey.

'Yes! Finally… I'm very thrilled, too. But keep this under wraps. Not a word. Not even a mention. And certainly not to that boy.' Tim winked, rubbing his hands in glee.

'Sagar?' Koena laughed.

'No, I won't. You can trust me on this.' Koena winked back and, as a gesture of total reassurance, patted his hand.

'I came by to show you this report Sagar and I have been working on for some time now. We would like you to go through it and give your approval. Also, it would be great if we could do prime time.' Koena knew she was treading on eggshells; Tim was extremely possessive about the prime-time slots.

He nodded thoughtfully. With a grunt, he took the laptop and started reading. He went through the report with the utmost focus and did not even glance at her once. He was also typing something.

Is he giving comments?

Koena sat silently, looking down at her phone. Shom had not messaged yet.

Would he have landed?

She typed a text message.

'Landed?'

No reply. But her message got delivered.

And then, two things happened at the same time, like how these things initially take time, make you wait. But when the providential ball gets rolling, it keeps rolling. And rolling.

Tim nodded and removed his spectacles. It was a sign; Koena knew from experience.

'I like it. I need you to make a few changes, though. I have made some notes. Go through them. I need you and Sagar to present this before the others tomorrow. Make it by 10. We will see where it goes.'

Koena's heart fluttered wildly. It was over. Approved. Just like that. Tim had agreed immediately. *What luck!* She had been mentally prepared for a battle, but there had been no need. The others–meaning the members of the committee that approved prime time programs–never opposed anything that Tim had pre-approved. After all, he was the one with the stash in the bank.

No one opposed a capitalist.

Once Tim agreed for the slot, Koena gushed with excitement, visualizing her show. Thanking Tim, she happily made her way to her desk to give the exciting news to Sagar.

Her phone beeped just then, and a text message arrived. She didn't look at it immediately. She knew it was from Shom. Walking briskly to her desk, she could not quell her curiosity, and opened the text message with one hand, giving it a quick look.

And her guess was correct.

Shona, will be late. Held up. At the police station.

Three sentences. Three solid knives that pierced her heart and stopped her in her tracks, freezing her blood.

She held on to a work station table to let the dizziness pass.

Police station! Why is Shom in the police station? Is he in trouble? Oh god! Please, please, please keep Shom safe.

Panicking and momentarily forgetting the joy of landing a prime-time slot, she called her husband. The phone rang several times, but Shom did not pick up.

She texted him instead. Her fingers flew over the keypad, life around her momentarily suspended. She looked around frantically. Searching for some solace–a glance of pity or a smile of empathy. People were in their own bubbles, worrying about their EMIs and their routines. They had no time to deal with Koena's worries.

Which police station? What happened? Pick my call.

No reply.

In full panic mode, Koena's legs pumped ahead, and she nearly ran to her desk, her heart thudding and her mind conjuring up weird and scary images of dingy police stations culled from trashy Bollywood movies. She imagined Shom hung upside down, stripped to his underwear, hanging like a piece of dirty meat....*Damn!*

Recollecting with a start that Sagar was sitting at her desk, she stopped near an empty cubicle and composed herself. She held on to the laptop tightly till her knuckles turned white.

Breathe in, breathe out. Yes. Again. Breathe in... breathe out. I will call him later. I need to first update Sagar about the slot. Breathe in... breathe out.

She walked into her cubicle wearing a forced smile. Sagar was looking intently at his laptop. She laid a hand on his shoulder, gently shaking him. He sat up, surprised.

She placed her laptop on the desk and beamed at him. Waving her hands like a conductor, she announced, 'I think you should leave early today and take rest. We have a big day tomorrow.' She smiled some more, raising her eyebrows and doing a little jig.

Sagar's eyes bulged, and a large smile broke on his face, lighting it up.

'He agreed? Oh my! Wow! Koena, you are a magician, I tell you. There is nothing in this world that you can't do. Nothing.' Sagar repeated and made an elaborate bowing action, making Koena giggle.

Smiling, Koena sat down at her desk. They had a presentation to make. She gave the downloaded notes of the meeting with Tim to Sagar and told him to prepare for the presentation.

'The committee members might ask a few important questions on the format,' she informed him ruefully.

He nodded, sulking.

'I can handle those oldies. Curmudgeons, all of them.' Sagar winked.

Koena cringed. The members were closer to her age, and she said so. Sagar bit his tongue and apologized. He touched his earlobes and mumbled apologetically.

'I don't mean that all people older than me are wet blankets. You are also older than me. But... You are so clever. You are so...gorgeous. You don't look a day older than twenty.' Sagar smiled widely, winking again. It was his way of smoothing ruffled feathers. Koena smiled, mentally agreeing that the committee members were indeed a bit uptight. Suppressing a giggle at Sagar's accurate mimicry of a committee member, Koena half-heartedly rebuked him.

'Okay, get back to work. I need to make an important call.'

Koena made her way to the reception area, which was bursting at the seams. There was no way she could have an intimate conversation there. She needed a private corner to have an uninterrupted talk. 'Uninterrupted', being the keyword.

Let me go to that landing. It is too early for smokers to congregate.

Koena called Shom once she reached the staircase landing. The call connected immediately, but someone else came on the line.

'Yes, this is Inspector Das from the A1 station. Who are you, madam?' A gruff voice asked. Koena's heart sank.

Shom was in trouble. But why?

'Uhh, I'm Koena; I mean, I am his wife... Shom Mahapatra's wife. Where is he? Why have you arrested him? What has he done? I think you're mistaken. He would not have done anything.' Koena blabbered nervously.

She clenched and unclenched her fist, trying to calm her jumpy nerves.

'See, Madam. We have not arrested your husband. We just need to ask him a few questions. We will let him go after we're done. You have to come here, too. We need to ask you a few questions as well. Note down this address. It is good that you called by yourself. We were planning to come to your office to pick you up.' The inspector said.

Koena's knees buckled. She slumped on the stairs, unmindful of the fine layer of dust that made way for her and merrily settled on her pristine off-white dress. *Ugh*! She would have to remember to dust herself.

We are being questioned. Why? What has Shom done? Thank god she called!

Unable to form coherent thoughts, Koena sat on the stairs for some time after the inspector disconnected the call. She looked once again at the text message from Shom's phone. The station was not far from the office.

Should I leave now?

■

MAY 2, 2000
TNN Office
4:00 p.m.

REALIZING THAT SHE could not do any more work, she decided to leave early and reach the police station. She didn't want anyone to come to her office in search of her. She took a few deep breaths to calm herself. Her frayed nerves weren't helping. Maybe it was about the boy Shom had taken to the clinic. Maybe the boy was a burglar or some petty criminal. Since Shom had been kind enough to help him, the police were questioning him. Maybe it was about the burglary that had happened last week at the next-door mall. Or maybe it was something else. Something very lame. Frustrated, Koena decided to just see for herself. She rushed to her desk.

'Sagar, I must leave right away. Something has come up.' Koena said, looking at Sagar for a reaction.

None. He stared at her blankly.

She shook his shoulder slightly. He shuddered as if he was suddenly brought to life.

'Yes, Yes… I understood. Okay, no problem. Go ahead.' Sagar replied, nodding and shrugging.

This boy!

Before leaving, she left detailed instructions with Sagar for the presentation the next day and extracted a promise from him that he would email her a copy of the presentation by night.

'I will email it to you… Don't worry, get going.' Sagar nodded furiously.

'Ok, thanks.'

Picking up her huge backpack, Koena left after saying a hasty bye. She had sent out an email to Tim saying she wasn't feeling well and was leaving early. By any standards, 4:00 p.m. was early.

He had replied with a single word. Ok.

Once Koena left, Sagar returned to his desk and continued working on the presentation.

■

MAY 2, 2000

Laxmi Sagar Police Station
4:15 p.m.

KOENA RUSHED TO the parking lot and took her car out. She made her way to the Laxmi Sagar police station. Within fifteen minutes, she reached the sombre building, tucked away in a dusty by-lane. She parked her car at a distance and walked to the station after furtively checking around for familiar faces. Their house was close by. They knew people who lived in that area. They still lived in times when a visit to the police station was deeply frowned upon.

Thankfully, there were no familiar faces to embitter Koena's moment of extreme panic. Paranoia was her inborn quality, and she deeply despised that characteristic. She looked around multiple times and stared at strangers to ensure nobody knew her or had even noticed her.

None. People were minding their businesses.

Emboldened, she straightened her shoulders and walked towards the station. It was milling with people. Koena immediately started perspiring in the high humidity. Sweat poured down her shoulders and armpits. She dabbed her forehead in an attempt to keep the sweat from pooling around her eyes. Inside the station, it was chaos. A group of women were talking at the same time, while a harried-looking constable was trying to write down their complaint. Four sets of tables and chairs were placed at right angles, all vying for the real estate in the small, crowded station, occupied by police officers of different grades: constables and sub-inspectors. Koena looked around, confusion clouding her mind.

Where the hell is Shom?

Straining her neck to see beyond the crowd milling around the constable, she noticed a set of rooms, their half-doors painted in olive green. A few constables made their way into one room, pushing the door flaps as they went in. Koena looked around and found a target.

She made her way to a constable who was sipping tea, perched on a table bulging with files and folders of all shapes. He was the only one who looked approachable.

'Sir, where can I find Inspector Das?'

His head jerked up at Koena's voice. Either nobody had addressed him as 'Sir', or he had probably never spoken to a woman who looked like her. In the constable's case, both statements were true. With a sloppy toothy grin, he directed her to a door set in the far corner of the packed room. Thanking him, Koena made her way to the door and knocked.

A gruff voice asked her to come in. When she stepped inside the room, Koena sucked in a breath.

There he is. My god! He looks like shit. Thankfully, he is not hanging upside down!

Shom was looking dishevelled, distraught. The inspector was staring at him, a stick loosely dangling from his right hand, his left holding a smouldering cigarette. Koena had never been inside a police station, and she momentarily wondered if the man would try to stub it on Shom's skin.

Easy, darling. This is real life. Sigh! I should not watch too much TV.

Pushing the morbid thoughts aside with extreme self-directed scorn, she cleared her throat and politely mustered, 'Hello, Sir. May I come in?'

The inspector turned and waved her in. He also managed a half-smile. Koena tried to smile in return. Her heart *was* thudding in her ears. She smoothened her black trousers and tugged at her scarf in an attempt to look less harried. Nothing worked. Her mind was in complete turmoil, her throat was parched.

'Come, Madam. Please take a seat. This will take just a few minutes. I have a few questions… Please answer them, and we will let you go.' The inspector had a jovial face, fair skin, and wide eyes, like a dancer. Koena noticed his thick shapely eyebrows and wondered if he was a part-time dancer.

She turned to look at Shom. One look at his condition and her funny thoughts about the inspector's appearance vanished. Poof.

'Sure, I'll answer any question. I'm sure there is some misunderstanding. We're normal tax-paying citizens, Sir.' Koena tried to reason with the inspector, her voice coming out like a squeak. She coughed to clear the congestion threatening to clog her voice.

The inspector smiled, his eyebrows doing a weird dance. Mouth wide open, he banged his open hand on a file and said, 'Madam, let us not go there, okay? I have all your details here.'

The dust resting on the file jumped a few inches above the files and resettled. The inspector continued, unfazed, 'Now, I just want to understand what you guys were doing last Thursday. Where was your husband yesterday and the day before? If you can answer this truthfully, you are free to go.'

Koena gulped. She had not missed the stress placed on Thursday. She gulped harder. Nothing helped. Her throat was dry, and it pained like hell to even try to swallow.

Why did he say 'let us not go there'? Was there an issue in their tax submission? Oh god! Had Shom done some terrible financial crime? Like evasion or something like that?

'Sure, Sir. So, let me see. Shom had a shoot in Kolkata. He was supposed to return today, which… he has. And I was at work, as usual…' Koena managed, clearing her throat. She looked at Shom, who was staring at an indeterminate point on the wooden desk. Koena reached out and squeezed his hand, reassuring him. His hands were freezing.

Like those of Sagar's. Why am I thinking of Sagar now?

'Madam, are you sure about this? Can you recall all your activities this week, till today?'

Koena gulped harder.

I can do this.

'Of course… So…it was a Wednesday. Shom left in the afternoon. Probably around 12:30. On Thursday, he said he had some important work in Kolkata. I'm not sure what it was. He was supposed to take the late afternoon flight while returning. This afternoon he messaged me around 1:00 p.m. saying he was boarding the flight. Here, I have the text message from him. I even have the flight details. You can take a look, Sir.' Koena took out her phone and showed the text message from Shom. The extra stress on Sir did not go unnoticed.

The inspector's answering grimace said it all. He took a cursory glance and waved it away. His focus did not waver. He kept looking at Koena and Shom, in turns. Koena dropped her phone inside her bag.

'Well, that is all I have to say,' Koena said and took a sip of water from her bottle.

'Madam, you are right about two things. Let me explain.' The inspector smiled and leaned forward. Koena tried to quell her nervousness. She could smell his cologne.

Had she missed anything?

The cold hand in hers didn't stir. Shom kept staring, *apparently* unmindful of anything happening around him.

'Shom Mahapatra did leave your home by 12:30. You are right. He also took the flight back here today. You are right again. Apart from these two facts, the rest is a blur.

'Shom Mahapatra, *apparently*, did not go to Kolkata. Instead, he went to Delhi. He was *apparently* seen with a few people suspected of being behind this blast. He also *allegedly* helped a guy get some medical help here in Bhubaneswar. We have witnesses who saw him that day. So, the open questions are: If Shom Mahapatra was supposedly in Kolkata, what was he doing in Bhubaneswar on that day? Had he come to Bhubaneswar and returned there in a day? Had he come here to help the guy? Doesn't make sense at all. If we assume that Shom was not in Bhubaneswar, we need to figure out who the liars are. These liars happen to be well-heeled members of society. This is why I want to understand who is lying. Is it Shom or our well-heeled friends? And, if either of them is lying…why are they lying? What are they trying to hide, and why? Madam, I hope you understand that I am doing my duty and trying to solve a high-profile case which has a connection with our sleepy town. You may wonder why I am concerned about a blast in Delhi that you just covered, right?'

Koena nodded to assure the inspector of her cooperation. *He is thorough… And knows everything!*

'So, it is very important that you tell me everything you remember, anything at all—even the smallest detail. Though I would very much want to grab the culprit as soon as possible, I certainly do not wish to harass an innocent person. Hope you understand.'

'Sir, I totally understand. I do appreciate that you are trying to be as fair as possible. Koena continued. 'I have recalled and recounted everything I know.'

She quickly looked at her husband and asked him, 'Shom, isn't this what you told me?' Getting no reaction from him, she turned to the inspector and said, 'No, Sir. This is exactly how it happened. I remember clearly.'

A niggling thought troubled her; a flash of memory crossed her conscious mind, and worry stabbed her heart.

Had Shom even gone to Kolkata? Hadn't Dr. Partho met him the other day? Oh god! What was happening?

'Madam, I'm sure you're right about the chronology of events. Events which *you are aware of*.' The pause and the stress on the last few words sent a cold shiver down Koena's spine. The hand in hers shook a bit, making her shiver more pronounced. A sense of terrible foreboding hit her. Her heartbeat plummeted, making her feel light-headed. She held the arm of the chair to steady herself.

'Shom did catch a flight. Not to Kolkata… But to Delhi. We received some intelligence reports that a prominent restaurateur was involved in the explosion in Delhi that happened yesterday. I know what you're thinking. It could be anybody. Yes, it could be someone else, also. I'm being honest with you. My job is to investigate and grill anyone on the radar.'

'Are you…' Koena's voice caught in her throat while her rational mind grappled to make sense of this new shred of information. She cleared her throat. 'Are you suggesting that you do not have conclusive evidence that Shom was behind the blast?' Her mind was already clearing and making sense of the entire incident. The hand resting in hers became still once again.

Oh god! Thank you so much. They were questioning him only because he had a fucking restaurant in the city. God!

'Yes, madam. I'm afraid so… It is pure speculation, and we're questioning everyone. We have rounded up a list of probable suspects, and your husband is one of them. He has already shared his flight details, which we have cross-checked. He did travel to Kolkata. But I also have a report and a few witnesses who say that a man matching his description travelled to Delhi and was seen in the Civil Lines area. This man bought some suspicious items and paid by cash. When asked, he reportedly threw the name of a restaurant and said he owned it.'

'If it was Shom, why would he reveal his identity? And what was the name of the restaurant?' Koena asked, her hands still trembling. She squeezed Shom's hand and waited with bated breath.

'You're correct. We're not sure about the name. Our witness is not able to recollect the name.' The inspector agreed, adding, 'Unfortunately.'

He suddenly seemed unsure and looked almost apologetic.

Koena reassured him. 'I understand you're just doing your duty, Sir. We're honest citizens. We will cooperate in any way we can. Let me assure you that we are strictly against such anti-national and anti-social elements and have absolutely no compassion for such people. I speak for my husband, too. Shom is an honest and law-abiding citizen. We have never done anything to harm anyone. I assure you that we will help you in any way we can. Wouldn't we, Shom?' She finished, wishing that he would wake up from his slumber and say something, anything at all. She pressed the hand harder, nudging him to rouse himself up from the stupor. His silence was scaring her.

Why is he so silent? Is he guilty? Does this have anything to do with that useless friend of his who he had accompanied to the clinic?

'Uh, yes... Yes, inspector Das. I have already told you what I had to. I have... nothing more to say. If you don't mind, I want to go home. I'm not feeling well.' Shom finally managed.

Koena turned sharply to take in his condition. His voice sounded hoarse. His eyes were unfocused and he looked sick. She took out the water bottle from her bag and passed it to her husband. He gladly took a large gulp and smiled at her.

For the first time since she had arrived.

'Okay, in that case... I guess I have nothing else to ask. But let me warn you. This is just the preliminary questioning. We have just started the investigation, and we may have to call you several times for questioning. Please cooperate with us. And one more thing...' The inspector paused for effect. His tone and expression did not match, making Koena shudder.

Koena and Shom had stood up but waited for him to complete his sentence.

'You cannot travel outside the country or even leave town without my explicit permission. Written permission.' He nodded for effect and to reinforce his authority.

Koena and Shom nodded. She was still holding his hand. It was warm now.

'So, may we leave, Sir?' Koena asked, using her sweetest voice. The drawled out 'Sir' lingered in the air.

'Yes, you may.' The response was immediate. The inspector had started looking at some files and had already mentally dismissed them.

The couple left the station, hurrying through the late evening crowd milling around the area. They walked in silence until they reached the car. After surreptitiously checking the surrounding area, Koena unlocked the car and they got in. Koena locked the doors immediately. Shom didn't say a word as he got in. He closed his eyes and lay his head on the headrest. Koena put the car in gear and made her way to the main road. After the harrowing experience, she needed something strong.

Whisky! Whisky! Whisky. Her mind repeated.

Some whisky would be ideal. *Sigh. On the rocks, please.*

I need to drink something hot to make me feel human.

On their way, she pulled over at a small café, bought two strong cappuccinos, and handed one to Shom. He sipped his coffee and thanked her. Nodding, Koena sat silently, staring at the passing cars. She knew the 'thanks' was more for her presence and not only for getting him coffee.

'Shall we go?' Koena asked gently, collecting the empty cups and throwing them in the bin.

Shom nodded, still not meeting her eyes. His silence was torturing her. His eyes looked dead.

Is he hiding something?

The familiar feeling of foreboding returned. With a vengeance. Koena tried hard to focus on the road. They were just ten minutes away from home. She wanted to compose herself before attempting to speak with Shom.

■

MAY 2, 2000

Ashiana Apartments
7:30 p.m.

WHEN SHE FINALLY parked the car in their apartment's parking lot, she heaved a sigh of relief. Finally, they were home. It was already evening. Her shoulders were aching, and her head was throbbing again.

She got out after picking up her backpack from the rear seat. Shom had gotten out as soon as she had pulled into the parking, without even waiting for her to turn the ignition off. *Strange.*

Koena mused as she made her way to the elevators.

When she reached home, the door was ajar. Shom had left it open. She entered and moved in. The shower was running in the master bedroom. Sighing, she plonked down on her bed.

The cook had left after preparing dinner. In the Mahapatra household, it was always roti and two types of vegetable curries for dinner. The familiar smells and sounds soothed Koena's frayed nerves. She realized she needed a hot shower, too.

She grabbed a towel and her night-dress and went to the bathroom in the guest bedroom.

The hot water shocked her initially. The spray eventually felt nice on her warm and sticky skin, and she stood under the showerhead without moving a muscle. She closed her eyes and let the water wash away the day's stress. After enjoying it for a few more minutes, she finished her bath and stepped out.

Is there a way to cleanse my mind? And my soul?

Shom was sitting on the bed when she came out. He looked like a little boy; his wet head bent over his chest. Her heart went out to him, and she rushed to hug him, 'I love you, Shona. You are my lifeline. Without you, I am nothing.' Shom whispered in her hair and kissed her silky wet head.

'I love you too, baby,' Koena whispered.

'Let's get some food. I will go, set the table' Shom suggested, gently releasing her. Koena nodded.

The mention of food made her realize that she was famished. She could hear Shom pottering around in the kitchen, getting plates and spoons. By the time Koena dressed and emerged from the guest bedroom, Shom had laid the table. She pulled a chair and sat down.

Shom lovingly placed two rotis and served some curry in a small bowl. Koena waited for him to join. He took three rotis and curry and sat down opposite her. Chewing a mouthful, he looked at her and said, 'Shona, we will talk. We have to talk. First, let us finish dinner.'

Koena jumped; a bit startled. Shom had this innate ability to pluck thoughts out of her brain and put them into words. She mutely nodded. He smiled and held out a hand. She placed her hand in his, and he squeezed it, reassuring her.

After dinner, they silently cleared the table. Shom got busy making two cups of hot chocolate while Koena arranged the cushions on the floor in their bedroom to set the stage for what, she imagined, would be a long discussion session. Shom came in carrying a tray loaded with cookies and hot chocolate.

It was a ritual in their household. Any important discussion, be it Koena's job offer, their son Kit's admission to a boarding school, or even seemingly inane issues had been dealt with, and discussed late into the night in this set-up. The drink was varied. The ritual didn't.

There were only two rules:

1. Each person had the right to speak their mind without using expletives or getting touchy or emotional.
2. The other had to listen carefully without judging or interrupting.

Shom smiled and handed a cup to Koena. She sighed and took a sip, relishing the heavenly concoction, which travelled smoothly down her throat, leaving behind a chocolaty feel. Shom then slumped down on the floor and took a sip, his eyes fixed on his cup.

'So...' Koena started, placing her cup on the tray and reaching out for a cookie.

'So. Where do we start?' Shom replied, taking a large sip of his drink. He took one cookie and dunked it in, putting it in his mouth before it could melt. Koena nodded and munched on a cookie, noticing for the first time that it had blueberries – her favourite.

'There are blueberries in this. Wow!' She exclaimed.

'Yes, Shona. I made them before leaving for Kolkata. Forgot to mention.' Shom continued munching on the cookie, his brows drawn, making him look serious. He then gave a lopsided smile, making her heart flip.

Koena waited.

'Shona. Whatever happened today at the police station was very unfortunate. I'm sorry you got dragged into it. I really am.' Shom paused.

Koena nodded.

'I did go to Kolkata, and we did have a shoot. I had to return to Bhubaneswar to take care of an urgent matter. Then I flew back the same day.' Shom said and waited for her reaction.

'Well. That was short.' Koena sighed, chewing on a cookie. 'Now, what was this urgent matter?'

'Hmm. So… There are a few things you do not know about me.' Shom paused to take a sip and dunk another cookie.

Koena stared at her husband. *Things I did not know about him…what does he mean?*

'I work with an organization, besides running my restaurant. You know about my politically communist leanings. You might also be aware that I am a Naxal sympathizer. Few years back, when I was in London, I met a guy who introduced me to some people… some like-minded people who have come together to achieve an objective. I have been working with them for a year now. I don't want you to know anything more than this. I don't generally discuss this part of my life because you know how people look down upon communists and nax… others…' Shom took a long sip from his cup and scanned Koena's face for a reaction.

'That's quite an important part, I must say.' Koena stared at him, her heartbeat rising. 'Is that all?' She demanded, her raised eyebrows vanishing into her hairline.

Did he just say that he was a Naxalite? Oh lord! Could she just rewind the day? Please, God!

Shom nodded. 'Yep, that is it.'

His soft voice soothed her fears. and she almost felt normal. Almost.

'So, what were you doing in Bhubaneswar the other day? And why didn't you call me? Why didn't you confide in me at least?' She asked, not willing to let it go that easily. The remaining portions of her questions hung in her head, unsaid and unformed.

Like an unwanted foetus.

'Shona, I really was in a hurry. I just didn't have the time. I had to complete a task and rush back.' Shom looked upset; something about that face confused her. Koena decided not to press further. His cryptic replies were leaving her flabbergasted.

What kind of organization is this man working for?

'I got your parcel from Dr. Partho's Clinic.' She diverted and waited for his response.

'Oh, great. He called me…Where is it?' Shom asked.

Koena leaned over and dragged her backpack from near the bed, where she had dumped it earlier. She took the parcel out and handed it to Shom. He unwrapped it quickly and checked the contents. She watched his face for tell-tale signs. Out fell a folder.

What did the folder contain? Not that he is going to tell me…

'So, what do you do in this organization, Shom? Is it dangerous?' Koena asked gently, willing to know more details.

'There's no need for you to know, Shona. All you need to know is what I have already told you. I told you all this because we ended up at the police station today. It will never happen again. Even this slip happened because of that silly boy – a new boy who joined us last month…He ended up injuring himself. Since I am in charge of recruits in Bhubaneswar, I had to personally attend to the situation and take him to Dr Partho. I didn't realize the police were watching me. I revealed myself. Unnecessarily.'

Revealed! What does he mean by that?

Koena nodded. It was more of an automatic reaction rather than an acceptance of his statement.

'So, are we okay?' Shom leaned forward and cupped her face, his eyes warm and open.

Koena sighed. *No, it is not ok.*

Then she nodded slowly, hugged him, and closed her eyes, inhaling his musky smell.

I am going to wake up anytime now, and all this will have been just a big nightmare.

But reality did intrude.

Ok. I am not dreaming. What else is he hiding?

She opened her eyes, but nothing had changed. Shom got up and sat on the bed. Koena pulled up a chair nearby and plonked on it, exhausted. Slowly, they drifted to regular domestic topics. Soon after, they went to bed.

Broken hearts and dishevelled thoughts do not make good bedmates, though.

Koena turned on her side and closed her eyes. Tears flowed softly, staining the satin pillowcase. Their relationship had changed irrevocably. She knew it would never be the same again.

I know. I know it in my heart. There is more, and it has always been so.

She couldn't sleep at all and kept tossing and turning the whole night. Shom started snoring softly as soon as his head hit the pillow.

■

MAY 3, 2000

Ashiana Apartments

5:30 a.m.

THE NEXT MORNING, when the cook came to wake them up with coffee, the couple was already up and about.

'Shona…hope you remember that we have the Deys' pool party today. We missed Guptaji's party yesterday!' Shom said, his back turned towards Koena. She was sitting at the dining table, her brows knit, fingers flying over the keyboard. She looked up, startled, at the mention of the pool party. Shom was going through some messages on his laptop.

Don't I have to meet Shreya in the evening? How did I forget?

'Hmmm. Deys' pool party. Oh yeah… Is it today? It slipped my mind. I haven't even selected my dress. I have put on some flab… on my tummy, I think. But you know what, Shom? I am so excited! It has been almost a month since we attended a party. We missed the one yesterday also… hmm… let's take the BMW.' Koena rattled, visibly distracted from work, patting her non-existent tummy as proof.

Shom briefly glanced at her tummy, then up at her face with a funny expression. He strode up to her and shook his wet head vigorously, dislodging some water droplets that promptly landed on her, making her squeal.

'No, Shona. You're just perfect. Even I was thinking of taking the BMW out. It has been a while since I was driven around.' Shom added, grinning at her.

'Cool. Will come early from work, then. I need time to dress up.' Koena got up and rushed out after pecking his cheek.

I will meet Shreya also sometime during the lunch hour. I will send her a text from the car.

Mr. Dey was an important man in the scheme of things for Shom, and he didn't want to let go of any opportunity to mingle with the high and mighty of Bhubaneswar's Page 3 circuit.

Koena was more worried about the garrulous Mrs. Dey, who would pounce on her and pester for arranging an interview. Koena had told the woman many times that she was not a print journalist and therefore could not do an interview, but Mrs. Dey failed to register this piece of information, infuriating Koena further.

The day swept by in a daze of haphazard meetings and unaccounted for hours spent in deep contemplation about how things had supposedly panned out, leaving no doubts about the contents of the near future. During lunch hour, Koena called the familiar number and asked for an appointment with her therapist, Shreya Basu. A quick chat with Shreya, and she felt at peace with whatever Fate had thrown at her.

Koena had met Shreya at the insistence of her gynaecologist when she was going through post-partum blues. But after the initial sessions, when she noticed the improvements, she clung on. Over the years, Shreya had helped Koena navigate very tricky paths.

She had even taught Koena some tricks to handle her inner demons that arose occasionally, threatening to upset her carefully orchestrated life.

Shreya knew her so well and could understand the deepest of emotions running in her mind; like how she had caught up with the demons running amok.

That afternoon, Koena rushed to Shreya's clinic.

'Demons are troubling you too much, K?' Shreya asked, gently pushing Koena back on the couch and urging Koena to close her eyes. In a hypnotherapy session later, Shreya gave Koena advice on how to handle the latest upheavals in her life, and how Koena had to train her mind to stay away from the effects of the traumatic childhood incident. She made Koena intone, 'I am a whole person. I am healed, and I have the right to live a happy life.'

Shreya urged her to repeat the sentences even when she felt better or was at work, explaining that it was very easy for her subconscious mind to pounce on her unannounced. Shreya reiterated the fact that Koena's urges and unnatural attractions were just a way of her subconscious mind attacking her. Shreya had explained during the initial sessions that childhood trauma usually caused such unnerving emotions to surface and force the subjects to take rash decisions. Shreya made Koena promise that the latter would keep strict tabs on any runaway thoughts. Thanking Shreya profusely and promising to meet her soon for the next appointment, Koena made her way back to her office.

Now, I can go on for some time. I can focus on mundane issues like dresses, socializing... and my Naxalite husband. Sigh!

On her way back home that evening, Koena's brain kept going over her wardrobe, sifting, pausing, and reflecting on the appropriate dress to be worn, befitting the occasion: Mrs. and Mr. Dey's anniversary party being held at The Resident, a swanky five-star hotel that was in the news for its grandeur. By the Poolside—as the stylishly designed invitation proudly proclaimed.

Koena zeroed in on a black sleeveless gown she had picked up from Paris the previous year. And while making her way upstairs from the parking, she mentally matched her dress with the appropriate accessories.

When she turned the key, she could hear the TV blaring in the master bedroom. Shom was up and about. She kicked off her sandals and walked into the bedroom.

'Hey sweety, I'm back! Oh my...Somebody is looking very handsome...' She threw her bag on the bed and gave a quick peck on her husband's neck. He was standing in front of the mirror, adjusting his tie.

Shom never needed any guidance with selecting his clothes. He somehow always knew what worked best to impress the party-goers in his circuit. The elites of Bhubaneswar were a picky lot. They were not impressed with the mere presence of Hermes ties or Gucci apparel on anyone's body. They demanded contemplative attention to every detail when it came to accepting members into their erudite fold. Shom had wined and dined with these people, elucidating the appropriate responses at accurate times and ended up in the list of must-have invitees. Always.

A proud proclamation of this fact had become the highlight of a recent impromptu party thrown by a certain high-flying media baron and his journalist wife.

'How do I look?' Shom turned smartly, an eyebrow raised in an amused sort of way.

Koena showed a thumbs-up sign and blew a kiss in his direction before rushing into the bathroom for a shower. Dressing quickly, Koena and Shom rushed out of their flat to their car, and their smartly dressed chauffeur opened the door after saluting. Shom used the services of a chauffeur when he wanted to impress people or wanted to reinforce his standing within the circle.

For that evening, both reasons were applicable.

Mr. Dey had a certain stake in a certain deal, and this percentage was known to a select few in his inner circle. Shom had been trying to break into this inner circle for a while now to grab a piece of a certain lucrative pie.

Koena knew all about this deal. Shom had been fostering a keen interest in inking a deal with Mr. Dey in order to further his business interests in the international arena after a successful home run by opening a couple of outlets of his restaurant abroad. By the time they reached the venue, it was jam-packed with the who's who of the Eastern city. Rubbing shoulders with the moneyed and the powerful, Shom glided in and out easily, with Koena following close behind, making heads turn in her elegant ensemble. She knew where she had to focus today. Weaving in and out, effortlessly air-kissing, dropping hellos and smiling, they made their way to the hosts of the evening.

A tall and lanky man, holding a fine cut glass half-filled with expensive scotch, was blocking Koena's way, grinning down at her. Koena looked up at the six-footer, stretching her neck. Frowning, she looked around and craned her neck to locate Shom, who had vanished suddenly, melting into the crowd of well-heeled gentries. She realized that signalling won't work for obvious reasons. He had gone ahead and was deep in conversation with someone.

After waiting a few seconds for Koena to catch up, Shom started getting impatient. He could see a man blocking her way. Excusing himself, Shom made his way towards the man and lightly touched his shoulder. 'Excuse me, do you mind?'

He held out a hand to Koena, who grabbed it gladly. The man turned around, too, making Shom exclaim loudly. Much to the unexpressed surprise of the assembled guests and those within immediate proximity.

'Bro!' Loud back-slaps followed by exuberant exclamations of eternal friendship bonds and reminiscences followed. Other guests soon lost interest in the gleeful reunion and moved away, refilling their glasses and their brains with idle gossip.

'Shom?' Koena cleared her throat after a while.

Shom turned to her. 'Babe! This is Chary… Err… my college buddy. I'm meeting him after a long gap. Isn't it wonderful?'

Koena nodded sagely, wondering how quickly the emergence of a long-lost buddy could initiate the dissolution of goals that had seemed set in stone until a few minutes ago. Nodding warmly to the guest and enquiring after his health, Koena soon reconfirmed her worst suspicion —that Shom was planning to leave the party early to catch up with his friend. Whoa! Now, that was something unheard of.

'Are you saying we have to leave now? We just arrived, honey.' Koena eventually managed, on the verge of losing her composure. She had been looking forward to an evening of good food and quality alcohol.

'Babe, I'm just going to go, catch Mr. Dey and excuse ourselves. Are you cool with that? If you want to stay on, I'll totally understand. I'll leave the car behind. You can come by yourself.'

As soon as Shom suggested this, Koena shook her head. 'No, no, not done. I am not staying without you. I have no interest in hobnobbing with these guys without a purpose. Remember, we had a purpose when we came here.' Koena gently reminded him, looking at the guests to check if there were any curious onlookers. None seemed interested. The disappointed look on Shom's face made Koena change tactics.

She shrugged resignedly.

Why did I even bother to dress up?!

'Babe, I just want to catch up...' Shom was almost pleading now. His expression could melt a rock. It brought a smile to Koena's lips.

'Fine,' Koena agreed and broke into a wide smile. The three of them quickly said their byes to the hosts and left the party. The trio then headed out to a cosy Thai place near the couple's apartment and found a secluded corner. The men got into a hushed conversation even as they waited to be seated. The maître d' ushered them in.

'So, what do you do, Koena? Where are you from? You don't look like you are from Bhubaneswar.' Chary asked, pulling a chair out for her.

How sweet! Koena gave him full marks for the chivalrous behaviour.

'I work with a TV network...' She paused, seeing Chary's pleasant face morph into a strange expression.

'What?' Koena asked, unable to bear the suspense.

'Well, I was always sure my dear friend would marry somebody who believed in reaffirming the capitalist mentality…I never expected him to get into bed with the media.' Shom's loud guffaw made Koena realize that Chary had pulled a fast one at her expense. It hurt her ego to be referred to in such a demeaning, condescending manner. Trying hard not to take offence, she countered, her cheeks flaming red, blood rushing to help her in her reaction, 'Come on. I'm not a part of the bourgeoisie, and you know that. I'm just a normal working woman, trying to earn her bread.' Koena then shrugged, looking at Chary and Shom in turns.

Chary stared at her, taking in her face and then slowly nodded. 'Worry about the working class, ever, Miss?' He asked, eyebrows raised, tone questioning, and eyes demanding. He crossed his lean fingers and rested his chin on them, his eyes fixed on her face.

'Why should I worry about the working class?' Koena demanded, staring back at Chary. She suddenly felt warm. Blood was rushing to her temples, giving her an overall warm feeling. A dull throb had formed in her skull.

Oh no! Not now. Not now.

'Am I the government?' She continued, unfazed by the sudden sullenness she had noticed on Shom's face. 'Why should I worry about somebody who doesn't contribute to the working of this country? I work my ass off, and these people live off my hard-earned tax money. All some people do is just blow up buildings in the name of some obscure movement, or some stupid belief. Why should I pay for all that drama? Do I look like I care? I'm sorry, I don't give a damn about the workers or the working class. All I care about is my husband and my son. And my life.'

'Well. Koena, all I'm trying to say is that people like you and Shom should do more for the working-class people. Work with us. Together, we can ensure we move towards a pro-proletarian approach. I'm not seeing any involvement from people like you, Koena.' Chary paused and looked at Shom first and then at his phone, quickly checking his messages.

Koena opened her mouth to counter when she felt a gentle tug on her arm. It was a sign. To let go. She shot an angry glance at her calm and collected husband. Shom cleared his throat and said, 'Let us order food first. Koena, what would you like?'

'A scotch, please… on the rocks. Make it double. Please.' Koena said, rubbing her forehead lightly with her fingers. The dull ache had finally made its presence known and was threatening to make a cozy home. With his insolent questioning, Chary had managed to arouse her deep curiosity about many things. Koena sometimes hated her curious streak, especially when there were troubling outcomes. She threw a murderous glance at both men and focused on the menu.

Suddenly, the evening seemed to drag, and she felt her energy levels moving southwards. This man, Chary, had managed to stir deep unrest in her. An unknown feeling that Koena was unable to nail. She stared hard at Chary, wondering what about the man was disturbing her.

While Koena engaged her furious brain in scrutinizing Chary, the men were in a deep conversation after a brief spell of silence. Koena forced herself to notice the other diners. The restaurant was quite crowded, and she observed various people, like the lovey-dovey couple next to the pillar, or the man sitting by himself, reading the papers. Chary kept pulling Koena into their conversation, asking her opinion on different topics. Shom seemed a bit uncomfortable about this forced intrusion but didn't say anything aloud. Koena kept Chary humoured by responding to his curious questions. Her responses in no way reflected her true beliefs or ideologies related to the questions that Chary threw at her.

"Koena, what do you feel about the Government's bill on child trafficking?" "Would you like to visit our workplace some time?" "Have you ever lived in the collieries, Koena?" "Koena, do you like your fish steamed or grilled?" "Where are your parents from, Koena?"

This man! How many questions he has! Sigh!

They placed their food order soon enough, and Koena resigned herself to being a silent spectator, nodding occasionally when the men looked in her direction. After the food arrived, she found herself suitably occupied. The rice preparation was subtle, and the flavour reminded Koena of a dish she had eaten on a trip to Indonesia. Shom and Chary ate in silence, and Koena kept herself busy by browsing through her phone.

Chary's next question threw her off guard.

'Koena, what are your thoughts about the Naxal movement?' His eyes seemed cold and distant. Koena spluttered and coughed. Her eyes urgently sought out Shom's, but he had conveniently gotten busy with the menu card. *Again!*

What is the man seeing in the damn menu card?

Chary offered her a glass of water, which she took gladly. After gulping some of it, she decided to handle his curiosity once and for all.

'I have no particular opinions about the movement. I actually do not have any idea about it, nor have I been interested in learning about it. I feel they are a huge strain on our economy. All they do is kill people, ruin existing infrastructure, and create chaos. I've never heard of Naxalites who have done anything good. Take, for example, this incident that happened in Delhi. Who was responsible for it? Naxalites, right? They are a huge, unnecessary burden on our system.' Koena felt awkward after the outburst. She quickly scanned Shom's inscrutable face for a reaction. Any reaction at all.

None. It is as if the man wants me to be grilled.

The only reaction was from Chary, who gave her a lopsided grin and shook his head. Koena decided to pull her husband into the duel.

How dare he drag her into this silly debate?

'Shom, your friend seems very keen to interview me. Hope he does not work with a rival channel!' Koena chuckled, staring at her husband, invoking a loud guffaw from Chary.

Shom finally reacted, 'Well, shona, I'm sure you are very much capable of handling any such discomfiture that lands on your plate. That said, Chary and I go back a long way... And let me tell you that such difficult conversations are Chary's way of getting to know you. I'm just allowing my best friend to become friends with my wife.'

Shom's smile seemed to say much more than he had allowed himself to verbally express. Koena slowly raised her eyes to look at Chary, who was staring at her with an indeterminable expression on his handsome chiselled face.

Koena gulped. A strange feeling enveloped her.

Why is he eliciting such a reaction from me? There, there... don't overreact. He must be the whacko type who likes to grill people before deciding whether to like them or not.

She drank some cold water, her mind whizzing with disturbing thoughts.

'Okay,' She managed to mutter, her throat dry. She gulped some more cold water nervously. Chary's eyes never left her face. Koena picked up her whiskey and gulped it down, ice cubes and all. It travelled fast inside her, burning a trail.

During dinner, she kept her eyes averted and avoided any chance of meeting Chary's inquisitive eyes. She kept herself busy by looking at Shom and the other diners. Eventually, Chary seemed to lose interest in her. After a while, Shom reached out under the table and squeezed her hand. Koena immediately felt better, and turned and smiled at her husband.

When they asked for the check, Koena excused herself and rushed to the ladies washroom.

Shom and Chary walked ahead and were waiting for her near the door. Shom took her hand and said, 'Shona, take care. Go home and rest. I will return as soon as I can. Alright?' Koena nodded mutely, unable to process whatever was happening around her. 'When will you come?' She blurted.

'I will... We have some business to settle.' Shom's face was impassive. Chary was busy with his phone.

Koena said her byes and got into the waiting car and didn't turn back to look. Even once.

When she reached home, she checked her phone and saw a message from Shom.

'Reached?'

'Yes…' she typed and added, 'Come soon. Love you.'

Pat came the reply: 'Sure.'

Koena changed into her night dress and started working on her project. By the time Shom came in, she had dozed off.

Somewhere around midnight, Shom tiptoed into the bedroom, so as to not disturb her. But his mere presence woke her up. And, try as she might, Koena could not go back to sleep. She was feeling restless and woke up upon hearing Shom pottering around in the bathroom. She got up and trotted to the bathroom, her head a mess, thoughts running in circles.

'Baby, who was he? Why have I never met him?' Koena murmured, engulfing Shom's shirtless torso with her arms and planting a soft kiss on his bare back.

'Shona, I told you, right? I am part of an organization. He heads it. We were friends back in college. I learned about this organization from him. He has come down to Bhubaneswar to meet some important people, and I offered to help him meet them.'

'Oh, sweety, I thought you were not going to pursue this… this organization thingie… Didn't you say something of that sort the other day?' Koena murmured, nuzzling her nose into his skin. She could not believe that Shom was still keen on continuing.

Why can't he be like normal people? He smells divine. Sigh! He has the best skin in the world.

'Babe, listen to me.' Shom said, staring at her in the mirror. His muscles tensed up, and Koena ran a soft hand over them, slowly kneading his tight shoulders. Shom brushed her hand aside softly and turned to look at her, holding her gaze. He held her firmly by her shoulders and shook her lightly.

'Listen to me, Koena!'

No babes, no shona, no honey. Uh oh. This was trouble.

'Yeah…' Koena murmured, fully aware of what he was going to say.

'I don't want to discuss this anymore. Never. You are to forget what transpired that day. Let me repeat. Never mention this to anyone. Do you understand?' Shom shook her a bit as if trying to drizzle the idea down into her stubborn head.

'Yeah, Yeah… I got it. Relax.' Koena murmured, softly rubbing the arm holding her. Shom turned around abruptly and finished washing his face before putting on a nightshirt. *Why is my life going southwards? Has somebody cast an evil eye? Sigh…*

With her mood successfully dampened, Koena wished a hushed goodnight and plonked on her side of the bed. She could hear Shom tidy up and check the locks in the living room. She closed her tired eyes to rid herself of the rising sense of doom. She forced her tired brain to visualize a pleasant scene. Her mind refused to cooperate.

Ugliness rears its head when you least expect it. Some moments lie dormant – forgotten almost – but they remain steadfast in their stickiness to the hosts, our brain cells, creating a newer schema and getting kicked into the consciousness when the opportunity presents itself.

When Shom finally came to bed, she lay motionless and did not stir when his hand landed on her belly. She forced herself to breathe softly, and as expected, he took his hand away, turned to the other side, and fell asleep.

Lying wide awake for the rest of the night, Koena kept churning the new information in her mind.

What were they discussing at the restaurant? Are they planning some attack?

Sigh! I am a mess.

■

MAY 3, 2000

Ashiana Apartments

6:00 a.m.

THEY ATE AN early breakfast in silence. The cook came to check twice, and both Koena and Shom wanted a refill. After eating heartily, Koena asked the cook for some black coffee, her all-time favourite. Shom preferred to make his special herbal tea by himself.

While sipping her coffee, Koena recollected that she had an important presentation to focus on. But her brain refused to cooperate. She was feeling drained and sleep-deprived and decided to take a small nap. She informed Shom, who simply nodded.

Lying on her bed, Koena slowly stretched out her legs. Her muscles felt sore. There was also a dull ache in her legs. She pulled the comforter over her head and closed her eyes, falling asleep almost immediately. When she got up, it was 8:30 a.m.

Hurriedly, Koena got ready and rushed to work. She could see Shom in the study, typing away furiously at his computer. She didn't want to disturb him, so she just peered in and waved. He threw a flying kiss at her and waved back.

That was that. Sigh. This man can get really involved in his work.

Strangely, the office parking lot was practically empty even at this hour. Koena gleefully tried out two slots before finalizing one. She quickly rode the elevator up to her office, which was nearly empty. She could see a few people here and there, working at their desks. Laila was in, looking resplendent, and wished her a cheerful morning. The watchman was also around, sipping his morning chai as he wished her and let her in.

She reached her desk and pulled out her laptop. While it booted, she craned her neck to see if the coffee guy had arrived.

He had.

Thank God for small mercies. Of course, he comes in early.

She got herself a cup of coffee and a plate of cookies and got to work. Sagar had sent her the presentation as promised, and he had done a damn good job of it. Koena smiled at his perfectionist streak. She made minor changes to the presentation and saved it in a local network folder.

Koena checked if Sagar had sent out the meeting invites. He had. She verified the date and time. Everything was perfect.

Koena looked around for Sagar, who was nowhere to be seen. The boy usually came in early. Shrugging, she returned to her desk.

At around 09:45 AM, Sagar walked over, looking anything but fresh. Koena clucked her tongue and enquired sympathetically, 'Tch, tch! What happened to you? Why are you so late? We have to go over the deck once, remember?'

Sagar slumped into a chair and massaged his temples. 'Yesterday, it was you. Today, it is me. I have a terrible headache. Is it okay if you make the presentation all by yourself?'

Koena retorted, 'No, it is not okay. This is a golden chance for you to impress the members. I won't let you throw it away. Come on, take a tablet, wash your face, and come to the meeting room.'

Koena got up, gently patting his back. Sagar groaned and pushed himself up from the chair.

'Okay? Will see you in the meeting room!' Koena said after ensuring he was carrying a tablet.

He nodded, reaching out into his pocket and pulling out a strip. Gobbling one with water, Sagar freshened up.

Finally, at 11 o'clock, the presentation got over. The members seemed pleased with the idea and the effort, and they promised that Koena would get a prime slot for her program. Sagar and Koena high-fived after the members left.

Now, they had a bigger task ahead—the actual implementation of the program! It looked like making Tim have a baby would have been easier! They knew they had to plan it meticulously. No other regional channel had done such a talk show, and Tim had sounded quite encouraging.

But Koena knew that in no time, he would be shitting bricks. She felt nervous excitement coursing through her limbs. Strangely, the nervousness remained in her lower extremities and did not travel to her head. Her mind was frightfully calm. Crystal clear.

While they were packing up their stuff, Tim stopped by to discuss the members' thoughts.

'Guys, it is on.' Tim declared with a thumbs-up. Koena and Sagar let out a whoop of joy.

Tim continued, 'We are launching in a month, and we got the 10 p.m. slot. You know we have the saas-bahu thing running at 9:30, so our program is immediately after it.'

'Sure, Tim, that is great news.' Koena gushed, her mind methodically going over nitty-gritty details. Pushing the thoughts aside, she asked, 'So when do we shoot?'

'ASAP, Koena.' Tim replied, looking all energetic and pumped up. 'We have to shoot two episodes first. We will use the studio for the shoot, and that's about it. Call if you have any questions. Ciao.'

Koena was perfectly fine with the conditions. Tim smiled for the second time in a day. Koena knew that within the concrete, tough exterior was a gentle human being. Though she was mainly in awe of Tim, she was also quite fond of him.

Tim excused himself, and Sagar and Koena got down to their task. They had a lot of work and very little time. They grabbed a cup of coffee each before huddling at Koena's desk to work out the program details. While Koena went through the notes Sagar had made, she looked up, startled.

How had she missed this?

'Sagar, how can we invite Gordy? You know who he is, right?'

Their show was about people who had braved odds and fought against abuse to make a name for themselves. Sagar had suggested that they invite a fiery communist activist called Gordy Raghav to the show.

'Yeah… I know.' Sagar looked at Koena with a strange expression.

'Then? Why the… Why have you invited him? Has Tim seen this? I don't think we had given his name in the presentation. Why and when did you add it?' Koena was getting worried now. *What was Sagar playing at?*

'Tsk, tsk… Koena, listen to me, I have thought about it. I feel Gordy would be a great addition to this show. Make it more… umm, let me see… scandalous. He will help us deliver the bang. And you know very well that any new show needs some bang to make it big. Anyway, we will be giving him a script that he has to follow. So why are you worrying?'

'No way. This man is a social pariah. We cannot have him on our show and give him credibility. Tim will never allow…'

'He knows, Koena.' Sagar interjected softly, waiting for her reaction, staring at her unblinkingly.

'What?' Koena's shock was complete. Her hands shook a bit with anger.

How? When? Am I missing something?

'When did you speak with him?' Her head was spinning now.

Is he working behind my back?

'When you were on your call, Tim came by and wanted to see the list of invitees. I just casually asked if I could invite Gordy too. He liked it and immediately agreed that it was a great idea.'

'Sagar, are you by any chance making this up?' Koena could still not believe it.

Sagar shook his head. 'No, Koena.'

'I need to verify this. I'll be back. You wait right here.' Koena warned Sagar before storming off to find her boss. She found Tim at the water cooler, filling his water bottle.

'Hey there.' Tim waved when he saw her.

'Hey, Tim. I wanted to know if you have okayed Gordy as a guest on the show.' Koena asked directly.

'Yes. I did. Sagar said you had given him the idea and wanted to confirm if I was fine with it. I am. So, I said go ahead. It is indeed a great idea. Let us get this show on the road and light some fireworks.' Tim said and walked away.

Koena's head was reeling. *Why did Sagar lie to me?*

'Oh, thanks, Tim,' Koena mumbled at the receding figure.

When she reached her desk, Sagar was busy working on his notes.

'Sagar, why did you lie to Tim that it was my idea?' Koena put her hands on her hips and demanded angrily.

I hate liars.

'Koena, sit down, please.' Sagar said, pulling her onto a chair. 'Listen, if I had said it was my idea, Tim would have shredded me to pieces. You are his star employee, and I wanted your show – our show – to be a grand success. Whatever you suggest, Tim would just nod his head. I know him. So, a small white lie didn't look very significant to me. What matters is that we got his approval!' Sagar looked so earnest that Koena's heart melted.

Yeah, right. He did have a point. Tim would have never agreed if Sagar had told him, it was his idea.

'Fine!' Koena smiled. Sagar surprised her with his depth of thought, at times.

Some foresight the boy has!

'Now, let us get to work and finalize the other two invitees. I say we go for this socialite and the schoolteacher apart from Gordy. What say?' Koena asked, circling the names on the print-out with a red pen.

'Sure, sounds good,' Sagar nodded and typed out the names in the sheet that he was preparing.

'I know that the schoolteacher, Ms Rehman, is a die-hard fanatic and loves a good debate. I have seen her speak before. She hates the likes of Gordy. It will be a great session. Communist activist pitted against the idealistic schoolteacher, and the socialite butterfly making her presence felt by her strong perfume and fluttering eyelashes.' Sagar concluded, making a few funny faces mimicking the socialite.

Koena laughed aloud, and Sagar joined her.

'I think we should also call Mrs. Mehta, the hypnotherapist, as the fourth guest. She is popular and can throw some light on the after effects of abuse and trauma. She has written a couple of books also on abuse victims.'

Sagar nodded and keyed in Mrs Mehta's name.

After a quick lunch, the colleagues wrapped up the initial draft. They had to pass it through Tim, and Koena took that responsibility. By 7 p.m., they were ready to close shop. Sagar left to pack his belongings. Koena wrapped up and waited for him at the reception. While waiting, Koena checked her phone. No missed calls and no messages from Shom. *Strange.*

She sighed. Everything had been strange since yesterday. That one revelation had changed their easy camaraderie. Koena was scared even to go home and face Shom.

Would he still be the same loving husband? Can I trust him again?

'I'm done! Come. Are you sure you want to drop me? I can walk back, you know.' Sagar asked, adjusting his backpack.

'Of course, I want to. Let's say I'm dying to drop you home. Now, shall we?' Koena stuck her tongue out. Laughing, they left the office.

Carefully taking her car out, Koena left the office building and turned left towards Sagar's house. After dropping off Sagar and promising to come to work early the next day, Koena slowly made her way home. Her mind had gone back to masticate on the disturbing conversation with Shom, and she realized that she was still coming to terms with the shocking facts. Despite having a fruitful day at work, the usual productivity-induced high was missing. Depression was setting in like a damp fog. Somewhere deep down, Koena knew that she wanted all this to be a bad joke. Not being a religious person, and at times even doubting the theistic philosophies thrust on her by the kind nuns she grew up with, Koena did not have the least inclination to reach out to the Almighty. With a heavy heart that threatened to plummet further into the depths of her bowels, Koena shuffled up the stairs. She wanted to keep as much distance as she could between herself and the place she had called home for the past decade.

■

MAY 3, 2000
Ashiana Apartments
8:00 p.m.

WHEN KOENA FINALLY reached her floor, she paused in front of her house's door and searched for her keys. Eyebrows knit, she wondered about probable places where she might have dropped her keys. Eventually abandoning the search with a loud sigh and a sinking heart, she rang the bell.

The intricately carved door immediately swung open. A surprised Shom stood at the door, wearing an apron, his Chef's hat, and a heart-warming smile. Koena's heart soared.

He looks so dishy! Was it all a nightmare, then?

'Hey, shona! You are back. Why are you ringing the bell? Where are your keys? Okay, never mind… look who's here.' Shom exclaimed without a pause and made a sweeping motion with his free hand. Koena strained her neck to see beyond him and let out a shrill scream of joy. 'Kittu! When did you come?'

She rushed inside and hugged their only son, showering him with kisses. Kit responded warmly. After a few seconds, he realized the overwhelming maternal outpouring was not going to stop soon, and protested, 'Mom! I'm a teenager now. Enough.'

'Shut up, boy. You will always be my child, come what may.' Koena pulled him closer and hugged him to her heart's content.

Kit laughed, hugged her back and said, 'Yes, Ma! I love you too. I missed you too,' winking at his bemused father.

'May I?' Shom cleared his throat, spreading his arms out.

'Of course, head of the family, come in!' Koena said, pulling her husband into the circle of love. Releasing each other, they heard the details of Kit's sudden holiday plan and his decision to visit his parents. He would be staying for two days, he informed happily.

Koena felt deliriously happy to see her boy. She knew Kit's presence would act as a balm to smoothen the crack that had wormed its way into her relationship with Shom. After listening eagerly to Kit's plans, she freshened up and helped Shom with dinner. She offered to make the salad.

He handed over the cucumbers and tomatoes with a sloppy grin plastered on his face.

She stared at him blankly, her heart unable to forget the incident. Shrugging, Shom got back to laying the table. Kit was lying on his belly on the living room floor, watching a football match. He turned, asking, 'Ma, can we visit the lake? I heard they have some cool stuff there.'

Koena turned and looked at Shom, who nodded.

'Sure, we can. When do you want to go?' Shom asked, removing his chef's cap and folding it perfectly.

'Umm… Tomorrow evening, maybe?' Kit was sitting up now, paying complete attention to his mother. She looked at Shom for affirmation. He came by and side-hugged her, making her heart do a little jiggle.

'Sure, let us make a list after dinner… What say, young man?' Shom asked, tightening his hold on his wife's shoulder. Kit nodded eagerly and switched off the TV.

'I will get the plates,' Koena said and tried to escape.

'You sit. I will get them.' Shom said and went into the kitchen.

'Kit, come over,' Koena placed the salad plate on the table and called her son. She then slumped on the chair at her usual place. She wasn't hungry, although the chicken curry looked yummy. Shom served her first and then served Kit.

The couple ate silently while Kit regaled them with stories of life at his boarding school. He kept glancing at his parents in turns.

'I'm thinking of taking a day off tomorrow.' Koena exclaimed, looking at her son, expecting an excited reaction. Instead, she saw confusion in his young eyes. Kit looked at Shom, who stared at Koena. He cleared his throat and began, 'Shona, err… well… Kit and I have made some plans to go shopping. While you are at work, we will wrap up things here. Anyway, we are heading out in the evening, right?' Shom's explanation made Koena wince.

Her face fell and her shoulders drooped. *They don't need me.*

'So, you don't want your mother anymore. I know you are an adult… almost an adult. You need your father, not me. I can live with that.' Koena grumbled without looking up, pulling her lower lip down.

'Oh, Mom! You are such a drama queen.' Kit laughed, jumping up to hug her. 'I just want to spend some time with Dad alone, Ma. That's all! Is that ok?' He asked sweetly, placing a soft kiss on her cheek.

Koena's heart melted and she readily agreed. *He is a charmer—like his father.*

Lightening up her mood, Kit ensured his mother didn't feel left out. He promised to spend a day with her when he visited next. Koena hugged him tightly, feeling both proud and amazed.

My little boy! When did he become so mature?

After dinner, they bid goodnight. Kit slipped into a peaceful sleep almost immediately. While the adults tugged at the dainty strings of dreamless sleep—the night went by in a swoosh.

When the next day dawned, Koena went to work while Shom and Kit went shopping. That evening, they downed ghee soaked Parathas at the nearby Dhaba to their heart's content and chilled at the lake as Kit was to leave the next day.

■

MAY 4, 2000
Ashiana Apartments
7:00 a.m.

THE NEXT MORNING, Koena bid a teary goodbye to Kit. She was already dreading the time she would be left alone to deal with Shom's other side. And, most importantly, her reaction to his truth.

How should I react? What should I say?

■

MAY 4, 2000
TNN Office
11:00 a.m.

KOENA MANAGED TO keep her interaction with Shom to the minimum and reached office by 8:00 a.m. Sagar was also in by then.

They started working feverishly on the details of the new talk show. They wanted to pull out all stops to make it a huge success. The shoot for the first two episodes was due in a few days, and Koena had to finalize the script. She had even considered asking for help from a writer in the Creative team. At the last minute, she decided against it and did it herself.

The show was to be called 'Prime Nights with Koena'.

Though she felt squeamish at first to have her name on a show, Koena also knew that in order to go up the work ladder, she had to shed her inhibitions. In the past ten years, Koena had worked on several programs but always in the background, with the design team, or giving ideas for the look and feel, or writing the script. She had once co-hosted a news show with another anchor. This was the first time Tim had shown enough confidence in her to give her a solo show.

'I have full confidence in you. Go fly, my bird.' Tim had said with a hearty laugh.

What if something went wrong?

Koena had wondered during the initial talks about the TV show. Later, she got used to all the attention and even basked in it. Now that the show had been announced and the trailer was being telecast, Koena was developing cold feet. It was a unique concept. Never had a TV channel– that too a local TV channel—aired a talk show on such a sensitive topic: Effect of abuse on kids and adults. There was huge speculation about it.

Sagar had somehow pre-empted her discomfort and had been a huge support. He kept encouraging her. Sighing, she got back to work. Sagar was silently making notes. Nowadays, he would come straight to her desk with his backpack instead of going to his desk. Koena saw no reason to suggest otherwise. After all, they did have to work together the whole day.

'Sagar, shall we go over the script one last time?' Koena asked, pushing her relentless thoughts aside.

'Sure,' Sagar nodded, keeping his notes away and giving her his full attention.

Koena went through the script slowly, intermittently looking up to see if Sagar was following her. In a few places, he made some comments, which she noted down. By the time they wrapped up, it was lunchtime.

'How is Shom?' Sagar asked suddenly, seeing her concerned face.

'He... he is fine, thank you, Sagar,' Koena gave a forced smile.

'Is everything okay? Have you guys been fighting?' Sagar knew her enough to ask such a personal question.

Koena shook her head. 'Nope. It is fine. We are just... just something we need to sort out between ourselves.'

'Hmm, well, do that before the shoot. Else, you will not be able to give your 200%. Like Tim says.' Sagar said, his brows strung together, looking pensive.

'Yes, sure... I will.' Koena felt better after hearing the concern in Sagar's voice. True! *Work should not be sacrificed at the altar of personal anguish.*

After lunch, they wrapped up the script and moved on to the other aspects of programming with the relevant teams. In the evening, Koena sat down to call and directly invite the guests to the show. All of them confirmed their participation. With just a few last-minute items remaining, Koena decided to call it a day.

■

MAY 4, 2000

Ashiana Apartments

8:30 p.m.

WHEN KOENA REACHED home, she deeply inhaled the familiar delectable aroma wafting from the kitchen. Her mood perked up instantly. Food did that to her. She felt almost orgasmic when she was in the company of good food. Especially food cooked lovingly by Shom. The cook was away and Shom had smoothly stepped into her place.

Tip-toeing, she made her way to the kitchen and observed Shom rustling up her favourite dish: grilled fish. She leaned on the doorframe and watched silently as Shom went about chopping coriander and spreading it evenly on the dish. Next, he neatly cut the tomatoes, cucumbers, and carrots, arranging them on a plate and adding a sprig of cilantro for some jazz. When he turned to take off his apron, he smiled, sweat dotting his handsome face, his eyes gleaming with unadulterated love. He opened his arms wide, and Koena rushed into them, her eyes brimming over. He kissed her hair and face as he hugged her tight.

'I love you, shona; I missed you so much.' He whispered, his soft voice tickling her. Koena giggled.

What was I thinking? My Shom, my lover. He is the same man I married years ago. I know he loves me to the moon and back.

'Shona, are you hungry?' Shom asked softly.

'Hmmm,' Koena nodded eagerly, 'ravenous,' she whispered back, inhaling his musky perfume mixed with his heady scent. The cocktail hit her neurons, calming her almost immediately.

'Come, let us eat, then. I cooked your favourite dish.' Shom said, gently pulling back.

Koena nodded, tucking a stray tendril of hair behind her ear, 'Let me quickly freshen up?'

'Go, go, don't forget to scrub your feet.' Shom said and playfully slapped her buttocks.

Squealing, Koena rushed to their bedroom for a quick shower. After she had dressed, they sat down to eat. The house seemed empty after Kit's departure. Talking about inane things, the couple ate their dinner.

The Bloomsdale School at Ooty ensured that their wards had a safe stay, so they allowed only a few vacations in between the school semester. This time, it was an emergency at their end, so they had to ask all the students to stay with their parents or guardians for two days.

Their interaction was strictly confined to Kit's visit and whether he had reached safely. Shom also didn't say much after informing Koena that Kit's housemaster had called. Usually, Shom would drop off Kit at school when he went after vacations. But this time, another parent was travelling from Bhubaneswar and had gladly agreed to take Kit along. His son and Kit were classmates and friends. The day ended with as much unassuming simplicity as it had started.

■

MAY 5, 2000
TNN Office
7:30 a.m.

THE NEXT MORNING, Koena was up early. She got ready at breakneck speed, surprising herself. Shom was still asleep. His soft snores filled the bedroom. She threw a glance at him, tracing his sleeping figure with her eyes. Turning quickly, she raced out of the house and out of the building. There were very few cars on the road. Putting her car in fifth gear, Koena accelerated, with the windows rolled down, letting the cool morning breeze lift her hair and tickle her skin. When Koena reached the office in under twenty minutes, Sagar was already in.

He was early, even by Koena's standards.

'Hola, you are in so early! Did you sleep here?' Koena asked, grabbing the cookie jar from her desk and munching on a cookie noisily. She offered the jar to Sagar, who gladly helped himself to one from it. Chocolate chip cookies were her favourite, and she kept a jar of them in her desk drawer, often to be dipped into when she felt the lows hit her. Today was a chocolate-chip-cookie day.

'Yeah, had to work on something that Tim thrust on me. I feel like a aging, desperate clientless sex worker who opens herself to anyone who comes by. I want to be exclusive.' Sagar's doleful expression overtook the stunned silence that had followed his funny retort.

Ouch! What an analogy!

She nodded fervently, urging him to continue. The analogy had hit hard. She gulped to keep the shock from showing on her face.

Oblivious of her agonized expression, Sagar continued, a gleam finding its way into his eyes. 'He asked me to do a piece on some Maoists hiding in the jungles of Bihar and Bengal. He wants me to write a one-pager on this one–a fugitive man called Bubai, who has a few lakhs on his head. Now, where will I find these Maoists sitting here in Bhubaneswar? Moreover, which self-respecting Maoist calls himself 'Bubai'?! Seriously, Tim sometimes just goes off the tangent occasionally. We're a small network. I'm not sure our audience will even understand what or who a Maoist is. All they are bothered about are the various similar-sounding soaps with sob stories of daughters-in-law and their abusive mothers-in-law. Crazy, yaar.' Sagar slumped down further into his chair, massaging his temples.

He continued muttering angrily. 'I hate Tim. I tell you. One of these days, I'm going to murder him. When I asked him where I would find Maoists to write this piece, he asked me to go to the jungles and search. Is he kidding or what?'

First the analogy now Maoists! What's happening?

Koena imagined white fumes coming out of Sagar's ears and nostrils. She had managed to arrange her face muscles to project normalcy.

'Tch, tch! It's okay. He just wants you to do an investigative piece. I don't see anything wrong with the request. I'm sure you can come up with something if you put your head to it. Anyway, why are you being so uptight? Maybe it will turn out to be a brilliant piece. Who knows? Maybe someone somewhere will notice your work, and your career might take off on a different tangent. What say?' Koena sympathized, juggling her eyebrows to shoot a quizzical look at Sagar.

'Yeah, right. And they will hand me the Pulitzer.' Sagar pouted, bowing with a funny smile pasted on his face.

Koena laughed out aloud.

'Now, you are also making fun of me.' Sagar's pout became pronounced.

'Arrey, baba, it's ok. Let me see the sheet. Now, what does Tim want?'

Koena put on her reading glasses and tried to focus. She had hardly reached the second paragraph when Sagar's abrupt question froze her blood.

'By the way, would you know any Naxalite, Koena?' Sagar asked, his face still, his eyes steady and unblinkingly focused on her. The question hit her like a ton of bricks. She faltered ever so slightly before curbing the quiver in her voice. *What the...*

'What? Wha... what kind of question is that? Do I look like the type who knows Maoists... or... Naxalites? What nonsense are you blabbering, Sagar?' Koena fumed nervously, the hand holding the notes shivering ever so slightly.

Her anger grew when Sagar's eyes were still steadily trained on her face, watching her reaction. She averted her eyes, looking down and trying to focus.

'I am a decent tax-paying citizen. I do NOT know any Maoist, nor do I know any terrorist—I don't even want to know about them anyway.' Koena repeated. Her face, flushed. She knew she was getting angrier. Her feeble attempt at deep breathing wasn't helping. On top of that, Sagar's gaze was unsettling her further.

Koena, control yourself. Take a deep breath. He is just simply asking a question. He has no idea…

'Chill, Koena. I just asked in case you'd have an idea, yaar. You have a strong network *na.* I didn't mean anything. Anyway, my brain isn't working. I need caffeine. Do you want some? Shall we?' Sagar suddenly stood up and pointed towards the office canteen.

Koena nodded, placed the sheets on her desk, and followed him. Her cheeks had grown warm. She needed a whisky on the rocks. But coffee would work, too. After sipping their black coffees, both felt a bit calmer. Waving the white flag, albeit a bit grudgingly, Koena flashed a tiny smile, her dimples playing peekaboo. 'I thought you were being a bit offensive back there. Sorry for snapping. Didn't mean to.'

'It is okay. My question was quite stupid, I agree. I'm truly sorry. Do forgive me. I mean how would you know aout…' Sagar shook his head and touched her arm with his cold index finger. Koena shuddered at the cool touch. Goosebumps formed where Sagar had placed his finger. Absent-mindedly, she rubbed the area subtly after Sagar moved away.

A subdued Koena and a hyperactive Sagar returned to her desk, deciding to concentrate on finer details. The shoot was beginning soon, and they had to wrap up their planning rapidly. That was the mandate from Tim.

A guy from the production team called them to inform that they were ready and that the crew had set up their equipment, ready to roll as soon as Koena was. As the head of the show, Koena was calling the shots, taking orders only from Tim.

Mrs. Mehta arrived first, followed closely by the socialite and the activist. Gordy looked like a Maths professor in person. He shook hands warmly and thanked her for inviting him. Koena responded equally politely and ensured her guests were comfortable. Ms Rehman arrived a bit late, uncharacteristic for a teacher. She apologized profusely for the delay.

The socialite, Mrs. Tanuja Roy, with her cropped hair and a flowing sleeveless gown in shocking pink with a plunging neckline, ensured she had everyone's attention, Especially all the men. Tim welcomed her with a huge hug and air kisses. Koena and Sagar rolled their eyes for effect at the gesture, knowing well that Tim hated the air-head types. Mrs. Roy had been invited only for her glamour quotient. She also had a novel to her credit–ghost-written, needless to say. The buzz was that she was being considered for the Sahitya Akademi award for her novel about a pilot and his dead lover.

Koena noticed that the woman had brought a few copies to the set. She winced, wondering if her show would become a promotional event instead. She decided to keep careful tabs in case the socialite-author decided to run riot.

Ms Rehman shook hands warmly with Koena, apologizing again. In response, Koena congratulated her on winning the coveted Padma award and wished her many more years of popularity.

'Ms. Mahapatra, I truly am honoured by all the attention I have been getting. Actually, I never expected to get nominated. For ages, my family has been doing this service. I am just another cog in this huge wheel. And, I am touched at being invited to your talk show.'

Koena smiled widely, her heart doing a little dance. She thanked Ms Rehman profusely.

Koena had prepared all of them for the debate, and they were ready, looking excited at the prospect of being part of a new show which had gathered a lot of interest due to the brilliantly shot teaser videos.

Koena stepped into the spotlight. Her heart was hammering in her chest, but her mind was composed. It would be a cakewalk. She had it all figured out in her head. Subtly, she gulped some air and began. 'Hello, viewers. Welcome to the brand-new show, 'Prime Nights with Koena'. I am Koena Mahapatra, your host for the evening… and here are our guests. Before we begin, let me introduce them…'

She pointed out each participant as she called their names. 'Mr. Gordy, a well-known orator, actor, and social worker. Seated next to him is Ms Rehman, a Padma awardee, renowned teacher, and a great inspiration to us. We also have a very talented author and actor, Mrs. Roy. Last but not the least, we have on our panel, Mrs. Mehta, famous hypnotherapist, who will share some amazing insights on how hypnotherapy has helped many child sexual abuse victims regain their hold on life.'

Koena turned to face her guests, welcoming them warmly. Each of her guests smiled at her. Turning to face the camera, Koena continued. 'Let us first ask what Mr. Gordy thinks about the sexual abuse of underprivileged women. Have you known of any such instances, Mr. Gordy?'

'Hi. Well, in my line of work, I have seen many such instances. To say it deeply pains me would be an understatement. I have interacted with multiple affected people. specially, in the coal mines; it is such a sad state of affairs.'

'Thank you, Mr. Gordy; let me ask the same question to Ms Rehman. So, tell me, Ma'am, have you come across any such instances?'

'Hello everybody. Yes, Koena, I have. It is so disheartening to see that the system does not have any provisions to curb this horror. Little girls unwittingly become victims when they cannot even comprehend what has happened to them. So many kids come to see me. Their mothers bring them, asking if I can do something to heal them. I get them primary first aid, some therapy, and a lot of confidence to get on with life despite the crippling trauma. The mothers, surprisingly, are very strong. They put their foot down and decide to get their girls educated, not wanting them to face the same struggles they have themselves faced.'

'Thank you so much, Ms Rehman. Let us ask Mrs. Roy about her views on this subject.'

The socialite-author turned towards the camera and preened. Koena cringed inwardly and rolled her eyes in her mind. *Damn fool!*

'Hello, beautiful people. I love you all. It is nice to be here. It has been such a long time. Being away from the camera makes me feel edgy, you know. Well, coming to the point, I haven't seen any such instances. You know, if I do, I will put my foot down and immediately ask Ramu to do something about it. I will not keep quiet. I will ensure the culprit does not get away. Only last week, Ramu was taking me to the parlour, and we saw a very old woman trying to cross the road. All by herself, poor thing.

'My heart went out to her. I immediately asked Ramu to help her, which he did. God bless him. So, whenever I come across any instance, I do try to help people. I am like that, you know. It is genetic. Even my mother, God bless her dead soul, was like that. Very sweet. She would even give food to her maids, you know. Such a sweetheart. I…'

Koena interjected softly. 'Thank you so much, Mrs. Roy, for sharing your thoughts about this subject. Now, let me ask Mrs. Mehta.' She made eye contact with Sagar, and he deftly switched off the input from the socialite's collar mike, rendering her inaudible for a while. Mrs. Roy tried to butt in with a few words, but the others ignored her.

All eyes were on Mrs. Mehta.

'Hi, everyone. I'm glad to be here. In my practice, I see, almost on a daily basis, people with traumatic pasts, mostly related to sexual attacks. Children are extremely vulnerable and are victimized often. I have participated in many research programs where we tried to help the victims heal. I must say we have achieved quite a lot of success. I would love to share some insights today.'

'Thank you so much, ma'am. Your thoughts are invaluable.'

Tim's voice boomed into Koena's ear. 'Make her talk a bit about her hypnotherapy sessions. Or ask her to do a demonstration. I can see the eyeballs rising in the audience.'

In response, Koena turned towards Mrs. Mehta and asked, 'So, ma'am, are there any special methods you use to help your victims heal? Would you please describe a method for us?'

'Ahh, well, the methods are quite simple. But, yes, I can do a demonstration. I was actually planning to ask you if I could.'

Koena's heart jumped.

What! Her talk show was becoming something else, and she had to stop this now. No demonstrations!

Tim was nodding furiously. Koena noticed him in her peripheral view. She was just about to refuse politely when Tim's voice boomed into her ear. 'Allow her. Say yes.'

Ignoring his irritating voice, Koena smoothly called for a commercial break, and the set crew moved in to prepare the stage for the next session. She glared at Tim for forcing her to divert from the script.

While the other guests retired to the visitor's lounge, Koena approached the hypnotherapist and asked, 'Mrs. Mehta, our Producer is quite keen to have a demonstration, and as we speak, we are arranging for the session. So, who would you like to hypnotize?'.

'Of course, you, my dear.'

Her answer left Koena stunned.

What! Me? No, no... It had to be someone from the audience.

Koena shook her head vigorously.

'Er, no, ma'am! I am the anchor. I can't do this. I suggest we call someone from the audience. Else I will call my colleague, Sagar.'

'No, my dear. Don't you worry, it will be fine.' The therapist's reassurance did not work. Koena became extremely nervous. She knew how these sessions worked and the effect they had on her mostly delicate psyche. On several occasions, her therapist had discussed repressed emotions that had come to the surface. So, she was afraid of what she might blabber.

What if she blabbered about her recent issues with Shom? Or worse, her past...Oh god! No, she could not do this.

'Sorry, ma'am, I really cannot do this. You are not getting the point. I'm the anchor... I have to constantly guide the show; I cannot lie down on your couch, unaware of myself for even a few minutes.' Koena protested.

The older woman simply smiled. 'Koena, my dear, there is no need to worry. I promise, if you start saying something personal, which might not be suitable, I will stop. Isn't that what you are actually worried about?' The woman's smile was magnetic.

Koena caught herself nodding as if agreeing to the idea. After the short recess, the shoot began. Koena lay down on the couch. As explained earlier, the therapist swung a pendulum and asked Koena to observe it. Soon Koena went into a trance-like state, her rational mind numbed as she went down an unknown memory path.

There were lights on both sides—bright, colourful lights. Koena watched with wonder as she zoomed across. She was flying. She knew that. She looked down to see her body. But there was just a pillar of light. She tried to move her arms. Nothing! It was just air—empty space. Then suddenly, there was a strong smell. A very familiar smell of mustard oil. It burnt her nostrils. She tried to hold her nostrils closed, but her hands would not move. They seemed stuck. She kept zooming ahead; her eyes tightly closed, the smell following her, enveloping her and entering her pores. She kept floating, slowly, then picking up speed. Then she became still—a calm spread through her body. And abruptly, she felt cold, goosebumps forming on her skin.

Suddenly, she was being pulled into a strong white light. It was bright, brilliant, and expanding. She went straight in. The core was warm like the summer sun's rays. Somebody was calling out her name. She heard it clearly. She turned her head a bit, but could not move her neck. She opened her mouth to reply, no words came out.

Koena?! Koena! Koena...

A snap! She was sucked into a vacuum. A loud whoosh followed, almost deafening her, as if she was breaking the sound barrier in reverse. And then, she could feel her senses returning all at once. Her eyes shot wide open. Koena looked around; her mind muddled.

She was in the studio.

'How are you feeling, my dear?' Mrs. Mehta asked gently.

Koena tried to sit up. She looked around, startled. There was nobody around. Tim had probably asked everyone to stay outside, even Sagar.

'Slowly, dear.' Mrs. Mehta's soft drawl fell on Koena's ears.

'I'm okay! What happened? What did I say? Did the session work?' Koena stammered, sitting up, her heart hammering in her chest. 'Is it over?'

'Yes, it is over. Now, I need you to rest a bit. Drink some water. Do not think too much.'

'Why? What happened?' Koena felt uneasy. *Had she blabbered something?* 'Did I say something odd?'

'No dear, you did not say anything about anyone. You just spoke about yourself,' Mrs. Mehta whispered. The camera was obviously off, and the unit members had gone scarce.

'Did the shoot happen?' Koena mumbled, still trying to get a grasp.

'Yes, yes, it went just fine. Take a break, and then we can resume.' Mrs. Mehta gently led Koena towards the door.

Staggering, Koena made her way out of the room. Both Sagar and Tim were nowhere to be seen. Smoothening her skirt and adjusting her hair, Koena stepped out of the studio. There was no one in the corridor, either. Koena made her way to her desk. She needed to freshen up. The office was the usual hum of frenetic activity. She crossed Sagar's desk – he was not there, either. Then she walked past Tim's desk, where she saw him in deep conversation over the phone. He did not raise his head when she crossed. Koena decided she would tackle him later.

She grabbed her bag and rushed to the washroom. In the mirror, she noticed her dishevelled look. Horrified, she tried to recollect the moments of the past hour. Nothing came to mind. Zero.

I have done some major damage to my career. Shit! Where the fuck is this Sagar?

Almost absently, Koena ran a brush through her silky hair. Once her hair was in place, she washed her face and re-applied her makeup. She felt a lot better with that sorted. Spraying some perfume on herself, she stepped out of the washroom and collided with Laila, the buxom receptionist, who rushed inside and got busy with her vanity case.

Koena apologized as Laila replied, 'Happens, darling. You must be so upset...'.

Laila preened, looking at her reflection. Then she turned to look at Koena, who stepped right back in, trying to catch her breath. *Now, what did she mean?*

'What do you mean, Laila?'

'I just heard you created quite a ruckus inside... Must say, you don't look the type, you know.'

Koena's blood froze when she heard this. Unaware, Laila continued colouring her voluptuous lips drawn in a lovely pout.

'What? What are you talking about?' Koena asked, scowling at Laila's reflection in the mirror.

'I'm not gossiping,' Laila shook her head, glancing at Koena and quickly looking away.

'What did you hear?' Koena pressed, her heart hammering in her ears. She grabbed Laila's arm lightly, almost pulling her away from the makeup. Laila shook her head after inspecting her lips carefully in the mirror.

'Sweety, I am not too sure of the details. One of the unit members was saying that you were out for an hour or so, and were recollecting some weird things. I don't know what exactly happened.' Laila declared. 'Are you alright?' She added, almost like an afterthought, her false eyelashes fluttering.

'I'm okay, thanks, Laila.' Koena said, rushing out. She needed fresh air. Laila kept staring at her till the door closed behind her back.

I have done some major damage to my career, maybe even my life. What a foolish decision it was, to agree to this shit!

Koena returned to her desk, her legs heavy and her heart heavier, wondering if the whole office was gossiping about her outburst. *Her terrible past! Oh lord!*

Tim came by at that precise moment. Hooking his arm on the cubicle wall, he raised his eyebrows at Koena's woebegone expression.

'Heyya. What's up? You seem rattled. The man giving you issues, eh?'

Koena looked up sharply and shook her head, coming straight to the point. 'Well, what happened inside? Can you please tell me?'

Tim shook his head before replying, 'Well. Nothing much. You went into a trance, as expected. You relived some painful memories, again, as expected. You said a few things. These were quite… umm… let me put it this way; they were… unexpected.'

Tim crossed his arms over his chest, looking almost apologetic.

Koena slapped her forehead, wincing at the pain, 'Oh my! What did I do, Tim?!'

Tim placed a reassuring hand on her shoulder, trying to calm her. But it didn't work. Her heart was racing, and her blood was sloshing around like a juggler on drugs.

'See, Koena, pushing you into this was my idea. It backfired. I'm extremely sorry. As soon as I realized things were getting out of hand, I stopped the shoot and shooed the crew away. So, if it provides some succour to you, only Sagar and I witnessed the complete session. Well, he insisted; I did try to shoo him away, too, though.'

Tim said earnestly, trying to calm Koena's fears at her meltdown being witnessed by strangers.

'And Mrs. Mehta was very kind. She signalled to us discreetly, saying you were talking about deeply personal issues, which should not be publicised. We stopped shooting at once.' He assured her, watching her face carefully.

'So, do you have the recording of the first few minutes? Can I see it?'

'Sure. Come to my desk.'

Koena got up and followed Tim. On their way, they met Sagar, who wanted to trail along. But Koena shooed him away. In his office, Tim played the video on his laptop. Koena's heart sank when she heard her voice. She gasped, clasping a trembling hand over her mouth. The shock turned to fear, and her legs gave way. She fell into the nearest chair.

She had blabbered big time. Had she spoken about...?

Looking at her ashen face, Tim shook his head and placed a reassuring hand on her shoulder. 'No worries. I am not going to use this. We will do a reshoot. This time, you will lie awake, and we will do a mock hypno-session. Also, we don't care what or who you were...for me, you will always be my star reporter. Koena, you need not worry...please don't...' Tim let his voice trail off.

His promise managed to permeate the stunned layers of her mind. Eventually, she managed, 'Will you do that for me? That is extremely kind of you. Thank you so much.'

Then she asked, 'And, who else...'

'Well, the cameraman was there, of course. And Sagar.' Tim replied, knowing what Koena was about to ask.

The cog fell into place. 'Oh. That is how Laila knows.'

'What does Laila know?' Tim asked, surprised.

'Well, she asked me how I was feeling... Of course, I didn't say anything.' Koena muttered, distracted by how many other people would be knowing this by now.

Tim nodded, frowning. 'I see... hmm. You carry on... I will think of something and get back to you. Meanwhile, don't overthink this. Nothing has changed. Nothing.' He gave a quick pat on her hand to reaasure her.

His words and gesture warmed Koena's heart. *So sweet.*

'Sure. Thanks, Tim.' Koena felt a little better but was still worried about the telecast.

Tim had explained that they had gone on a recess and shown only that part of the session when Mrs. Mehta started hypnotizing Koena. Coming back to her desk, Koena met Sagar again. He'd probably been hanging around nearby to talk to her as soon as she emerged from Tim's cubicle.

'Heya. So, are you feeling better?' Sagar asked, his concern seeming genuine.

'Yea... sort of. Well. No, Sagar. I'm in deep shit. Crazy. Such a stupid duck! Why did I agree to this? Oh no. I just flushed my career down the drain.' Koena cribbed, her eyes welling up. The recording she had seen in Tim's cubicle was disastrous. It was playing in a loop in her head.

'I know. I saw everything. Well, if you were to ask me, it doesn't look that bad, speaking objectively. You know... I suggest you calm down and watch the video again. I'm sure you will feel differently about this.' Sagar shrugged.

Koena looked at him in shock. 'You're kidding. I blabbered so many things about my childhood. Crazy things... I don't even remember all that. Where did they come from? I...' Her voice trailed off, her mind in a mess, like a stuck cassette's reel.

'C'mon, relax now. Let us do this. We will watch it together again and decide what needs to be done. Okay? Now, we must wrap up this shoot. Cheer up.'

Sagar always knew the right things to say. Koena felt o bliged to smile even though her heart was not in it. She wanted to call up Shom.

'You're right. Let us wrap up the shoot first, and then decide what to do.'

They retraced their steps to the studio, which was in a separate wing. They called in the guests after the crew got ready. Mrs. Mehta smiled warmly at Koena, enquiring if she was feeling better. Koena merely nodded, unwilling to speak much. In a few hours, they wrapped up the shoot without any untoward incident. Mrs. Mehta and Koena reshot the hypnotherapy session with a rehearsed script and satisfactorily covered the main aspects relevant to the show.

Happy with the day's work, Koena thanked each guest profusely for making time to participate in the program and promised to inform them of the telecast date. After bidding them goodbye, Koena and Sagar returned to Tim's seat to update him. Her heart felt heavy. She wanted to speak to Shom and hear his warm voice.

■

MAY 5, 2000

Ashiana Apartments

When Koena wrapped up all her pending tasks, she was ready to drop. Koena pulled onto the main road, and she realized it would take a long time to reach home. There was a bad traffic jam, and she had waded right into it. When Koena reached home, it was almost 9:00 p.m. Her stress had worsened with the drive.

The faint strains of Jazz reached her ears as she opened the door with her keys, which she had eventually found beneath the spare scarf she had stuffed in her bag.

'What a wonderful world…'

The singer's soulful rendition made Koena's heart flip. Removing her shoes, she walked straight into her bedroom. Shom was lying on the couch, his eyes closed, immersed in the music. He was moving his hands to the tune and singing along in his mellifluous voice, obviously relishing the moment.

Koena leaned on the doorframe and watched as her husband soaked himself in the lovely number, unaware of her presence, or the world around him. His eyes fluttered open when the song ended. He caught sight of her then, and smiled at her – a wide, happy smile, Shom's special smile. He opened his arms and invited her in for a hug. Koena's heart thudded fast at this vision of perfection.

Isn't he dishy?

She rushed forward and allowed herself to be engulfed, her heart overflowing with affection. They had been through a lot.

We will get through this storm, too. We. Will.

■

MAY 6, 2000
TNN Office
4:00 p.m.

THE DAY HAD been pleasant. Her show was the most talked about topic and many wondered about her guts to do this spill-it-all. She had gallantly smiled through all the questions throughout the day. Tim had swung by twice to check if she was doing ok. Sagar had also been extra nice.

Why are they treating me like this? Shit!

By the time Koena packed up for the day, most of the female staff had congratulated her, giving her a mental high.

She drove out of the building, humming to herself, playing all her favorite songs on the car stereo.

When she reached home, she literally ran out of the lift, eager to share her joy with Shom. *How thrilled he would be!*

■

MAY 6, 2000
Ashiana Apartments
6:30 p.m.

WHEN SHE LET herself in, Shom was standing near the table and working on his laptop. She rushed and gave him a tight hug, turning him round and round, till he put his hands up and asked, 'ohho, what is happening? Why am I getting attacked? Where is my sweet composed wife?'

'Sit down, I am very happy. Today was the best day of my life. My show is a hit!' Koena could not contain her excitement and blurted out.

'What! And you are telling me now?' Shom pushed her towards the kitchen, opened the fridge, took out a piece of long jamun and stuffed it into her mouth.

'Can we watch a repeat telecast, shona?' Shom asked, his eyes dancing in anticipation of partaking his wife's success.

'Sure, let me see the repeat telecast list…' Koena got busy with the TV remote while Shom made her a hot cup of coffee. While searching for the show, Koena described in detail about the show and how it had been a huge hit. In her excitement, she let it slip that Tim had congratulated her on her show, and the ratings were good.

'Let's watch it together,' Shom pulled her into his arms and they sat down to watch the show.

■

MAY 6, 2000
Ashiana Apartments
9:00 p.m.

'ANSWER ME, KOENA…' Shom's face was about to burst open like an over ripe papaya, or so, Koena imagined. *There he goes again!*

It had been a few hours since they had watched the show together. Shom had almost burst a nerve when they watched the hypnotizing session. Despite the anger bursting inside his head, he watched the entire show. A sullenness spread across his face, scaring Koena.

'Tomorrow, first thing, you will ask Tim to delete this. Do you get me?' Koena looked at Shom, stunned at his demand.

Shom went ahead and interrogated her about the show. Why had she maligned his family's reputation? Why had she even agreed to be part of the session? So many questions…

Koena's heart was doing somersaults. She could hear her blood playing squash inside her arteries, threatening to deafen her. She stared down at her fingers, fighting tears. Her sorrow at being questioned was so huge that she was finding it hard not to erupt in anger and sorrow. Myriad emotions continued to dance in her head, further hammering her sorrow into each pore of her body. She felt as if she was walking over broken pieces of glass, with each piece piercing her feet and going straight to her heart. Each word that Shom threw at her was like a shock pulse directly attacking her mind and heart.

'Shona, people do not forget things like this. It is pure gossip material. Why did you do this? How did you forget to tell me about this? Or did you choose to ignore me? Do I not matter to you anymore? When you told me about this incident, did I not tell you to never talk about it to anybody? You went and spoke about it all on television! What's wrong with you?'

'So, what am I supposed to do now, Shom? We went ahead and telecast it. It was me. I watched the video and decided that I was fine with how it looked. I did think of you and your parents and was genuinely worried about their reaction. I realized after a while that I had not mentioned anything wrong there. Well. Not exactly. So, I gave the go-ahead to use the original recording.'

She sulked, pulling her legs up and wrapping her arms around them. 'I didn't know I should ask you before taking professional decisions.' She added, anger rearing its ugly head, creating a veritable volcano inside her. She quashed it with a hasty gulp, a deep frown, and a dangerous sulk, signalling an impending outburst.

'What?! Shona, did you actually say that?' Shom shook his head, keeping his tea cup down. His eyes reflected the turmoil in his mind. He was livid. His outwardly calm appearance never fooled Koena. Not after all these years.

'Koena, never forget that I made you who you are today. Remember that I literally picked you up from the streets and groomed you into a lady. Look at yourself, strutting around in Versace and acting as if you were born into wealth. All your stylish, classy behaviour...remember who you were. I sent you to London to study in that expensive college. I gave you a name, an identity. Who are you without me, Koena? You better watch what you say to me...'

Koena listened to his outburst, stunned. *So, this is what he thinks of me. All these years. This is how he has always thought of me...*

■

MAY 7, 2000

Ashiana Apartments
6:00 p.m.

A GLORIOUS SUNDAY dawned, but Koena and Shom spent it scowling at each other. Each made separate meal arrangements to drive home the intense displeasure they were feeling. The cook was still away, adding to the simmering unpleasantness.

Finally, around evening, Shom invited Koena with a cup of herbal tea and cookies for their ritual. Koena was completely unprepared for this. He had caught her unawares when she returned home after a quick walk around their apartment.

I can't even disagree. He did create this new me. Oh god! I'm just a mere puppet in his hands…

She looked at Shom. A large portion of her heart had turned cold at his outburst. At the words he could use against her. At what he had thought of her. She pushed the obvious thoughts aside and decided to focus on the current things.

Later! I will deal with these later.

'How on earth would I know that Tim would keep repeating the first episode? I had assumed that he would just move on to the next episodes. And why on earth is Mrs. Dey watching talk shows on TV and happily recollecting them verbatim to your Mother in Kolkata? Quote, unquote. Pray, tell me, I am dying to know,' Koena retorted.

'Cut the crap and tone down the sarcasm, Koena,' Shom warned, his voice dropping low. He was a pure homegrown mamma's boy and could not tolerate anything being said against his mother. Or her friends. Or even her *bhaji wallah*. Not that Koena had ever done that before.

Mentally rephrasing the sentence, Koena delivered it in a nicer way. 'I just meant that older ladies do not usually watch such talk shows.' Then she hastily added, in a conciliatory tone, 'Well, see, I didn't say anything about Ma. I'm just cribbing about that old hag.'

Her mind was dizzy with the details thrown at her in the past hour and a half.

'Never mind. The point is, you were part of a talk show, where you got hypnotized, visibly lost control, and blabbered something about your childhood. You refused to pay heed to my words. It hurts. I feel ignored and unwanted. We argued about it the other day and you said you will talk to Tim about stopping repeat telecasts.' Shom stopped abruptly and took a sip of his insipid tea. It was cold. With a grimace that contorted his face, he got up, poured the remnants into the sink, and announced that he was going to make some more tea. 'Do you want some?' He asked brusquely.

He was angry. Koena could see that. She felt extremely uncomfortable with his anger. She always had a problem handling any kind of conflict. His words stabbed her right through her heart. She could feel blood oozing internally from her wounds.

Had I made him feel unwanted? Oh lord! When did I agree to talk to Tim? Uff!

'Yes, please,' she murmured. Tea would be nice, especially when made by Shom. Today's ritual was turning out to be difficult. They were going to be here for a long time. She recollected rule number 3. 'Neither leaves the room until the issue gets sorted.' It just meant that she would have to order dinner. It was a Sunday, and their cook was on leave. Neither of them would have it in them to cook after going through a grilling session like this.

I will personally whack that old hag if I lay my hands on her.

Koena absently noticed that she was edging dangerously close to planning a cold-blooded murder of that gossipy old woman. Shom returned with two cups of steaming tea and some more cookies. Koena loved cookies, and Shom knew that. Eagerly she grabbed a few and munched on one, looking dolefully at her husband. The cookies had the desired effect on her guilt-ridden, tired mind. The sugar rush was making her almost euphoric. In a much lighter state of mind, as if she had just smoked a pot of hashish, Koena threw a sweet smile at Shom.

'What? No, we are not leaving until you agree to revoke that stupid show. I don't care how you do it.' Shom snapped, refusing to be distracted by her sweet smile.

Koena gulped hard. The tea was hot. Damn! After munching on a second cookie, she set her cup down and attempted to reason with him.

'Shom, aren't you contradicting yourself here? You say you are a communist, a Naxal sympathizer. And the very basis of your leaning is freedom: freedom for people, freedom from the oppressive nature of society, from patriarchy, from the norms of capitalists, and working towards a classless society. Then how can you not be open to a portion of my life which I had no control over? Why is it such a big deal? Shouldn't you be sympathetic to my ordeals? Why do you have to behave like a typical patriarchal man? A chauvinistic opinionated man?' Koena's eyes blazed to match the furore in her words.

'Shona, I can't have the public talking about my wife's past. Period. You are free to share your arguments. This is what I have to say.' Shom sulked, silently sipping his tea.

Koena knew from Shom's body language that the conversation was over. Agreeing to continue after dinner, they broke up to order some of the usual fare of noodles and chicken curry from a local Chinese takeaway.

While they waited for their food, they chatted amicably about Kit and a local actor who had asked Shom if he could become a co-owner in the latter's restaurant. When Koena asked why an actor would want to join him, Shom shrugged. The bell rang when Shom was describing the actor's antics at his restaurant when he had come over for a chat.

Koena got the dinner parcel, balancing the packets carefully. Steaming hot and unmistakably loaded with MSG. Koena's mind registered the number of calories she had been consuming for the past few hours.

Sigh. I will do a double shift at the gym. I will have to.

They ate silently and settled down on the floor again, with more tea and a full jar of cookies. Koena continued where she had left off.

Shom looks less angry. Maybe he will come around.

'See, baby. The issue is not resolved in your opinion. You must understand that it is not in my hands to revoke the show. Besides, the clip has already been aired. It is done and dusted. And, in my opinion, after a few days, nobody is even going to remember it. Though the show did a lot for our TRPs—I'm sure like every other show, it will be forgotten. It has been, already. It is old. We wont replay the first episode anymore. We will move to the next episodes. Who remembers what was said in the first one, except for that old hag?' Koena finished, her temper rising slightly.

The dinner of Hakka noodles was in her stomach, and she felt doubly uneasy. Almost queasy.

'Don't cross the limits of decency, shona. She is much older than you and is Ma's best friend. I will not tolerate any kind of indecent talk about elders. You can argue without getting hyper or personal or abusive. You know my thoughts on these already.' Shom looked upset.

Koena's heart sank when she took in the sullen face and the crossed arms.

Yes, I was a little rough there. Should have been calmer—damage control time.

'I am sorry!'

'It's okay, Shona. Let us sort out this matter now. Decently.' Shom did not waver.

Koena was a bit shaken. *Why is he acting so weird? Can't he let go? What was the fucking harm in calling out an old hag, a silly gossipmonger?*

'I have nothing more to say, Shom. I cannot do anything about it. If the channel wants, they can telecast it whenever they want.' Koena pouted, her voice trailing off.

'Shona, you need to talk to Tim. First thing tomorrow. Top priority. Ask him to... er... destroy the recording. Yes, that is it. Ask him to destroy the recording. That would do. Or...'

Shom paused, staring at Koena long enough, to make her gulp harder.

'Or, you... do it yourself. At any rate, I want them gone.'

When she did not respond, he continued,'Will you do it tomorrow? Without fail.'

The last sentence had a deafening ring of finality in it. It was an order! A statement of power and one-upmanship from a man who wanted to use the power of the pecking order and that of patriarchy in a household.

Koena was unable to comprehend whatever Shom was saying.

Destroy the tapes! What's wrong with this man? How can I even do something like that? He has no interest in even hearing out my objections. Had their places been reversed, would he do it? Would he agree to comply? Just for her sake?

Almost as if she already knew the answer, Koena's mind pulled up an image of an obstinate Shom refusing to pull along. *Why should I listen to him, then?*

'No. I will do no such thing. I will not do anything illegal.' Koena replied, crossing her arms over her chest.

A dark cloud crossed Shom's face, frightening Koena. She observed the cloud masking his handsome features. She pushed the mounting fear down.

Shit. There I go again, shooting off my mouth.

'Well. Shona, did you just throw my ideology at my face?' Shom asked, his voice swinging dangerously low, indicating his increasing temper. He was practically glowering now.

Koena cringed some more. *Shit! Fuck my brain. And my big mouth.*

'No. No, not exactly, no…' She responded automatically.

'What did you mean, Koena?' Shom's voice constricted. His eyes bulged, making him look menacing. Koena gulped harder, reaching out to the bottle of water and taking a long swig.

'I just meant… that… it will be difficult for me to get my hands on the recording. I was wondering…' Koena's voice trailed off, her nervousness increasing. She kept gulping air to maintain her voice, which quivered like an old woman's teeth during winters. Her voice, now completely fraught with nervousness, shook audibly. Strangely, it was directly proportional to the depth of her husband's scowl. Shom had crossed his legs and was now sitting erect, his eyes focused on her face. Sharp, unrelenting eyes looked at her for any sign of assent. He looked like he would never back down.

Fucking crazy Capricorn. Why can't he let go? Shit. I am in a huge mess. Okay, let me plan something.

'Okay, I will do it tomorrow.' Koena finally nodded, making up her mind.

What the fuck am I agreeing to?!

Shom nodded curtly. 'Good. I'm happy. Finally, you see reason. Let us now go to bed. It has been a long day.'

It was. They had spent four long hours with the ritual. Shom collected the empty mugs and the tray. He walked out of the room without looking back. Koena heard him clearing up the kitchen. Koena knew that Shom was very much capable of handling the kitchen duties. She decided to go to bed instead and headed to the bedroom. She lay down on the bed, waiting for Shom to wrap up and come. He never appeared.

Soon, she felt drowsy. Her eyes closed. Her tired mind registered a gentle shift in the side of the bed next to her much later. She didn't stir.

Her mind had zoned out.

■

MAY 8, 2000
Ashiana Apartments
5:00 a.m.

MONDAY MORNINGS HAVE this effect on most people–turning them into unwilling, unbending asocial monsters. Being asocial came naturally to Koena. On most days, she wanted to just sit peacefully by herself and not interact with anyone. Sometimes, dealing with her own thoughts also took a heavy toll on her.

Also, she hated Mondays. Period. And after the previous night's discussion, she didn't feel like doing anything.

I hope I don't end up hating Shom.

There was nothing anyone–including herself–could do about that. After mulling over this mental maladroitness to wake up to a cheery self, Koena had reconciled with the fact that she might have to live her life with the painfully simple explanation that a few things were beyond her comprehension. This was one of them.

Grudgingly, she got ready for work.

A divine smell wafted from the kitchen, contributing heavily to lifting her spirits. She closed her eyes and inhaled the aroma, hurrying out to check what her handsome Chef had rustled up. Shom had made her a breakfast of hot toast, peanut butter and a fluffy happy brown cheese omelette that sat invitingly on the dining table, beckoning her.

Gleefully, she tucked in and smiled widely at Shom, picking up the crumbs from her plate and stuffing them into her mouth, closing her eyes in ecstasy. Shom smiled indulgently. He knew that the way to Koena's heart was through her stomach. She looked at him closely. With good food inside her, she could battle any war of any scale. His disarming manner unnerved her a bit. He had even given a day off to the cook.

Why is he being so gallant? Or is he trying to make up for last night?

But before she could entertain that thought, Shom spoke.

'Shona, don't forget the tapes. That is an action item for you today,' he sweetly reminded her, handing her a cup of steaming coffee, just the way she liked it. Hot. Black. Koena sniffed it and felt her brain start working. She could almost hear the gears and locks whir and perform an opening dance. Clang. Clack. Brrrr. Thud.

There he goes again. The Tapes! God!

'Sure,' Koena managed to mutter, nodding vigorously to accentuate her understanding of the subject being drilled into her stubborn head.

'Good girl. I love you so much,' Shom whispered, kissing her head and inhaling the fresh scent of her hair. Koena stiffened up and then slowly let go of her fears. She hugged her husband warmly before rushing to their room to grab her backpack. After bidding a hasty bye, Koena left the house.

■

MAY 8, 2000

Ashiana Apartments

8:30 a.m.

THIS IS ALL so strange. Why am I acting? Is this how we are going to live our lives now?

On her way to the parking lot, she slowed down, sifting through her emotions. Her mind was in constant turmoil, and she realized that she didn't even have an iota of interest in going to work. Never in her career had she felt as demotivated as she did today. On top of all this, it was a Monday.

Shit. I hate Mondays.

Reversing her car from her slot, she slowly made her way out, switching on the radio. No channels were playing anything of interest. On one channel, they were playing an old song, and she let it run as she rolled down the window. The early morning breeze was cool and fresh. It tickled her ears and sent a shiver through her spine. The fresh air on her face dulled the effect of that morning's uneasy situation.

■

MAY 8, 2000
TNN Office
9:00 a.m.

SHE REACHED THE office in half an hour. After settling the things at her desk, she went to get some coffee. Koena's mind idly registered a fact. Of late, she had been guzzling too much coffee. She looked down at her cup and hesitated.

Am I drinking too much coffee?

No, there is no such thing as too much coffee.

Shrugging, she happily took a sip while walking to her desk.

Shom's advice played in a loop, and Koena felt distressed. The momentary high caused by the caffeine crashed, dragging her enthusiasm into a bottomless abyss. She would have to wait for Tim to come, to understand where they usually stored the recordings.

Am I really considering destroying the recordings? Why can't I simply lie that I did?

'I can't lie to Shom.' Inadvertently, she spoke out aloud, startling herself.

'Lie about what?' Sagar's voice startled Koena, and she almost spilled her coffee on her keyboard.

'Nothing. I was just becoming hyper about a small fight.' Koena managed a forced smile and greeted him.

'Did Shom say anything? About the telecast?' Sagar's harmless query sent a shiver down Koena's spine. She grabbed his arm to steady herself.

'How... how do you know?' Koena sputtered, her mind in a frenzy. Sagar's steady gaze unnerved her, and she looked away quietly.

'I know more than you give me credit for. Now, tell me, what did he say?' Sagar was insistent as if he had to know. At this precise moment, he was being a royal pain.

Sigh! *Guess, I have to tell him at least a bit, seeing as it is about the program, we are both doing.*

Koena then began, hesitatingly, 'Well... Shom was mighty pissed about what I had revealed during the program... about being abused as a child. And...' Koena paused, unable to proceed further.

'And he asked you to do something about it.' Sagar supplied, 'You realized that you were not actually ashamed of it after all, and told him so. Your guy threw a fit. Am I right, or am I right?' His eyebrows vanished into his hairline, faintly amusing Koena.

'Yes, you are right. Bang on.' Koena sighed, feeling the heaviness in her heart and mind lessen as if she had transferred all her stressful thoughts to Sagar.

'Koena, men often attach their honour to the... anatomies of their partners. Whether you like it or not; that is how Indian men are brought up and usually behave throughout their life. I would have been surprised if Shom had not reacted to this telecast at all, or if his reaction had been positive. Now I am certain that our Shom is a normal Indian man,' Sagar sighed, looking at his phone, checking his text messages.

Koena nodded mutely. Her mind was in a daze, and she was very stressed. *How correct!*

Smiling, Sagar continued, 'Do you know, men usually feel threatened if something like this happens to their wives, and they are expected to 'deal with it'. And they feel doubly annoyed if their wives seem to be fine with such incidents or find the strength in themselves to deal with it without coming to their men. Go figure. We are called simple creatures, but nothing is simple about us. Absolutely nothing.' Sagar shook his head vehemently, making Koena break into a grin.

'True, true... how poignant, Sagar.' She looked at the young man, wondering where he usually hid such deep thoughts. She had hardly seen such depth of thoughts in a man as young as Sagar. And Shom was refusing to let go.

'I'm sure you don't need me to tell you this. But to my mind, you are unsinkable, unstoppable, and unapologetic. I urge you to remain who you are, Koena. My mother used to tell me that it was okay to be not okay, sometimes.' He kept his eyes glued to his phone, and Koena looked away, trying to control her runaway thoughts and her tears.

Sigh. I have to figure out something soon. Can't I just leave all this and run away somewhere?

Shrugging off her escapist thoughts, Koena remarked, 'Let us ignore these personal issues for now and focus on work. What do we have on our plates?'

'So, let me see. More scripts, I think.' Sagar replied, helping himself to a cookie from Koena's jar.

The cookies and Koena were a thing in the small office; they were free for all. The only condition was that whoever took the last cookie had to refill the jar. It was a neat arrangement. The jar always seemed to be at least half-full.

'Hmm, yeah, maybe. Tim has asked me to work on a schedule for three to four episodes. I will need your help with that. After that, we are good to go.' Koena said, handing over a set of printouts to Sagar.

Eyebrows strung together in focus; Sagar started going over them. He sat quietly, still as a statue, only his chest rising and falling, until he finished reading. 'Hmm, I would like to make some changes, just minor ones.'

Koena shrugged and pushed a pen in his direction. 'Sure, go ahead.' Her mind was not allowing her to focus.

Sigh. I will not ask Tim to do anything. Maybe, I will just lie to Shom. There is no other way.

■

MAY 8, 2000
TNN Office
10:30 a.m.

HER CELL PHONE rang and she grabbed it, glad to be distracted. She would have spoken to a spam caller even. This was more welcome, since it was her bosom friend, Asha.

'Of course! I can do it on Sunday, babes. You know how we love to spend time with you both. Is Madhu coming, too?'

Life seemed to be going on track. Shom had stopped bothering her about the recordings when she had lied to him that Tim had deleted the video at her request.

Briefly distracted, Koena fiercely nodded, confirming her presence. She was longing for a holiday. A couple friend of theirs, Sunil and Asha, had planned a vacation to Seychelles and had invited Koena and Shom over. They had planned a small intimate party to celebrate their twentieth wedding anniversary, falling on the 13th, a Saturday. They were to go to a small resort in Seychelles, where Asha promised a weekend of complete fun and frolic with unlimited booze and choicest of gourmet food with close friends for company.

'I'm in, babes. I'm sure Shom, too, would be excited. Don't you worry, I will handle him!' Koena cooed into the phone. After bidding goodbye, she looked at her phone and smiled.

Seychelles. After so many years. I love vacations! A week to go. Yippeee!

Just then Tim came by. 'Heya, where is that boy of yours?' Tim queried, seemingly in a jovial mood. He never called Sagar by his name. Ever. It was always either 'that boy', or 'that boy of yours'.

A startled Koena turned around hastily to greet Tim. He had this habit of appearing suddenly, like out of nowhere. This freaked her out sometimes.

'He was here…must have gone to the restroom. Should I buzz him?' Koena asked, her curiosity going through the roof at this sudden piqued interest in 'that boy'.

'Well, there has been an incident. I need Sagar and you to travel. The usual expectations, you know… get information, talk to people, blah

blah.' Tim nodded so vigorously that Koena feared his head might get dislocated and roll away. Pushing her morbid thoughts aside, she nodded to denote rapt attention. Her mind had wandered onto a different dimension, gearing up for the adventure in store.

'Get going,' Tim said, before hurrying away, almost trotting, his ample chest flesh heaving. Koena sighed and looked at her watch, longing for a power nap.

Where is this boy, now?

■

MAY 8, 2000

Ashiana Apartments

11:30 a.m.

WHEN KOENA HAD planned to pack for the trip, she had not expected it to take such a long time. She had time only to grab a few dresses, her bathroom essentials, her voice recorder, stationery, and of course, her mobile phone. As she was about to step out of her house, a familiar feeling enveloped her. She shook her head, gripped it with both hands, and moaned, 'No, no, not now… I don't have time.'

The demon refused to go away. It had to have its feed. Sighing, she succumbed. The demon smirked and receded into the darkness, satiated, to rise again and catch her unawares some other time.

Koena lay down on the bed, exhausted. Her mind pushed her to wakefulness.

It was time to go.

An insistent honk jolted her out of her self-indulged pitiful state, and she sat up, smoothing her dress down. She hurried into the bathroom, rinsed her hands with soap, scrubbing them thrice with the pumice stone, and splashed water on her face, once, twice, examining herself in the mirror. The woman staring back was a stranger.

I am too far gone. Sigh. I am good….I am healed…I am…

Her mobile rang, springing to life suddenly. Insistent, like a petulant child.

It jostled her out of the self-inflicted reverie. It was Shom. He had gone to Kolkata for a meeting and was flying back the next morning.

She answered the call and rattled off, 'Baby, I'm going off on an assignment! I'll be back in two days. It's urgent. Tim just told me. I thought I will call you on my way…'

Silence.

'Shom… baby?' Koena asked, looking at her screen to check if the call was active. It was.

'Two days? Koena, I think you forgot… We've promised Kit that we will take him to Seychelles with us. Remember, we promised him a vacation. I called to remind you to buy any essentials for that trip. And now, you are running away! When will we pack? How can you agree to something else at this time? Please call up Tim and ask him to send Sagar instead. You cannot go, Koena, We have just got over a rough patch. Don't you want to iron out our issues?' Shom's voice betrayed his emotions.

She visualized his long, irritated face and kicked herself.

Shit! I do want to get back to our normal routine. And how did I forget! I could even ignore Asha's invitation, but how did I forget Kit's vacation time?! I am a terrible Mother.

'Please, Shom, try to understand. I know… I... we have to pack… But this is work, and it is very important to me. We are flying to Seychelles only on the 12th; I will be back on the 10th. We have a full day left to pack. And, anyway, I'm sure you will take care of all that,' she tried to sweet-talk her husband.

'Nope, not done. Please ask Tim to send someone else.' Shom's voice had an odd ring to it.

'I'm so sorry… about Kit's vacation plan; I totally forgot. This Tim, you know how he is, right? He just thrust this assignment on me,' Koena replied, her voice soft, manipulative.

This sudden change in tone, which only married men can understand, had no effect whatsoever on Shom.

'Koena, I will not say anything more. You decide what you want to do. But I do not want you to go on this trip, if you respect my wishes, you can call up Tim and ask him to let you off this.' Shom concluded.

Having delivered what he had to, he disconnected, leaving Koena miserable and almost in tears.

Sometimes, Shom just doesn't get it! He goes all patriarchal and stupid.

Another voice surfaced inside— a more aggressive one.

Isn't he always like this? You bend before him, listen to him, saying 'yes, Shom', 'no, Shom'. You allowed yourself to become his puppet. You were better off as…

Koena let out her breath in short puffs to calm her mental agony. Her mind had split into two. Instead of one, she had two mind voices now, telling her things. She then sighed, looking at her reflection in the bathroom mirror and asking out loud, *What do I do now? Should I ask Tim to send someone else?*

Her reflection remained pained and silent. Deciding to call Tim, Koena picked up her phone and dialled his number. The call went through smoothly.

'Tim, hey! I forgot. I had promised Kit that I would visit him. Is it okay if Sagar goes alone? I will coordinate with him and ensure everything goes well,' Koena rushed over her words.

'Koena, I'm sending you there for a reason. If I could send Sagar alone, I would have. Please leave immediately.' He said brusquely.

'But, Tim, listen to me…' Koena tried to reason, but Tim had already disconnected.

Just before the conversation ended, Koena overheard a voice in the background, asking, 'Is she not going?'

After pondering over the weirdness of the situation for a while, Koena decided that she had to leave. She just had to. There was something amiss, but there was absolutely no time to waste if she had to catch that flight.

Shom must understand. I have to do this myself. I will make peace with him later. I will also speak to Tim about springing these sudden trips on me once I return from this one. Anyway, it is just a two-day trip.

She picked up her bags and left, locking the door behind her. The note to Shom, which was stuck to the computer screen, fluttered slightly in the impact.

■

MAY 8, 2000
On the flight
1:30 p.m.

INSIDE THE GIANT jet, the air hostess was her usual self: calm, cool, and painfully polite.

Why doesn't her smile reach her eyes? Has she fought with her husband, too? Does she even have one? Maybe she has no husband, only lovers. Is she happy with what she has? Does she like her job? Maybe she loves to fly to different places and meet new people.

Koena kept chewing over the details of her recent tiff, her eyes stuck on a particularly svelte air hostess, her mind drifting in different directions. Aeroplanes did that to her. She had to have these unending monologues to keep herself from jumping at every turbulent rumble.

'Ma'am, hot towel for you?' whispered the air hostess, softly jolting Koena out of her daydream.

'Oh, yeah! Lovely, thanks.'

'Ma'am, would you like tea or coffee?' asked another honeyed voice from a woman pushing a burly cart that looked like an eighteen-month pregnant woman.

'Do you serve whisky?' Koena asked in a fierce whisper.

Why do we have to fly? What if the plane crashes? Shit, there I go again. Shut up, mind.

'I'm so sorry, ma'am. We do not serve alcohol on this flight.' The voice did not seem apologetic at all. Koena had a fleeting desire to slap the woman. Instead, she smiled sweetly and said, 'No problem, coffee would do. Make it black. No sugar. Thanks!'

Once the caffeine hit her bloodstream, it rushed to do its job and calmed Koena's jumpy nerves. Relaxing just a bit, Koena made a mental note to call Shreya, her therapist, after returning home. After today's incident, Koena felt that she might need a few more sessions. It had hit her suddenly, without warning. But Shreya had warned her about such incidents and asked her to set up an appointment as soon as something of the sort happened. Koena sipped her coffee, looking out at the pale afternoon sky.

By the time we land, it will be evening.

The plane had three-seaters on one side and two-seaters on the other. They had got a two-seater in the middle of the plane. She had requested a window seat, and the man next to her had slept as soon as the plane took off. Maybe he doesn't dream, Koena thought. Sagar, who sat in the aisle seat, had immediately started snoring after the plane took off.

How does this guy sleep anywhere and in any position?

Sagar had managed to curlup in his seat without breaking any rules of the aeroplane. Koena bent to check if his seat belt was on. Sagar was certainly weird. She shook her head in amazement before drifting off to her thoughts. She doubted if he had a personal life. Many times, she had wondered if he even went home. Every day, he surely changed his dress and looked neat, but on certain days, his bloodshot eyes indicated that he had pulled an all-nighter.

A busybody in the office had once remarked that Sagar was besotted with Koena. Even Koena agreed (to herself) that it was probably true. Sagar did have that puppy-dog-expression when he looked at her.

Sigh. He will get over it. Boys of his age do get crushes on older women. It's natural.

She sighed, closed her eyes and tried to take a nap. The plane gave a small jolt, and the speaker came to life. The sleeping figure stirred a bit and murmured, 'Have we reached?'

'No, not yet.'

'Oh, okay,' Sagar murmured again before softly slipping back to his previous state.

'This is your captain speaking. Ladies and gentlemen, please fasten your seatbelts till the sign is on. We're going through some turbulence due to bad weather. Please keep your seats erect and remain seated. The cabin crew will help you with this.'

A pretty air hostess came around, checking all the passengers. She reminded Koena of a headmistress checking for errant children and pulling them up if found lacking.

The voice repeated the message in three different languages and went silent. The sleeping junta remained unaware of this little incident. The bad weather continued for a while. The plane flew and hovered over the Raja Bhoj International Airport for thirty minutes before getting permission to land.

■

MAY 8, 2000

Raja Bhoj International Airport

2:30 p.m.

THE WEATHER WAS quite a shocker. It was drizzling. The cold raindrops felt nice on her skin during the short walk from the plane to the waiting bus. The bus ride was bumpy, and the exhausted duo arrived at the terminal.

Koena allowed Sagar to carry her hand-baggage while she tried to locate, among the waiting crowd, a placard with their names on it. There was none. It did not rattle her much. She was used to latecomers, and she looked around for a place to sit and wait for the driver. She found two empty seats and plonked down on one. Sagar sat down beside her.

'Driver has not yet arrived?'

'No.' Koena shook her head, declaring, 'I am calling Tim.'

'No use… I tried already. There's some issue with the network here. The call is not going through. We will have to try that one there,' Sagar said, pointing towards the yellow STD/ISD booths lined up neatly next to the airport that proclaimed 'TAXIS.'

They dialled Tim from the telephone booth.

'What do you mean you don't know?' Koena cried into the receiver. She had to shout to make herself heard over the din of the loudspeaker nearby.

'Koena, Koena, listen to me, please,' Tim cooed over the phone, his tone oscillating between cajoling, soft, and manipulative.

Don't you try that on me! I am a master at this. Koena thought angrily.

'No, Tim, you listen to me,' she snapped. 'We have had one of the bumpiest flights and want to reach the venue as soon as possible and settle down. Now, you are coolly telling me the driver has the flu, and we have to make alternate arrangements. Tell me, when did you get to know this?' Koena demanded.

Sagar thought she looked particularly menacing when she stood like that, with her hand on her hip. From experience, he knew she was in a bad mood. Tim had better have an alternative solution, or Koena would bite his head off soon.

'Fine,' shouted Koena before banging the receiver down. Tim had pleaded with her to find an alternative source of transport and reach Chirimiri latest by the next day.

After paying the guy at the phone booth, the duo started walking towards the taxi stand. There was a serpentine queue, and they wondered when they would get to Chirimiri.

■

MAY 8, 2000
Taj Bengal, Kolkata
7:30 p.m.

SHOM RETURNED TO his hotel room a long time before his wife's plane had landed. His head was still caught up in knots over her sudden flight to that god-forsaken place, sighing over Koena's obstinate demands. Why did she have to run away on this assignment?

This woman! She has a mind of her own, is obstinate, and never listens to me! Of all the places, why did she have to choose this one?

Shom felt angry and humiliated. He had categorically asked her not to go. But, remembering her smiling face, he let out a sigh. His anger dissipated slowly. And frustration set in.

I love her! Whatever makes her happy! Let me do some damage control.

Shom made a phone call and spoke briefly, making necessary arrangements. He thanked the person at the other end and disconnected. He felt better.

It is just for two days. I'm sure he will manage to keep her out of trouble.

Thoughts about Koena nagged Shom.

When he needed her the most, when they had planned to take a family vacation, she had run off on some assignment! And to which corner of the Earth had she gone? Chirimiri, for god's sake!

Shrugging his melancholy, Shom decided to wait it out. He called up his friends and confirmed their presence for the vacation. Koena would be back by the 10th, and they could fly off on her birthday, May 11th.

After mentally ticking off items to be purchased for Koena's surprise birthday party, Shom freshened up, ordered dinner, and booted his Mac. He worked for a while, then checked his watch and realized it was too early to call Koena.

'Will call her in some time… She would have reached her destination by then.' He decided to take a small nap. He lay down but was so tired that he woke up only the next morning.

■

MAY 8, 2000

Nirmal's House, Chirimiri

4:30 a.m.

WHEN NIRMAL MAHATO woke up that day, the sun was behind clouds— a hidden message from the elements around about impending danger, of grey clouds masking the glory of a sun-kissed life. His wife, Neeta, brought him his usual cup of strong ginger-flavoured tea. Nirmal looked fondly at his eight-month pregnant wife, caressing her arm lovingly. Any time now, they would have to visit the hospital. He had already applied for leave. They had been married for so many years, but their romance had not dimmed.

She handed him his cup. He held it with his left hand, and with his right, he pulled her towards him, urging her to sit on the cot beside him. As she demurely sat next to him, he realized with a fondness that she still had the same shy smile and demeanour she had had when she had come to this house as a young bride.

Nirmal was a nice man. He took good care of his wife and son. After Nirmal finished his tea, Neeta packed lunch for him and rushed to wake up Anand, who always wanted to stand at the doorway to wave at his father. Nirmal and Neeta lived in the settlement behind the *babus*' quarters.

From the house, Neeta could easily see the yawning entrance of the mine and the mammoth iron and steel structure that stood ominously over the opening. It beckoned to her many a time, teasing her to come and see what lay underneaththe seemingly solid ground. Neeta knew that her husband's profession was fraught with dangers.

When Nirmal waved at her from the gate, she waved back, as usual, urging him to take care. Nirmal nodded his head before donning his yellow miners' hat. At the gate, he turned to wave at his little son one last time.

The little boy broke into giggles, wrenched his hand away from his mother's and ran to his father, his silky hair waving in the wind. Nirmal easily caught the boy and swung him in the air, making him burst out in giggles. He then fist-bumped Anand, gave him a peck on his nose and went off.

He would be back soon, he promised. The boy nodded eagerly, his toothless grin warming his father's heart.

After some time, when Neeta was sipping her tea, sitting on the rope-strung cot outside the house, she heard a deep rumble near the mine's opening. She didn't give much thought to it as these noises and rumblings were part of her daily life. When the rumbling didn't stop even after a while, she hesitated and looked up.

The emergency alarm went off just then, shrieking to make its presence felt.

An emergency!

A thick black trail of smoke was winding up from the opening, making its way towards the heavens, as if building a path for souls to cross over.

Frowning, she kept her cup down, crossed the threshold of the house, and stepped into the sunlight. When she came to the narrow road, she heard soul-chilling screams and howls of women. And men. Panicked, she started walking fast. Her son had gone to school and would be back by noon.

The sinking feeling in the pit of her stomach was distressing. Her feet flew over the sand and stones, and she reached the wire fence that separated the settlement from the entrance to the mines. The whole place was shrouded in thick black acrid smoke making its way towards the settlement, bringing with it the news of death: the death of loved ones—the death of husbands and breadwinners.

The smoke and the sunlight together threatened to subdue the rising yelp from the deep confines of Neeta's swollen belly. Bile rose to her throat and gagged her. She tried to swallow it down, and, with it, curb the fear of losing Nirmal. She kept walking, determined, hoping. In her right hand, she clutched her mangalsutra, her lips muttering prayers to all the gods she had been taught to please. She crossed the wire fence and stepped over the opening to enter the mine area.

A foreman saw Neeta and came running towards her. His contorted face made Neeta feel sick. She could see the chaos around her like it was happening on a film reel, removed from the reality of it all. He gulped his sorrow now and then while his eyes chose freedom and expressed their solidarity with Neeta's once he brought her up to date with the shocking accident. Finally, he blurted, 'Neeta… Nirmal… Nirmal is no more.'

Registering the mortal blow, she gave up the struggle to stand and slipped down onto the warm, soft sand. When she slumped down, dust rose slightly, made space for her, and settled on her, covering her in its motherly embrace, comforting her.

The cloud of smoke settled around her slowly, but the clouds of dust hovered around. Neeta stirred after some time and raised her head. The foreman had gone on to deliver the news to others.

Neeta could not see anyone, anything, beyond the dust. Suddenly, everything—men, jeeps, blaring sirens—everything was tuned out. Everything around merged into the greyness within her. She kept staring at the grey cloud, wishing it all to be a nightmare. She came to her senses when a worker crossed her, asking if she was alright.

Nodding, she slowly got up and walked towards the cordoned area. A thought struck her. Was her baby alright? Would she have inadvertently hurt it when she fell? God could not be so harsh! She rubbed her belly and felt for the baby's movements, her heart beating faster—as if to reassure her that it was okay: her baby gave a strong kick. Neeta cried out first with joy, then tears of sorrow.

Exhausted by the effort, she sat down on a broken discarded vehicle piece, staring into the distance where the rescue workers were pulling people out of the mine. Her mind had blocked every thought and had just become calm. Still.

After a while, the rescue team finished pulling out the charred remains of the unfortunate miners. They laid out the remains on plastic sheets, waiting to be identified; by shoes, rings—by instinct, anything.

Nirmal had been wearing a bangle given by a Sadhu. For longevity – the Sadhu had promised.

Neeta stood up slowly and walked towards the heap of bodies lying near the gate. A rescue team member saw her approaching and asked, 'Are you looking for someone? What is his name?'

It was always a 'his'—since women were not allowed inside the mines.

Neeta, rooted in the Indian tradition and age-old customs, found it very difficult to say her husband's name aloud, that too to a strange man. She swallowed a few times before mumbling her husband's name, 'Nirmal…Nirmal Mahato.'

'Hmm… let me see. Nirmal Mahato. Any identification marks? Like a ring, his ID number?' the man asked kindly. He had soft understanding eyes. Neeta kept her eyes trained on the bodies, furtively looking for some identification, any sign that maybe the calamity was just a huge misunderstanding. Something that had happened to others, and not her loving man.

In the heap of charred bodies, only the helmets had escaped the inferno. They boldly sat there, near the heads of their owners, proclaiming to the world their invincibility.

Neeta nodded. She knew the number by heart.

'Yes, 130522.' Neeta said.

'Okay. Let me see. 130520, 134561, 130532, and… yes, here it is, 130522.'

'Listen, come here,' the man urged. He had large hands and bow legs. Neeta looked at his eyes; they were compassionate, she thought. He pointed at a corpse covered with a white sheet from head to toe. White was the colour of the dead. Neeta wondered if Nirmal minded being covered like that. Her rational mind reminded her that he was in no position to mind anything. White was a colour Nirmal had never worn, though.

He liked red, the colour of life, the colour of blood. The white sheet had some red marks on it, making it look like a designer bedsheet.

When Neeta walked towards the corpse, about to lift the sheet, the man held her hand and softly said, 'Umm, maybe you shouldn't see it. You won't be able to bear it, especially in this condition, please.'

'What else can go wrong, tell me, *dada*? I have lost my husband: my child has lost its father before even meeting him…I'm completely helpless! What else will go wrong? I can do this, *dada*. I can do this. I will…do this.' Neeta added after a pause, resolutely squaring her shoulders. The man nodded and left her alone to her sorrow.

With trembling hands and steely nerves, Neeta slowly uncovered the face. A scream left her bowels and traversed upwards, gaining velocity as it travelled. Sorrow compounded the process of slow sufferance. The face of her husband—her lover, her partner for life, looked gory.

Where was the face? The mass of flesh staring back at her with lifeless disdain was that of a stranger, a mound of flesh waiting for time to take over.

The man hovered somewhere in the distance, waiting for her to internalize the situation and unhinge him from the acceptance of her new reality. Her breakfast travelled back upwards and made her stomach lighter. Neeta felt dizzy. She steadied herself and beckoned to the man standing at a distance.

She identified Nirmal's body–what remained of it–by the hand that was still wearing the bangle. Neeta stared at it, her head reeling with images of a day when they had visited the 'famous' Sadhu to foretell the future of their unborn child. He had gallantly observed Neeta's enthusiasm and Nirmal's stoic silence before claiming a hundred years of life for the man and two more kids in the near future.

She caressed the hand gently, running her fingers on the bangle, the fake godman's fake bangle for longevity. *Sau saal jiyega!* He will live for 100 years; the Sadhu had claimed.

Nirmal was just forty-two, and he was dead. Cold. Gone.

At forty, she was a widow with two children.

Sobbing, she slowly sank near the body. Her beloved husband, now only mangled, charred body parts, was missing a hand–the other hand was saved probably because of the lucky bangle–and a leg. The face of the father of her children was burnt, but not so much that she could not identify him. Nirmal looked peaceful in death. A portion of his handsome face, his right cheek and eye, was intact. She bent down to kiss it. She would not have dared to do this some other time. It was not proper to express affection like this, in public, where others might see. Neeta wondered if he had thought of her when death came.

She would have been glad if she knew, somehow, that Nirmal had thought of her and their kids before he breathed his last. Neeta sat there for some time with her hands on her belly, near the heap of bodies, watching silently while people worked around her, until a warm hand pressed down on her thin shoulders, shaking her out of her reverie.

'Neeta...get up...it's over...Come...' A soft voice permeated Neeta's shocked brain.

When Gariya had seen Neeta running towards the blast site, she had followed her. Gariya was Neeta's neighbour for the past few years and a close friend. She had heard about the blast from her husband, who had taken leave due to illness. She now promised the Elephant God a hundred coconuts for saving her husband's life. She had just finished bathing her youngest when she heard the explosion and saw Neeta running out of her house. She called out to her daughter to take care of the boy and blindly started running after Neeta. When she reached the site, the area was so dusty that it took her a while to spot the dust-covered, hunched form of Neeta.

Gariya sat on her haunches near her friend, put a hand on Neeta's shoulder, and said, 'Everything is over. He is dead. You have to be strong.' A sudden flash of light made Neeta look up in surprise. The source of the light moved, and her eyes focused on a thin, gaunt, dark face. A leering smile pasted on the face made Neeta wince.

The man with a camera, looking for the perfect angle, bent to take a picture with Neeta in the foreground, the corpses and the smoke-filled mine in the background. Incensed, Gariya screamed at him, 'Are you mad or what? Have you lost it completely? Do you have no humanity left? Are you even human? She has lost everything, and you are taking her picture?'

The man nodded nonchalantly, motioned her to move out of the frame, and continued to click. Gariya looked around, found a big piece of coal, and threw it at him. It caught him bang in the eye, and he yelped like a mad dog.

'*Haraamzaadi*!' He yelled and kicked Gariya in her stomach while holding a handkerchief to his rapidly swelling eye. He grabbed his camera and scurried away.

Gariya fell in a swoop, holding her abdomen, doubling up in pain. Neeta kept staring straight ahead, mindless of whatever was happening around her. She gently rocked, willing herself to vanish. She just wanted all of this to go away. The baby in her womb gave another kick, trying to jolt the body outside its sac to come to its senses, and, in a way, make her understand that life goes on, come what may.

The kick from the occupant inside her pulled Neeta to the reality of being a husband-less woman— a widow. She slowly got up, supporting her belly and back with her hands. She stood up and massaged her stomach to reassure the baby that she was alright—that she was alive and would live on—keep them both alive—come what may. She helped Gariya get up. The friends slowly made their way home, each lost in their pain.

The photographer was nowhere to be seen.

When the blast happened, a local freelance photographer had been waiting to click pictures of the DGM (Operations) for the latter's interview slated for a local paper. The photographer had hit gold when he heard the blast of his luck, and he quickly snapped hot and happening pictures of the blast and the affected people. Later, he made a lot of money selling the exclusive snaps.

A trusted source had passed on one of the pictures to Tim, who had then passed it on to Sagar and Koena.

■

MAY 8, 2000

Bilaspur Railway Station

12:00 p.m.

SAGAR AND KOENA were getting increasingly frustrated, waiting for the train to arrive. Koena kept staring at the picture of the woman and her research data. A face that could have easily sold any cosmetic products in the city was now the grief-stricken face of a woman who had lost a husband—a friend, the father of her children and a breadwinner. Koena shuddered to think what the woman would have undergone.

A few hours ago, they had hailed a taxi and got off at Bilaspur railway station. They had planned to take a train from there to Chirimiri. The train's ETA was midnight. The distance of 600 odd kilometres seemed to stretch out further than they had thought. An easy trip was beginning to look more like a crazy adventure. They had wasted so much time waiting for transport in between.

The train chugged in and offloaded scores of weary passengers and bright-eyed foreign tourists clicking away at anything that seemed remotely exotic. Koena glared at a foreigner who was eyeing her interestedly, seeming quite keen to take her picture.

Bone weary, Koena and Sagar gobbled some oily poori-aloo in the railway station's canteen. Koena had the forethought to buy a few bottles of mineral water. The passenger train made umpteen stops at smaller towns, but none sold drinking water. At least, not the type of water that city folk like Koena and Sagar could consume without worry.

What kept Koena awake for a while were the sights and sounds of the small quaint towns and villages they crossed. With the soothing cool air on her face, Koena eventually started relaxing and dozed off after some time. She woke up when she realized that someone was shaking her.

Sagar looked at her quizzically when she sat upright and held her head in both hands. 'Are you alright? Do you want a tablet? Did you have a nightmare? You were crying in your sleep.' Sagar shot questions at her.

'No, I'm alright. I just need some coffee.' Koena replied.

Soon,the train halted at a station with a loud proclamation of pausing for a while before resuming. The dimly lit station proudly proclaimed: *Paradol.*

Chaa, chaaa, chaaa.

The incessant announcement registered in Koena's tired brain, and she peeped out of her window. A young boy with a rotund friendly-looking face came to their window and offered tea for five rupees. Though Koena was craving for a cup of hot coffee, she decided to adjust with tea. After all, caffeine was caffeine, be it in tea or coffee. She took the mud cup gladly and took a sip. The strong, sweet brew hit her palette with varying degrees of taste, and she felt her mind relaxing.

Sagar took a sip of his tea and addressed the boy, 'Nice tea. How old are you?'

'I'm twelve. I want to become like Abdul Kalam once I grow up. This is just a temporary job.' The boy, Chotu, informed them and his face lit up with a bright smile.

He held out a packet of Parle G biscuits. 'The biscuits are free for you...' Chotu said and flashed another toothy grin at Koena. She gladly took the packet, pressed a ten-rupee note into the tiny reluctant hand, took the biscuit, dipped it in the tea and ate it, relishing the sweetness of the tea and the crispiness of the biscuit. The train blared and slowly started pulling away from the station. As it was making its way out, Koena and Sagar waved to Chotu.

■

MAY 9, 2000
Chirimiri
7:00 a.m.

AFTER CROSSING SEVENTY-FIVE stations, the train finally halted at the small, neatly maintained Chirimiri station. Koena felt rested, having caught up on sleep. Tim had thankfully arranged for their stay in a small but clean lodge called Sri Krishna Inn. The owner was the father of a special correspondent with another channel who was one of Tim's ex-girlfriends.

When the train rolled into the small platform, Koena stood near the door and peeped out, firmly gripping the handhold. She noticed that there were very few people at the train station. She had expected a decent crowd at this hour.

Weird.

After getting down, Sagar and Koena walked quickly out of the station and hired a rickshaw to the Inn. Koena noted that the town was small but neatly laid out. She admired the area as they passed the neat houses, the magistrate's office, the primary health care centre, and the post office.

Their rooms at the Inn were cosy and comfortable, with attached bathrooms. Since they were special guests, the owner had let out his best rooms to them. He had also arranged breakfast for them in their rooms once they freshened up.

After breakfast, they decided to recce the area and find out about the blast from the panchayat and other government offices. They also spoke to people in the market and made a quick trip to the local police station.

By noon, they were ready to give up. The town was uptight, and even the papers with Gandhiji's smiling face on them failed to elicit any response. They returned to the Inn, had lunch, and then decided to figure out how to reach the miner's *basti*. Maybe the actual scene would give them some clue.

■

MAY 9, 2000
Chirimiri
1:30 p.m.

KOENA AND SAGAR boarded a bus from the town bus-stand, which took them directly to the mines. The bus stopped, and all the passengers alighted. Most were miners, some were vegetable vendors, and some were carrying hens in baskets. They started walking towards some far-off sand dunes.

The duo got down and looked around, adjusting their backpacks. Koena spotted some huge lorries near the dunes. Many workers were loading sand onto them.

'Sand dug out of the mines.' Sagar whispered into Koena's ear.

'Hmm,' Koena nodded. 'How do we reach the *basti*?'

Sagar nodded and asked one of the miners getting off the bus (in what sounded like chaste Bangla), 'Where is the worker's *basti*?'

The man, probably a migrant from Bangladesh or rural West Bengal, smiled, showing his betel-stained crooked teeth and pointed in the direction of the sand dunes.

Koena's jaw fell open.

This boy is something. When did he pick up Bangla?

'Whoa! You are something, aren't you?' Koena exclaimed while the worker hung around, looking at them in awe. Sagar stuffed a few rupee notes into his hands and saw him off. Koena ruffled his hair proudly, making Sagar blush.

He certainly knows how to get his work done. How did he learn Bangla?

She quizzed him about the newly picked-up language. Sagar merely shrugged and smiled before saying, 'Oh, just like that, Koena! I like Bangla. After living in Bhubaneswar for twenty years, I can speak Oriya fluently. Bangla seemed easier to pick up.'

'Oh, I didn't know you grew up here. I thought you grew up in Mumbai.' Koena raised a surprised eyebrow while they made their way to the mines in the hot afternoon sun. It was more than a kilometre away. From the main road, it hadn't seemed that far.

Koena looked around. There were no trees or buildings: just a vast stretch of landas far as the eyes could see and heaps of coal. As they neared the dunes, the coal mines came into distant view.

I am happy I decided to bring only jeans and T-shirts. I would have suffocated in my trousers. I should have gotten another tube of sunscreen. Anyway, it is just for a day.

Sagar smiled sheepishly. 'Okay, you got me there! I did migrate from Mumbai, but when I was in school, I had a few Bengali and Oriya friends… And I am good at picking up new languages.'

'Now, that makes perfect sense, Sagar.' Koena remarked, grinning as she studied the workers walking ahead of them. They wore what looked like a uniform: half-pants covered in coal dust and torn vests. All of them were wearing similar boots, some yawning near the toes. Koena looked down at her fairly new sneakers and felt a bit ridiculous. As if to distract her, a miner who was walking alongside, commented, '*Babu*, most workers in these mines migrate from West Bengal or Bihar. Some are from Bangladesh also. Where are you from?'

Koena looked at the miner curiously, but he kept his eyes averted and focused only on Sagar, who Sagar chatted happily with him, placing an arm over his shoulder. The men moved away while she trailed behind, the heat catching up with her. She took out a cap from her bag and wore it. *Some respite from the heat!*

They could see some buildings in the distance now and a huge wire fence going around. They spotted a settlement at the far end. Koena took a few pictures, making heads turn. She had been attracting a lot of attention and sly smiles from the workers while they had been walking. She knew they didn't mean any harm; it was idle curiosity.

'That's the settlement... most workers live there. Some of us live in the town.' Their miner-friend informed Sagar.

Raucous giggles distracted the group. Some boys on bicycles came into view. Their legs pedalling furiously, they emerged like little warriors from the side of the open cast mines. Grubby and covered in coal dust, their clothes had patches. Their faces were determined. Each bicycle had a pillion rider, who was balancing a huge bag of coal on his lap.

Koena raised her eyebrows at Sagar, who bid goodbye to his new best friend and came trotting towards her. The miners made their way into the office buildings.

'These boys dig up coal from the open cast mines and sell them in the market for some quick cash.' Sagar observed.

Koena nodded, a sudden realization dawning in her head. *Aah! They sell sand; they sell coal.*

'No wonder so many accidents happen.' Koena shook her head sadly, wondering about the state of the mines.

Sagar placed a hand over Koena's elbow and stopped her. 'What do you plan to do? We need to speak with the Manager and visit the settlement to meet Neeta. Which do we tackle first?'

'Let's meet the Manager first. Then we will go to meet Neeta.' Koena already had a plan.

The meeting with the Manager went off peacefully. Tim had informed him to be as helpful as possible. Koena was amazed at Tim's networking abilities.

They made their way to the worker's settlement, which was a small village – complete with a well and closely-packed huts. Each hut had a mud wall running around its periphery. Some huts had a small temple built inside the compound. Koena could make out a small dispensary, which was padlocked. Koena and Sagar did a quick recce and got to work. They learned that the village had around seven thousand homes. Most workers of the Chirimiri mines lived there.

They approached the miners sitting on the chowk and smoking beedis. The chowk had a small circular stage with a large stone umbrella offering some shade from the unrelenting sun. Koena asked the questions, and Sagar took care of the rest. He acted as the cameraman too. The miners were quite eager to share information about the blast. Koena nodded when Sagar asked if she had gotten enough to move on. They had decided to start with the miners, then talk to Neeta, whose picture they had seen from Tim. After that, they would go to the blast site and talk to some Managers, if possible.

Sagar got some great pictures of the miners' huts and the smoke still gushing out of the blast site. They walked towards one of the huts and asked the man sitting outside on a thread charpoy, 'Do you know her?'

The man looked at the picture and shook his head.

'See again, please. This is Neeta. We want to talk to her.' Koena squatted near the man and urged. He threw a careless glance at the picture and shook his head before hurriedly looking away. Sagar shrugged and motioned to Koena to move on. It was already 3 'o clock, and they had to be back to the Inn before sunset. The Inn owner had been quite concerned about traveling at night.

Koena's eyes fell on a small boy playing with a ball near one of the huts. She walked up to him, showed the picture, and asked, 'Do you know her?'

The boy saw the photo, traced a finger on it, and broke into a happy smile, saying, 'Ma.'

Koena's eyes immediately filled with joy. *Gotcha!* She jumped and waved at Sagar, who jogged towards her, his eyebrows quivering in excitement. Koena managed to control herself and asked the boy if he could take them to his house. The boy turned and started walking, occasionally turning to see if they were following. Koena and Sagar kept walking and soon were standing outside another small hut.

The boy rushed into the ajar door, shouting for his mother. Hearing the boy's animated cries, a woman came out and looked curiously at the visitors. She pushed the boy inside the house.

'What do you want?' She asked, eying them suspiciously. Well-dressed strangers in these parts always meant trouble!

'Are you Neeta?' Koena asked pointedly, ignoring the glares that the village folk were throwing in their direction.

'No, Neeta is inside. I'm Gariya. What do you want? Who are you?' She repeated her questions. Her eyes darted around, taking in the curiosity that the two people were generating.

Koena folded her hands in a Namaste and said, 'I'm Koena, and this is Sagar. We have come from Bhubaneshwar. We want to interview Neeta.'

'She is not in a state to talk to anyone. You can go now. Come tomorrow, please,' Gariya replied. Her voice was surely polite but firm. She was a woman used to being firm.

'Gariya, please try to understand. We have come all the way from Bhubaneshwar just to talk to Neeta. Would you please let us talk to her? We won't take long, I promise.' Koena urged, her eyes pleading.

'Memsaab, it is you who is not able to understand. Are you married?' Gariya had now put her arms on her hips; her stance was almost threatening—she meant business.

'Yes,' Koena replied, wondering where this was leading to.

'What is his name?' Gariya asked, stepping down from the porch and standing in front of Koena. Her face was set, and a lone nerve was throbbing on her right temple. Koena took in all this in a split second, sensing trouble.

'Shom…' Koena replied, utterly flummoxed.

'If Shom dies this instant, and I ask you to talk to me about it, will you be able to do that? If you can… Neeta will talk to you.' Gariya folded her arms over her chest, glaring at Koena.

Koena felt as if someone had punched her hard in the gut. She could feel the pain coursing through her nerves. Her eyes blurred with unshed tears.

Sagar looked at Gariya and then at Koena, shocked. Flushing angrily, he stepped forward to take the woman head-on when a soft hand reached out and held him back. He looked at Koena with stricken eyes— a slight nod from her, and he understood.

'Uh, you… you're right. We will come back…later.' Koena hastily interjected, recovering. She looked at Gariya and saw a spark of compassion in the keenly intelligent woman's eyes.

'Thanks,' Gariya said with folded hands. Koena knew she meant it.

Koena and Sagar walked out of the compound and decided to head back to the Inn. They could come back in the morning the next day to talk to Neeta.

When they were walking back towards the bus stop, Koena suddenly announced, 'I have to talk to Shom!'

She dialled Shom's mobile. The call went through, but Shom did not attend.

'What is he doing?' Koena wondered. Her heart was racing after Gariya's comment, and she urgently needed reassurance to hear her husband's voice; she wanted to be sure he was safe.

When Shom finally took the call, he laughed and said, 'Someone is missing me bad. Baby, what's up?'

'Shom! Where were you? I was so desperate to hear your voice.' Koena cried, tears welling up.

'Baby, shh, shh… why are you crying? I am at home, darling. Where will I go? What happened, tell me?' Shom cooed, stirring soup in a pot. He could sense that she was in distress and needed comfort.

Koena related the entire incident and sobbed into the phone. Shom switched off the stove, sat down, and heard her out patiently.

'Koena, listen to me! I'm alright. That woman just gave you an example to make you understand, alright?'

'I know! But I'm so disgusted with myself for having been so callous. I should not have asked her that, right?' Koena asked, feeling rotten.

'No, it was your duty to ask questions… But your timing was terrible. Maybe you should have given the woman some time to mourn, at least. You can empathize with her. You know, do that heart-to-heart talking that you are so good at!' Shom said, bringing a smile to her face.

'Thanks, sweetheart. You know why I love you madly. You are the best. Will talk to you later!' Koena said and hung up. It was such a relief talking to Shom. He could make the worst disaster disappear just like that.

She then turned to Sagar, saying, 'I feel much better. Let us take a look at the blast site and then call it a day, okay?'

She was feeling more enthused after discussing her fears with Shom. Sagar merely nodded. Slowly, they made their way towards the mine entrance. They could see the acrid smoke making its way towards the sky. A fire engine stood nearby, and many people had gathered around it, discussing the incident.

Koena and Sagar walked towards some miners who were coming from the opposite direction. The miners were dressed in vests and shorts. They wore miners' boots made of canvas and a steel toe. A black coating covered their bodies. Only their faces were clean. Sagar took some pictures of the miners. Some even posed for him happily. Koena smiled at them, introduced herself and Sagar, and asked them about the blast.

'When did this happen? How many people were inside the mine?' Koena asked an old miner in Hindi.

The man was carrying a spade. He removed his miner's hat and answered, 'It happened when the shift was changing… I was about to go… But I didn't go. Before that, I heard the blast.' His friend nodded and put a hand on his shoulder, adding, 'Even I didn't go. Today, we got lucky.' Koena smiled at them. A few other miners were walking nearby, and Sagar turned around to engage them.

Koena held her recorder closer and asked, 'How many people were inside?'

'Around fifty.' The man seemed pretty sure of the number.

'Any idea what caused the blast?'

'A methane leak in the mine. It is common in these mines. Poor Nirmal… I feel sorry for the boy…' Another miner joined the conversation.

Nirmal! Who is he?

'Who is… was Nirmal?'

'Our supervisor… His wife, Neeta… poor girl…'

Nirmal was Neeta's husband! Now, that is some angle.

She motioned to Sagar, who started talking to another group about Nirmal. Koena continued with the miner, who was eager to be interviewed.

'Did you see the explosion?'

'Yes, I was walking towards the village. My son was with me. The explosion was huge. There was dust and black smoke everywhere.' The man circled his head with his arms to describe the impact. He had tears in his eyes.

'How many times has this happened before?' Koena turned to ask other miners who had surrounded the duo. Some of them looked pensive; a few looked unsure if they had crossed some hidden line of protocol. In their excitement to talk about the incident that had shaken their lives, they had forgotten about following the protocol.

'What is happening here?' A gruff voice distracted Koena. She turned sharply and noticed a man dressed in a black T-shirt and standard denims staring at the miners. Koena stopped her recorder and stared back at the man. The miners took off, not looking back even once. Sagar turned to follow them, but Koena held him back.

Now is not the time.

'We are from the TNN… The News Network, Bhubaneswar. May I know who you are, Sir?' Koena added the guy with some practised smoothness.

Not fooled by her charm, the man wordlessly turned away and walked towards the offices.

Her heart sank. *There goes my interview.*

They made their way to the village and decided to call it a day. It was almost 4 p.m.. When they were walking towards the nearly deserted chowk, Koena noticed a man, at a distance near the dunes, getting down from a jeep and looking in their direction with a pair of binoculars.

Now, why would anybody do that?

Koena kept her eyes trained on a miner while discreetly observing the guy with the binoculars.

Somebody is very interested in us. Wonder why? Something is amiss. What could it be?

She turned to Sagar, whispering, 'Hey... The guy at 12 o'clock. Don't move too much. Is he keeping an eye on us?'

Sagar nodded infinitesimally after putting on his sunglasses, taking a look at the man.

They were sitting on a stone bench under a tree, eating sandwiches that the Inn owner had packed for them. Sagar got up, stretched, and started doing sit-ups, but Koena ignored him. After a while, he plonked down beside her and said, 'Maybe he is a ruffian who keeps an eye on these workers, you know... part of the management.'

'Hmm, but he seems to be keeping an eye on us, particularly. Look at his clothes, like he is some forest officer. Don't miss the rifle, though. Naxalite?' Koena stared at the man's bottle green uniform, not missing the rifle hanging innocently at his hip.

'Must be. They're everywhere. I saw a guy talking to the miners after we moved away. One of the miners pointed at Neeta's house. While you were talking to Gariya, I noticed that a man was keeping an eye on us. Let's ignore him,' Sagar said, munching on his sandwich.

With the material they had, a story had already taken shape. They took the same rickety bus back to the town centre and walked back to the Inn.

They discussed the day's events, ate an early dinner, and retired to their rooms. Koena could not sleep. She got up, and after switching on the light, sat down to write the day's entry into the network's database.

She kept thinking about the blast. Something was amiss.

There was one large piece missing in this whole puzzle. Till now, she had deduced that the explosion in the mine was not because of a safety issue and looked more like a plot. But if it was a plot, why did they kill so many innocent miners?

Why would anyone try to blow up a coal mine with coal worth obscene amounts of money? Either the perpetrator had taken a bad risk or did it deliberately to derail some other bigger plot.

'Or it was a ploy to distract people from something more sinister?' Sagar had declared earlier in the evening. Koena decided to pursue that angle.

A miner had confessed in hushed tones about how the coal lobby had tried to unravel the government's efforts to regularize the workers' compensation. He had hurried away when she had whipped out her recorder, though. Recollecting that conversation, Koena wondered if the so-called lobby was behind the explosion. Or was it the Naxals? Or someone else?

Who would be the biggest loser if the plans had come through? That person, that loser was the culprit behind the blast.

■

MAY 9, 2000
Chirimiri
7:30 p.m.

'LAL SALAAM! WHAT news do you have? What is happening in the settlement?' asked the man with the revolver. Rana Haldar – Rana *da* to his loyal men – was on the run from the law for the past few years. He had a hideout in China. When things cooled off a bit, he would cross over to West Bengal through the porous border. He was a Naxalite, and the State Government had announced a prize of 10 lakhs to whoever could give some relevant information about him. He was known to be a ruthless barbarian. There were many stories to attest to that; some true, some rural legends.

'Rana da, the journalists are talking to the miners. They're asking too many questions. They visited Nirmal's house also. But Neeta didn't talk to them,' the man informed.

'Hmm, did you hear what questions they were asking?' asked Rana.

'No *dada*, I kept an eye on them from a distance. I didn't want them to notice me or take my picture,' the man replied, feeling quite clever.

'What crap! Are you Salman Khan that they will want to take your picture? Why didn't you pose as a miner to see what they wanted? I heard from *Babu* that a few others have also come here to cover the blast! Is it true?' Rana asked. He didn't want the area to get too much attention.

'*Dada*, it is true! Four media persons have come, out of whom two are staying at a lodge in the town,' the man informed.

'Okay, you keep an eye on these people...see that they don't talk to the miners a lot. Ensure that the miners do not blurt anything. If anybody says anything, bring them over!' Rana ordered.

The informant scurried away.

■

MAY 9, 2000
Tim's House
Around Midnight

BRRR... BRRR... BRRR...

The phone on the side table announced its presence with a loud vibration. The man sleeping on the bed nearby did not even stir. The phone kept vibrating. Tim was fast asleep. After a long day at work, Tim had put his phone on silent mode and had gone to sleep.

Then the landline started ringing. This time, Tim woke up and picked up the receiver.

'Damn,' he cursed, 'Why are you calling me at this hour?' Tim wondered, cursing aloud.

Choubey spoke without any perfunctory pleasantries, 'Tigmanshu, have you sent Koena and Sagar to Chirimiri?'

He was the only person who called Tim by his full name.

'Err, yes. You had gone to cover the worker's strike in Jharkhand... I urgently wanted someone to go there and cover the blast,' Tim said. He had a bad feeling in his stomach. He could sense a feeling of doom from Choubey's tone. 'Why, what happened? Why are you asking me this? Most importantly, you called me at midnight for this?' Tim demanded.

'Forget all that. You have sent them to their deaths! That area is teeming with Naxalites. I just heard that Rana Haldar himself has come down and is now hiding in those jungles bordering the town. I heard from my sources that he was planning to kidnap any media people who came to cover the blast. You could have at least checked with me or called me before packing them off. Couldn't you reach me on my mobile phone?' Choubey asked, frustrated with Tim's stupidity.

Tim's blood ran cold when he heard this. And he gulped. This news about Rana's presence complicated things. He cleared his throat, saying, 'Choubey, now what do I do? I… oh God! Should I call them back? I had forgotten about Rana. You did mention this to me a few weeks back.'

He slapped his forehead as the fear overtook him.

'No use. I will do something. I have some contacts, and I will ensure Koena and Sagar are unharmed. But please ask them to return as soon as possible. I will get you whatever information you need,' Choubey said and cut the call.

Tim sat down on his bed, wiping his perspiring forehead.

As promised, Choubey immediately spoke to a few of his contacts and extracted a promise from one of them to keep tabs on Koena and Sagar. The man promised Choubey that he would put in a word to Rana to ensure that he didn't harm Koena and Sagar.

■

MAY 9, 2000

Ashiana Apartments

6:30 p.m.

SHOM WOUND UP for the day and came home early. He had wanted to spend some time reading and relaxing at home. He undressed and took a hot shower. After dressing, he switched on the TV. His thoughts wandered…*Koena said she would return in a day, on her birthday. She had confirmed the vacation plans, too. I hope she likes my surprise party idea…*

Koena had called to inform him that as per the plan, they would be leaving Chirimiri late at night and reaching Bhubaneswar the next morning. Their flight to Seychelles was only at night.

Shom browsed through all the channels. None offered anything new. Shom browsed through the news channels daily to check if his wife or Sagar were reporting something. Even the TNN channel did not have any updates on the blast. Shom switched the TV off and sat down at his desk to work.

It was pretty late when he finally looked up and realized he hadn't heard from his wife. His mobile phone screen came to life. Shom picked it up, expecting Koena's call. An unknown number was displayed. Frowning, Shom took the call.

'Hello.'

'Shom *babu*?' A gruff man's voice asked.

'Yes. Who is this?' asked Shom.

'Ask your wife not to ask many questions. *Bou jivito chaii toh*? (You want your wife back alive, right?)' Warned the man and cut the call.

'What do you... hello... hello?' Shom shouted, agitated. The monotonous sound of the disconnected call hung like a thick, suffocating cloud over his head.

His mobile phone rang again. Shom looked at the display; it said, 'Koena.'

'Hello, Koena!' Shom said, relief evident in his voice.

'Hi baby, how are you? What are you doing? Why was your phone not reachable for so long? I came back just now and wanted to talk to you,' Koena gushed. Perched on the bed, she ran her hand through her hair, visualising Shom's face.

'Listen, *shona*... Listen to me carefully,' Shom said, dead serious. He hadn't liked the man's tone at all.

'Yes... tell me, what happened?' Koena urged, sitting up on the bed. She could feel the tension in Shom's voice. He was obviously troubled about something.

What was it? Had something happened at the restaurant? Was Kit alright?

Koena's mind went over countless scenarios in quick succession.

'Shona, you and Sagar have to return immediately! You guys get out of that place right now! I know you have a booking for tonight. But I want you both to start as soon as possible, do you hear me?' Shom ordered, his voice quivering slightly. He was scared for his wife. The call had shaken him.

A stray thought crossed his mind. *Am I overreacting? Should I talk to my contact? Who was this guy who had called?*

He shrugged mentally. *Even if I am, I don't want to find out otherwise. I don't know who these people are...*

'But why, sweetheart? We have not yet done the interview we were supposed to do. We will just meet that woman, Neeta, and board the train tomorrow,' Koena replied, perplexed at her husband's demands.

She could not understand what had gotten into him. In any case, their stay had got extended by only a day. They had initially planned to return on the 11th; now, they were returning on the 12th instead. Koena ruefully realised that she would spend her birthday on the field, probably with Sagar for company. Her heart sank, but she perked up at the thought that she could meet Shom the next day, at least. She had already started missing him so much.

'Listen, Koena... You do what I am asking you to do. Is that clear? You and Sagar get on the first train from there, goddamn it, and return home. That is an order. Do you get it?' Shom barked into the phone.

'Okay, okay, we will. Now you relax. I will call you tomorrow after I start!' Koena said soothingly and disconnected the call.

■

MAY 9, 2000
Chirimiri
7:00 p.m.

'WAS THAT SHOM? What happened?' Sagar asked, turning to look at Koena's worried face. They were going through the interview's responses and uploading the data onto their network's server. He was sitting in a chair and had his laptop on a side table. Koena's hmms were getting longer and angrier, Sagar could tell.

'Nothing! He wants us both to return home immediately. I think there is more to it. He is not telling me the whole truth...' Koena replied.

'Strange, you know. Tim called while you were talking to Shom... He also said the same thing. In fact, he begged me to return.' Sagar informed.

'What? Really?'

'Yes.'

'Then there is certainly something that is going to happen... or has already happened. These guys are trying to save us from something or somebody. I'm sure. Shom is not someone who gets scared easily.' Koena said, worry dotting her forehead. Chewing her lip, she continued in a whisper, reflecting the myriad emotions running through her.

So, in all certainty, someone doesn't like us questioning. I want to know who. That someone is the key to this whole mystery. This is certainly about the blast… And they are trying to stop us from finding out the truth.

Sagar and Koena finished their reports and sent them to Tim. They had skipped dinner. Sagar retired for the night after promising to get up early. Koena shut the door behind him and plonked down on her bed. She checked her phone for messages. There were 5 from Shom and 1 from Kit. She replied to all of them and closed her eyes, but sleep eluded her. Dreams flitted past, dancing, luring, and provoking her. Koena tossed and turned the whole night.

Tomorrow is an important day!.

■

MAY 10, 2000
Chirimiri
5:00 a.m.

WHEN SAGAR WOKE up, he felt very disoriented. He was unable to comprehend his coordinates. He sat up slowly on the small, strange bed and rubbed his eyes. Where was he?

Then his memory kicked in, and he recollected everything. He completed his ablutions and went out to check on Koena. When he knocked on her door, there was no response. He knocked twice more. Koena heard the knock in her sleep. She was admiring a woodpecker seated on a tree in a jungle, where she, Kit, and Shom had gone for a vacation. The bird flew away, but Koena could still hear its sound: Rat-a-tat… rat-a tat… rat-a tat-a-tat.

When she could not ignore the noise anymore, her mind woke her up, pulling her back to reality. Someone was banging on the door. She was at the Inn in Chirimiri! When she finally let Sagar in, he was looking worried. 'Why weren't you opening the door?'

'I was sleeping!'

'Yeah, right… I knocked a thousand times. Man, you must be tired.' He observed.

'Yeah… come, let us get some coffee and breakfast.' Koena said, shaking her head.

What a weird dream she had had!

■

MAY 10, 2000
Chirimiri
7:00 a.m.

SAGAR AND KOENA made their way back to Neeta's house after tucking into a huge breakfast and packing their things, ready to leave at a moment's notice. They had planned to finish interviewing Neeta, return to the Inn, grab their stuff, and leave for the station.

■

MAY 10, 2000
Chirimiri
8:00 a.m.

THE RICKETY OLD bus dutifully took them to the settlement. Sagar and Koena reached Neeta's house quickly. The village seemed quiet at this time of the day. Neeta's son was playing outside the hut. There was no sign of Gariya, though. Koena stepped forward and knocked.

■

The Daughter

Kosa, Chhattisgarh

KOSA, A BUSTLING slum near Chirimiri collieries, was like a railway station. It had people from different cultures; some settlers, some simply looking to make a quick buck. The slum-dwellers worked in either the chemical factories or the coal mines. Some also worked in the nearby slaughterhouse. Though all inhabitants were migrants from either nearby Bihar or far-off Nepal, those who worked in the slaughterhouse were usually from a lower caste. *Chamaars*—they were called. The coal mine workers lived together, sharing tips and work opportunities with each other. Looking out for one another was a given. One such female worker was Lokki.

■

MAY 11, 1960
Kosa
1:00 p.m.

ON A HARSH summer afternoon, in a derelict mud house, a teenaged girl of around fifteen lay on a torn mat, writhing in pain. Labor, they say, extracts its pound of flesh in full.

Two old women sat next to her, watching her with sullen, worried expressions on their faces. The girl screamed, her hands flailing at her sides, grabbing the shabby bedsheet as if to gather some hold on her circumstances. The shrieks cut through the stillness of the summer heat and pierced the women's ears. Accompanying the girl's pitiable screams were newer ones that almost got drowned out–that of the newborn. The women brought warm wet towels and bathed the unconscious girl's head.

The girl did not stir— she lay still, with her legs splayed.

A small creature, a product of the girl's pain and trauma, lay between her legs, bathed in her blood, urine, and faeces. It made guttural sounds, demanding to be cleaned. One of the women picked up the baby girl and cooed to it. The baby stopped her gurgling and turned her head. Her eyes were tightly shut as if she hated to open them to see the ugliness of the world.

The two older women took the baby into an enclosure in the hut and bathed her. They wiped the blood and gore off her small body and stared at her wrinkled but gleaming skin. The baby was fair, unlike her mother, who was dark. She had a head full of dark hair. And she had dimples like her mother.

The mother, still unconscious, lay on the mat. She had been named after the Goddess of wealth, Lakshmi. Most people called her Lokki.

Lokki worked in the coal mines as a *Kamin*, loading and unloading coal onto the waiting trains and lorries. She earned a meagre salary of five rupees a day. In her free time, she worked as a maid in the houses of the *babus*, the Managers of the coal mines. That fetched her a few more rupees.

The baby demanded cuddles and gave out guttural howls. One of the older women, the new mother's maternal aunt, put her on her mother's bosom and then cradled her, singing softly-a song to announce the arrival of a new life amongst hardships and sorrows. Meanwhile, the other older woman, the midwife, cleaned up the mother and left after giving post-delivery care instructions to the old aunt.

When Lokki eventually woke up, she looked around frantically, asking to see her baby.

But her baby was long gone!

She sobbed, 'Oh, my baby.'

Her aunt patted her back gently, saying, 'It is for the good of the baby. Don't worry; things will get sorted. You will get used to it, *shona*.'

'No! My poor baby!' Lokki wailed. She lay on the mat and cried for a long time; her face turned towards the thin wall of the ramshackle hut. When her tears had dried up, she turned her face towards the old woman and asked, 'Tell me, *Pishi ma*, is it a boy?'

'No *ma*, it is a girl. A beautiful girl with deep dimples, like you, and… with fair skin,' said the old woman, fondly kissing her wet and hot head. Lokki hugged her aunt and sniffled. What a terrible fate she had given her new-born—a bastard girl child brought into this unkind world! Lokki wept, thinking about the night the baby was conceived, behind the dunes, where the man had pounced on her.

Her aunt kept caressing her head, and in no time, Lokki slipped into an exhausted sleep.

Meanwhile, two nuns from the Missionaries of Charity, Kolkata, West Bengal, rocked the baby girl and took her away to a new future. The Holy Nun had created a wide safety net for all such babies born out of wedlock and to destitute women and then enveloped them into her warm embrace. Her organisation was an international not-for-profit, backed by very powerful people.

Nobody messed with the pious women. They went about quietly doing their work with a perpetual smile on their lips. Of such virtuous lineage were the two nuns who had come at the behest of the old aunt, who was part of their flock! They had a chance to improve their strength and had enveloped the newborn infant in their arms and cuddled it.

■

MAY 11, 1960

A Rickety Bus enroute to Kolkata

4:00 p.m.

THE BABY UNDERSTOOD intuitively that her life was changing. Barely in their twenties, Sister Sara and Sister Jane smiled their quiet half-smiles and cooed to the gurgling baby, the youngest addition to the overflowing orphanage at Kalighat. She was handed over to an *aaya*, who became the baby's foster mother.

■

KOSA

5:00 p.m.

BACK IN THE settlement in Kosa, Lokki wept for a long time. She refused to eat the rice porridge that her aunt offered.

'Lokki ma, eat something,' the older woman insisted. Lokki shook her head, refusing the outstretched hand.

The old woman shrugged her frail shoulders, ran a withered hand over the bent head, and pressed her palm on it for a few seconds. Lokki looked up at her concerned face for a few seconds before bursting into fresh tears. 'Pishi ma, why did you take my baby away? Why?'

'No, my child… No! She was not in your destiny. She will grow up in a better environment and go to school, as those nuns have promised. What would she get if you had brought her up, tell me?' The older woman reasoned, slowly settling down on her haunches. Old age was a curse, she bitterly thought to herself. Her legs and her back were killing her. All this baby delivery business was a strenuous job.

She hoped that Lokki, her niece, would quickly come to terms with her sorrow and move on… Maybe find a nice man to marry. She was certain that Lokki would have more kids, but she knew in her heart that the firstborn would always have a special place. Lokki looked at the wrinkled, wise face of her aunt and nodded, realizing the wisdom in the older woman's decision.

Even if I decide to raise my baby, would I be able to keep her safe from the predators lurking in these dark by-lanes? Bloody, I could not even save myself, how do I expect to save an innocent child?

Her heart shuddered to think of the gory possibilities.

No, pishi ma is right. It is best for the baby to grow up with the nuns. I will go fetch her once she grows up. Maybe by then, I will find some nice guy and marry him.

Feeling better at the bright prospects for her baby, she nodded, and laid down with her head on her old aunt's lap. Her aunt lovingly caressed her head, urging her to eat some porridge. Lokki agreed, and the two women sipped some rice porridge, silently enjoying each other's comforting presence.

■

FEW DAYS LATER

Kosa

A FEW DAYS went by. Lokki would often wonder about her baby. The old aunt would, in turn, worry about her niece. In their current state of utter penury, an unwed motherhood was just another incident to be forgotten and erased. There were more important and critical worries to fill their heads, like survival, for instance, procuring food or just staying safe.

■

1960

The Angel Eyes Convent and Orphanage,Kalighat, Calcutta

IN THE ORPHANAGE, baby Tia was fast asleep, blissfully unaware of her destiny, of her mother who pined for her and all the obstacles life was planning to throw at her. She looked angelic, wrapped tightly in a thin pink blanket, with only her face visible; her eyes tightly closed. Occasionally, she would open them to look at the nurse and the nuns but frequently slipped back into sleep, too drowsy to bother about the world. Whenever she swallowed or moved her cheek muscles, her dimples deepened, pushing the *aayas* into fits of ecstatic giggles.

A true performer, she often showed off her dimples. It went on, the game between the gurgling happy baby and the *aayas*.

■

1960

Kosa

IN THE RAMSHACKLE hut, Lokki recovered from childbirth and slept well, often dreaming of her baby. One fine day, when she got up early to cook breakfast, horror struck her heart. She found the cold dead body of her old aunt lying next to her on the mat. She gasped, realizing her predicament.

Left alone in the world, she wondered how her baby was faring. Her aunt had not even told her where her baby was. Lokki had always thought she would ask her aunt the address of the nuns who had taken her daughter away. In her mind, she had even given her daughter a name, Maya–the one who would have a magical life.

Lokki wept for some time and then decided to accept her fate. She gathered her meagre savings and arranged for a simple funeral for her aunt. Then she mourned first for her old aunt, then for not being able to be with her baby. Her mind oscillated; either she cried or stared at the roof of her hut.

For three days, Lokki lay in her hut, staring at the leaky thatched roof. At the end of three days, Lokki got up and decided to move on. She bathed and went out to find some work. She had run out of savings and needed to start earning to make a living.

A few enterprising guys had set up a small cart selling basic food on the way to the mines where the workers milled around for fresh lunch and snacks. These guys were looking for a *kamin* to help them out. They hired Lokki immediately when she approached them.

Lokki worked hard the whole day, cleaning vessels. In the evening, the owner gave her a hearty meal. He also asked if she would like to work for a few days at his shop in the town. Lokki readily agreed. She badly needed money. Living in utter penury was not her idea of a good life. She had decided to start building her life post her traumatic experience.

Her mind replayed that unfortunate night when she had been working at the loading docks, and the supervisor had waylaid her. The experience had left her paralyzed with fear. That night, she had just wanted to kill herself after returning to her hut. Her aunt had ensured that she attempted nothing of that sort. Hours dragged by as Lokki slowly came to terms with her changed life path. She felt distressed and considered reporting the incident. But practicality stopped her. Her aunt dissuaded her, too, saying there was no point in reporting such crimes. The police would be of no help as they knew from experience. After two months, Lokki discovered her unwanted pregnancy; she urged her aunt to move in with her.

The night still haunted her…

A few weeks later

Lokki moved on from the job at the shop to a better paying job in the Chirimiri collieries as a *kamin*. The collieries were not yet nationalized. They were privately run by Chandra Singh & Co. She made ten rupees per day by loading and unloading the coal dug up from the depths of the Earth onto waiting trucks, which would then transport the coal to trains. These trains were open and could be loaded from both sides.

A few years later

While working in the Chirimiri mines, Lokki found love. Keshto seemed like an honest and decent man, and Lokki liked him immediately. He was their supervisor who always addressed all the women respectfully. Even if he had to reprimand someone, he would do it gracefully. It was love at first sight for them both. They kept admiring each other from a distance, and Lokki kept weaving beautiful dreams after work, holed up in her tiny hut.

After skirting around each other for months, one fine day, Keshto proposed.

It was a glorious Sunday, and Lokki had her weekly-off. She had long since been planning to visit the Vishnu temple in Chirimiri. When she came out after prayers, she noticed Keshto waiting for her, holding a small packet in his hands. He smiled and offered her the packet–a box full of motichoor laddoos–her favourite. Seeing her dimples dancing and playing peekaboo with the warm sunlight, Keshto's heart overflowed with affection.

He blurted, 'Lokki… I want to keep making you smile… Will you marry me?'

The sudden proposal knocked the wind out of Lokki. Blushing, she didn't know what to say. It was what she had also wanted, but she was finding it tough to look up and just say yes. Instead, she managed to look at his shoulder and nod. A loud whoop took her by surprise. Keshto scooped her up, kissing her full on the mouth. Life seemed to have turned around for Lokki.

A week after he proposed, while they were looking at a larger house for themselves, Lokki started talking about the daughter she had never met. Keshto gently placed a finger on her lips and said, 'I know all that. If, in the future, you want to bring her back, I would be more than happy to adopt her formally. Okay?'

A mounting feeling of respect filled Lokki's heart.

■

JUNE 1965

Chirimiri

THEY MARRIED IN a few days and settled down in their new cozy house. Keshto managed to convince Lokki to study and finish her school education.

Several years went by in a wink. Despite Lokki's insistence, Keshto never said anything about his family. After a while, she assumed that he was an orphan like herself and stopped pestering him. They settled into a matrimonial routine. They had decided to postpone becoming parents till they were financially better off.

■

1970

Chirimiri

KESHTO HAD RISEN in rank, and Lokki had become a graduate. She planned to become a teacher in her village sometime in the future. Right now, they were happy with their mundane lives and their meagre income.

One day, Keshto returned early from work. His tense face scared Lokki, so she kept nagging him. Finally, just to get her off his back, he narrated the weirdest tale she had ever heard.

His parents had been killed in a freak accident, and he had to leave. Seeing his anguish, Lokki steeled her heart. All that she managed to say was, 'Come back soon. If you need me to help you in any way, tell me.'

Keshto's shock was palpable. He had hidden such a huge truth about his past, and his wife of five years was taking it coolly. He hugged her tight, feeling his burden of sorrow lessen. 'I'm so sorry, Lokki. I hid the truth about my family. I came to work here to ensure I could lead a dignified life to support my family. We used to live a happy life in Barali, my village. Recently, I came to know that the police have murdered our parents. Nobody knows where my brother and sister are…I must go.'

Lokki caressed her husband's head. She understood his pain.

Keshto's trip was short. But each second seemed like aeons to Lokki. She kept worrying about him and the unknown dangers he might face. She kept repeating the name of the village as if it would magically transport Keshto back to Chirimiri.

Barali, Barali…

■

1970

Barali, Chhattisgarh

KESHTO'S TRIP TO Barali was uneventful. Rana had come down, and he hugged his brother and cried. Their sister who stayed with their maternal aunt, was still in shock. Keshto did the final rites. Rana had vowed to avenge their deaths and declared this with firmness, making Keshto worry about his brother. He tried very hard to dissuade Rana from doing anything foolish. But that evening changed everything.

The brothers were in mourning, so they had shaved off their heads and were cutting some fruits for their meals when there was a knock on their door.

When Rana went to check, a man rushed inside, scared and anxious.

'It does not matter who I am… but what I have to say is that your lives are in danger. Tonight, they will attack. They are planning to burn down your house. Please leave now…'

The man rushed out and merged into the inky black night.

'Hey! Who is this 'they'?' Rana shouted at his receding back.

'What happened? Who was he?' Keshto rushed out on hearing the commotion.

'*Dada*, I do not know… Some guy wanted to warn us about some plot to kill us…' Rana said, annoyed.

'Let us go to Mashi ma's house then.' Keshto suggested, making Rana frown.

'No, *dada*. Let me stay here; you go. I want to see who will try to kill us!' Rana went inside his father's room and returned with his hunting rifle.

Seeing his brother, Keshto smiled, 'A handsome vigilante, eh!'

'*Dada*!' Rana exclaimed, smiling reluctantly.

Keshto was not planning to leave Rana behind in the house to fight some crazy gunslingers, so he stayed back, too, with his own set of ammunition and a rifle. Together, they guarded the house, taking turns to cover the perimeter. The night passed, but not a soul came by.

In the morning, when Rana went to make tea, he shouted, '*Dada*! Come here… fast!'

Hearing his cry, Keshto hurried into the kitchen. A disembodied chicken lay there… its blood smeared on the granite floor and the kitchen slab. They stared at the mess for some time and silently began clearing it up. Both had made up their minds.

Keshto wanted none of this.

But Rana wanted revenge.

After the mandatory mourning period ended, Keshto told of his plan to give his share of the house to Rana and their sister. Rana refused flatly. He had made up his mind about his life path. He confessed to his brother and made him promise that he would take care of their sister.

'She has two brothers. We both will take care of her. We will figure out a way, Rana.' Keshto hugged his brother and left after making Rana promise to visit him and his new wife someday. Rana also promised to ensure Neeta stayed comfortably in the Calcutta house and would be taken care of.

Keshto returned to Chirimiri with a boxful of memories and a heart full of sorrow. Lokki found it tough even to get him to talk. After a few day, he found his feet and told her about how he had to take care of his sister. Lokki was very supportive and understanding. She even offered to move to Calcutta to be able to live close to Neeta. 'Or maybe, Neeta could come to stay with us,' she suggested.

They kept postponing the decision to move.

In the next five years, all of their lives took a U-turn.

■

1975

Chirimiri

AFTER SOME DELIBERATION, Keshto and Lokki decided to move to Calcutta and have Neeta stay with them. Their baby plans had been stalled indeterminedly. It was time to get Neeta settled, they decided. Keshto's maternal aunt had passed away, and they could not leave the girl alone. That way, Rana also could stay with them all. Keshto decided to quit his job and prepare for their trip. He informed his manager about his decision.

TWO DAYS LATER

Manager's Cabin, Chirimiri Mines

'SIR, MY SUPERVISOR, Keshto, is planning to quit… I do not know if he has spoken to anyone…. No, sir, I don't think he is the type to squeal… he wants to go live with his sister in Calcutta… okay… Okay, sir. No problem, sir. I will take care. No, no… no need, I will call my men.'

The Manager stared at the telephone receiver with irritation. Now, he had an unwanted issue on hand. He placed another call and summoned his men. 'Come fast.'

■

AN HOUR LATER

THE MANAGER AND his three goons waylaid Keshto and Lokki while they were returning from the market after buying a few essentials for their trip.

'Keshto… you took a very bad decision. You should have just left. You did a very wrong thing by telling me your plans. Do you know why? Because I think you are lying… and now you will be punished for that…,' the Manager snarled.

'Saheb, you can't stop me from quitting. I don't want to cause any trouble for anyone. I just want to live my life peacefully. Please let me go… please, I beg…'

Lokki's scream fell useless… '*Ogo*, look out…'

Thud.

One of the men silenced Keshto's protest with a swift turn of his wrist, holding a thin metal rod. Keshto fell like a bag of potatoes, his head bursting open.

'Leave him alone,' Lokki cried, struggling with the men who held her. One of them deftly tied her hands before pushing her down on the dusty road. She screamed till her lungs threatened to burst. One of the men kicked her hard in her stomach. The pain radiated through her body, and Lokki thought she would die. She curled up and watched as they dragged Keshto's unconscious body to the other side of the road. One of them brought out a can of petrol and poured it generously over Keshto and the remnants over Lokki.

Just then, a distant honk and approaching headlights scattered the men. They dragged the couple into the shrubs and ran away. The headlights were from a jeep, which sped away faster than it had appeared.

Lokki managed to free her hands and rushed to her husband's aid. He was barely breathing. The blood had crusted around his head after colouring the brown sand crimson. She ran a shaking hand over his face, longing for him to stay awake.

'Ogo, wake up, wake up! I won't let you die; open your eyes… open your eyes,' Lokki cried, tears running down her cheeks.

There was no vehicle movement on those roads in the evenings. Keshto was slipping slowly into unconsciousness. Lokki dragged him to the road and frantically looked around for help. No one was in sight. A feeble sound escaped Keshto's throat, making Lokki panicky.

'No, no, don't go! You can't leave me alone, no!' Lokki cried, shaking her husband hard. Keshto opened his eyes slightly with great difficulty. He ran a finger down Lokki's face and managed to whisper, '*Bhalo theko*, be good.'

The hand fell to the dusty ground as Lokki watched, dread filling her heart. Keshto slipped into timeless oblivion. Lokki gasped and stared at

Keshto's lifeless body. She shook him hard, crying, but Keshto was gone. She slumped over him, wailing uncontrollably.

Suddenly, a siren pierced the stillness, making Lokki jump. A jeep came into view, and Lokki rose and waved to stop them. Two policemen got out. One of them adjusted his trousers over his ample belly, asking, 'What are you doing at this time? What happened?'

'Sir, this is my husband; some goons attacked us! Please help me, please.' Lokki cried and related the incident to them. She fell at their feet, crying, begging for justice. The constable whispered something to his senior. The other policeman, the Inspector, smirked, giving Lokki a hard stare. They both nodded and looked at Keshto's body.

On the Inspector's directions, the constable dragged Keshto's body and dumped it into the back of the jeep. He then dragged Lokki and pushed her into the back, too. He got into the driver's side while the Inspector sat beside him. The police station was located close to the panchayat office. There was no separate cell for women criminals (as women were not expected to commit crimes). Lokki was dumped into a cell while Keshto's body lay in the dusty jeep.

Lokki anxiously kept banging on the grill of the lockup. The constable came by and rapped her on her outstretched arm, making her cry out in pain. He warned her against making a sound. 'Shut up! Don't make a ruckus. Saheb will come and talk to you', he said and left.

Neither the 'Saheb'nor the constable returned.

Sometime after midnight, when Lokki was sitting still with numbness inside the cell, a sudden braking sound pierced the night. Several jeeps screeched to a halt outside the station in a melodramatic sequence. Dust rose and covered the entire area, and the clouds did not settle. Lokki got up, startled.

By the time the two groggy constables manning the station scrambled up to their tired feet, a neat bullet each untethered their connection with life. The other inmates of the police station cried out in unison, 'Lal Salaam, bhai.'

'Lal Salaam! Free everyone!' A man wearing a mask cried.

Lokki watched the scene unfold with wonderstruck eyes.

Who are these people?

A man with a black cloth tied across his face came up to her cell and peered into the darkness. He had a heavy voice. 'Come here! Who are you, and why are you here?'

Lokki dragged herself to the gate and narrated her ordeal.

'What was your husband's name?'

'Keshto… Keshav Haldar', Lokki replied, bursting into fresh tears.

The man turned and whispered something to a comrade, who rushed out to do his leader's bidding. Out came a rifle and a crowbar. The cheap lock gave up its valiant struggle after losing to the crowbar. The man opened the door and stepped in, gently reaching out to Lokki, who immediately shrunk back in fear. The man held out his hands and said, 'Lokki *Boudi*, you need not worry; I will take care of that. You come with us now.'

A startled Lokki stared at the man while he helped her out of the station. He procured a warm shawl and wrapped it around her frail shoulders.

'Who are you, *dada*? Keshto's body…' she asked, startled.

'As you addressed me, I'm your *dada*, a brother. Do not worry, I have taken care of everything! Now, please come with me,' the man said, gently guiding her out of the cell and then out of the station. His group slowly trudged behind. One of them hurled a crude country-made bomb inside the station, and when it flared, the station got wiped off from the face of Earth.

The jeeps started in a uniform tempo, and all of them bundled in, allowing Lokki to sit comfortably in the front seat, next to the man in the mask. Lokki kept stealing glances at him. She was completely confused about the turn of events. When they had travelled some distance, Lokki cleared her throat and managed to ask, '*Dada*, how do you know Keshto? And where are we going?'

The man pulled down his mask to reveal a handsome, chiselled face. He smiled softly and said, 'Boudi, I'm Rana. We are going home. I learned about all this *jhamela* only today when I returned from a short trip. If only I had been around, this might not have happened…I had not expected to see you here. I got a word that some goons had picked on you both. I expected Keshav da also…'

Seeing a man tear up, Lokki could not control her outpouring. Whimpering softly, she gave in. After a while, Rana wiped his eyes, looked at Lokki's confused face, and said softly, 'Keshto was my elder brother. You and I have never met in person…'

■

1967

The Angel Eyes Convent and Orphanage,Kalighat, Calcutta

A LANKY TEENAGED boy ran inside the huge kitchen of the convent and stopped before a huge wooden cupboard filled with various jars of different sizes and shapes. His eyes darted wildly until they found the plastic bottle. He raised on his toes lightly and picked it up. It was surprisingly heavy. Maybe the cook had refilled the bottle. He opened it carefully, keeping an eye out for any surprise visitors.

The Convent was in a *postho*-induced state of slumber. No one was around.

The boy poured some mustard oil into a small bowl and placed the bottle where it had been. He stepped back to check if he had changed the location of any other item on that shelf. Nothing. Perfect. With a small smile, he picked up the bowl and made his way stealthily out of the kitchen. He made his way to his room. The door was latched from the outside, and a huge padlock hung on it.

The boy entered the room and closed the door softly behind him.

In the small room, on his wooden bed, was a bed sheet with large embroidered pink roses. On it, a red coloured plastic mat–the ones used for infants to arrest their urine flow–was spread. The pink bed sheet fluttered noiselessly due to the air circulating from the soft whirring of the ancient fan. A girl was lying on the bed, her legs spread wide, waiting for him. She looked smaller than she was, lying on the big cot.

He removed his clothes without any perfunctory announcement. This was routine, and he had no compunctions in his heart. He went through the motions quickly taking care to apply the oil liberally. The girl kept staring at the slowly rotating fan. Blissfully oblivious.

Once the deed was done, the boy cleaned up quickly, remembering to dab the girl with some talcum powder.

He then picked her up in his arms and opened the door. He walked slowly out into the veranda, opened the wooden gates, and crossed over to the next building. Opening a similar set of wooden gates there, he walked in. A woman in her early thirties met him midway, and smiled, 'Oh, here you are; I was wondering where you had vanished with her,' said the woman, taking the girl by her arm.

'Nowhere… I was just playing with her,' said the boy, giving a half-smile.

The boy was seventeen, and the girl was five.

He affectionately ruffled the girl's hair and walked off, whistling a soft tune.

The little girl turned and hid her face in the soft folds of the nun's dress, scratching herself. The mustard oil made her tender skin burn, and the talcum powder didn't help.

Sister Sarah, a nun in the Angel Eyes Convent and Orphanage, led little Tia inside the children's ward.

■

1969

The Angel Eyes Convent and Orphanage, Kalighat, Calcutta

THE SOFT FOLDS of the nun's habit covered her ample bosom, making it easy for the seven-year-old Tia to hide her sorrow. The nun spoke soothingly to the frightened child and smoothed her hair. She noticed that the girl had started resembling her mother so much. The nun, Sister Sarah, was the one who had brought little Tia from the slum to the convent. In no time, the angelic Tia had captured the hearts of all the nuns and other inmates.

Monidipa Mondol – Moni di for short – was especially fond of the girl. She urged Sister Sarah to appoint her as an *ayah* for the child. There were many children like Tia. Wealthy benefactors from across the globe funded the orphanage. Tia had instantly become attached with the matronly Moni di and followed her everywhere. Sister Sarah took her under her wings and supervised her studies. Tia responded gladly to the affection and shone in her studies, making the nun proud.

Now responding to Sister Sarah's soft touch and soothing voice, Tia calmed down and looked up into her kind eyes.

'What happened, my child? Tell me.'

'I don't like Ismail da. He is not good,' Tia managed to describe her ordeal in between bouts of sad tears.

'That horrible boy! Let me handle him. You don't cry, my baby,' soothed the nun.

'Ismail!' Her shrill voice of the nun rang and reverberated through the old walls of the orphanage.

The boy in question – Ismail – aged about nineteen, was the son of the watchman, Ahmed. He did odd jobs around the orphanage and took care of the smaller children, mostly ensuring they did not fall off their beds or wander away. He was paid a token amount which helped him in his education.

When he heard his name being called out, he realized he was in trouble and meekly presented himself before the Senior Nun. He knew she had a kind heart within the tough exterior, so he hoped she would be lenient towards him, too. Mentally, he tried to recollect his mistake of the day that could have caused this avalanche. When his eyes fell on the small figure ensconced in the nun's habit, his blood ran dry. He instinctively knew. Tia tried to shrink further into the nun's dress as a reflex reaction to his presence.

He hung his head in shame.

The nun moved forward and slapped him hard, surprising him. It hurt, but Ismail could not bear to look into the eyes of the woman who had taught him to read and write. He knew he had wronged her, and in the eyes of the God she worshipped, what he had done was a mortal sin.

It was a grave sin in the eyes of anyone – be it a living being or the unseen God.

Ahmed was summoned next. The decision was final. Ismail had to leave; Ahmed could stay on or go with his son. Ahmed decided to stay. He was frail and old; he would not get decent employment in the outside world. His son, he was sure, could somehow manage to make ends meet.

When the nun sat back in her favourite chair with a cup of tea, her mind was in turmoil. 'What was the world coming to? How can men be so barbaric? After all, Tia was just a baby, a child. How could Ismail even think of doing something this heinous to her?' Tears ran down the nun's cheek.

Her heart went out to the poor child, who had complained that her favourite playmate Ismail *da* had forgotten to rub the oil 'there', and it hurt. The nun, being a celibate, took a few minutes to understand the situation. She called for their doctor, Dr. Maria, who examined the little girl. When they found traces of semen in the little girl's vagina and underwear, their blood ran cold.

Sister Sarah found it very difficult to control her surging temper. She said a few hymns to calm her mind, then looked at what had to be done, uncharacteristically shouting out orders. Ismail had to be punished. This was a heinous crime which had been going on every day for the past three years. The poor child had undergone so much trauma. Sister Sarah felt terrible. She had let down Tia by not being able to protect her.; she wanted to kill herself. She sat down to meditate on the Lord's word and then decided on the best course of action.

Ahmed sat stoically on the bed, his mind going over the horrid events of the day. It was like a nightmare. When the Sister had told him all about his only son's despicable act, he could not stand on his feet. He had just collapsed. Though a devout Muslim by birth, the convent had been his life since his mother died at its doorstep, leaving him orphaned. He had grown up here, gotten married, and had Ismail, the light of his life, whose mother, Sara, died at childbirth. Ahmed had brought up the boy by himself. The nuns had helped him with everything – money, food, shelter, the boy's education. He owed his life to them. And, now this!

How many dreams had he had for the boy! The wretch had shattered everything. Was he to blame for the perverted demon he had procreated? Oh, God! Was he to blame for the poor little girl's trauma? Ahmed felt so terrible and decided to punish Ismail in his own way.

He hung himself from the ceiling. Death, fortunately for him, came almost immediately.

When Ismail went to collect his belongings, he found the cold dead body of his loving, doting father. He gasped, realizing that his life would never be the same. By his own doing, he had upturned his smooth, calm life.

All for a few minutes of pleasure. Was it even worth it?

Now, within a few hours, he was an orphan and a homeless criminal. The crime he had committed for not being able to curb his passion, had continued for years; thinking that it was alright, that nobody would learn about it, haunted him for the next two days, tearing apart his heart. Ismail had never realized until this moment that he had committed a sin by defiling a child. Now, he could not undo the damage. He hugged his father's body and cried. His tears kept flowing slowly, like acid, washing over his sins, burning deep holes. That night, he did not sleep. Tia's young and trusting face kept haunting him. Finally, unable to face his sins, he jumped off the Rabindra Setu into the welcoming arms of the Hooghly to cleanse his soul of the filth that had turned him into a monster. His body was never found.

After this episode, strict rules were enforced in the convent. No males were allowed to take care of young girls – even the baby girls. It became, in the true sense of the word, a convent.

1972

The Angel Eyes Convent and Orphanage, Kalighat, Calcutta

Time went by, and Tia reached puberty at the age of twelve. A petite nun called Agnes taught her the basics and took care of her when she asked hundreds of questions about her continuously changing body. Tia was redirected to Sister Sarah when her questions became too 'intense' for Sister Agnes' comfort.

A red-faced Sister Agnes took her hand and led her to Sister Sarah's room. The older nun made her sit down and explained whatever she knew, theoretically. Dr. Maria also helped Tia understand the many natural processes as simply as she could. She also warned Tia of the additional complications that would arise now by letting any boy or man touch her private parts.

Tia finished primary school with good marks. Since the orphanage was not attached to a secondary or senior secondary school, Tia was forced to travel a bit to attend another school a bit far away. Initially, one of the sisters accompanied her till the school gates. But after a while, Tia felt confident enough to travel by public transport, and the charitable trust took care of her educational expenses.

The Mother in the new school was a kind and affectionate woman who instantly took a liking to the petite, thin girl with large brown eyes filled with the pathos of the entire world. Her heart went out to the girl. She gave Tia a warm hug the first time she met her and offered her some chocolate.

Tia liked this school. She made friends with orphans like her.

She was good at her studies and topped her class. The Mother gave her a gold-tipped pen as a reward. Tia was good in Maths and Science and planned to become a teacher. Since she was clear about her career and life goals, she opted for the Science stream at the undergraduate level.

Sister Sarah had planned to initiate Tia into the sisterhood when she attained the legal age of eighteen. They had big plans for her. Tia was a special girl, and they would be glad to have her. Sister Sarah often wondered whether they should let Tia herself decide to become a nun. She decided to let nature take its course.

Unbeknownst to the nun, Tia was also completely clear about her life path. She had made up her mind to devote her life to the service of Jesus Christ as his bride. But before that, she wanted to complete her graduation and serve as a teacher for at least two years before taking initiation into the fold.

However, Fate intervened, and Tia's life changed yet again.

Sister Sarah, Tia's benefactor, succumbed to a terminal illness she had been battling for a long time.

Her replacement, a stern-faced nun, made many changes to the convent's policies. Her first strike was on the disbursement of the trust-fund amount. She amended the rules a bit, and this hit the students dependent on the aid given by the Church; Tia among them.

Since she had scored good marks in her School Leaving Certificate examination, Tia got accepted into two colleges: The Bhawanipur Educational Society College and the Birla College of Science & Education.

She approached the new Mother with an application for student aid. The Mother took a look at her and asked her about her history. After listening to the girl's narrative, she replied, 'Tia, it is with great sorrow that

I have to tell you… that from this moment onwards, we have decided not to support beneficiaries like you. So, the question of you getting a student aid does not arise at all.'

Tia was so surprised that her mouth fell open at the rudeness of the nun. She gulped and cleared her throat before saying, 'Mother, I… I mean, I have always lived here, in the orphanage… I mean... This is my home. The Church is my family. Who will I go and ask for money?'

'I do not know. You are a big girl; you are, what? Seventeen? We can maybe try something else if you are ready to cooperate…' the nun said after referring to a file. 'Else, you can surely find a day job and educate yourself.'

'Mother, tell me, what should I do? I will do anything… just tell me.' Tia begged, not wanting to lose her chance to educate herself.

The nun stared hard at the girl. 'I do not wish to speak indirectly. So, let me be quite open. I want your kidney, my dear girl. Can you give it?'

Tia stared at the nun in shock, wondering if she had heard right. The kidney? Was she for real? A kidney in exchange for a life in the Convent?

'So… if I give my kidney, will you let me stay here forever?' Tia blurted.

The nun burst out laughing. 'Oh! You are quite naïve, I see. No, dear girl. You see, everything has a price. So, you can live here as many days your kidney buys you.' The laughter vanished and a thin smirk took its place.

Tia just stared at the nun and her cruel face. 'How can I sell my kidney? I won't… I can't, please… There must be some other way…' Tia begged.

The nun continued in the same cruel tone. 'When you are not ready to give us anything, why should we pay so much to educate you? I feel it is a waste of money. You are wasting my time. If you have no other questions, excuse me.'

'But…' Tia started but was herded out of the door by a nun who had materialized silently behind her. She looked new. She almost dragged Tia to her room, watched while Tia packed her few belongings, and shut the convent door after pushing Tia out on the road.

■

1977

Kalighat, Calcutta

TIA STOOD OUTSIDE the convent for a long time, not knowing where to go. Her worldly possessions were packed neatly in a box: four sets of dresses, a few books, her diary, and a framed photo of Sister Sarah holding her in her arms. Tia sighed and started walking. The world was waiting for her; the temple bells tolled just then;it was surely a sign. With a sinking heart, she looked at the beautiful dome of the Kalighat temple in the distance. Crossing herself, she prayed hard, asking for some divine intervention.

Oh, God! Where will I go now? Help me, God!

Exhilaration, fear, and trepidation enveloped her. Finally, she turned and started walking. Tia kept walking, never once looking back at the Orphanage that had once been her home. Now it stood like an old wretch that had shunned its inhabitants. Tears flowed unchecked. She did not want to wipe them.

Suddenly, it started pouring. 'Rains in this season were odd,' a passer-by muttered as he hurried to get shelter.

Everything is so strange, thought Tia as she walked slowly, hugging her meagre belongings close to her frail body. She kept walking until she reached the Rabindra Setu. The mighty Hooghly flowed merrily under the cantilever bridge. Beckoning Tia to mingle in her, the Hooghly flowed, leaving in Her wake the filth thrown by the milling crowds. In the distance, she could see the red-coloured Howrah station building looming large against the pale dusk sky.

Exhausted, Tia sat down on the wet steps of the jetty. The rains had stopped, and a pale grey cloud had covered the city. Tia looked around, wondering what to do. All emotions – except fear – vied for space in her mind.

A vendor selling the ubiquitous *jhaalmuri* was hovering nearby, looking at her, hoping to make a sale. She bought one packet, giving him some change.

The *jhaalmuri* tasted good.

The seventeen-year-old Tia sat on the banks of the Hooghly till late evening, eating the *jhaalmuri* slowly, trying to think of her next step.

I must somehow find a place to stay. Maybe I can sleep at the station. Tomorrow, I will…

A soft pat on her shoulder made Tia jump. A young woman of indeterminate age was smiling down at her. Tia got up hurriedly, clutching the small suitcase in her arms. The woman smiled warmly, held out her hand and said, 'Tia?'

Tia nodded, hugging her suitcase tightly.

'My name is Asha Francis, and I am Sister Sarah's niece. Come with me; let us go home.'

'Oh! How did you recognize me?' Tia asked, her brows knit, taught to be wary of even kind-looking people.

'Good question!' Asha said, smiling and nodding her head in a peculiar manner that made her curls bounce. Asha had shoulder-length curly hair that she had tied back with a bandana. Tia looked at her in amazement, thinking that Asha looked very pretty.

Asha continued, oblivious to Tia's admiring glances, 'Tia, Aunt Sarah is my mother's sister. She took the Holy Vow, whereas my mother got married and had me. My dad died when I was younger. The sisters kept in touch. Whenever Aunt Sarah visited us, she would talk about you. We have even seen you growing up – obviously in pictures. And I think you look prettier in person.,' Asha concluded with a smile, showing her the picture of Tia with Sister Sarah. Tia felt comforted. She smiled at the memory and looked up at Asha.

'Then I guess we must get going.' Tia smiled. The girls made their way to the Howrah station and took the narrow lane adjacent to it.

Asha led Tia through the narrow lanes of Howrah, and eventually stopped outside a small house. Tia had never been to this side of the city, as she had grown up in the orphanage. The house was small and neat. Asha said that her mother had gone out for work and would return in some time. The time was around seven in the evening.

Asha started making tea, telling Tia about how she found her.

'I got a letter from Aunt Sarah a few days before she passed. Mother and I went to visit her at the hospital. I don't think I had met you then.

After her demise, we got busy with our lives, and I totally forgot about her letter. Yesterday, we were going through her books and letters when we found this letter. She had written to us telling us to take care of you after she passed away. She was sure that the new Mother would not be kind to you and that you would certainly need shelter. My mother was just so happy to oblige her. On her deathbed, Aunt Sarah had made us promise that we would look out for you. Last week, I went to check on you at the orphanage. There were new people there, and none of them spoke to me well. Then, someone took pity on me and told me that you had gone to check on the admissions list and would be back in the evening. I left a message and returned. But, obviously, you didn't get the message. Today, I went again and barged into that nun's office. She literally pushed me out.' Asha laughed, making a face, recalling how the old nun had almost burst a nerve trying to throw her out.

Tia laughed, 'Yes, the old hag. Such an evil woman. I didn't know where to go, so I kept walking. Guess I didn't reach very far.'

'I asked a few people if they had seen you. I had a tough time, but somehow people had noticed you.'

'And I was under the impression that nobody was noticing me...' Tia said, and both girls laughed. Asha's full-throated laughter took Tia by surprise. Tia looked in awe—she had never seen a woman like Asha. In fact, Tia's exposure to the external world was very limited.

Older than Tia by a few years, Asha, twenty-three, worked in a beauty parlour to support her mother in running the household. Her mother worked in the office of a local daily as a front office receptionist.

Tia looked around the small one-bedroom house. So, this is how a house looks like! Having lived in a room with three other girls, Tia had never even been to – or seen – anybody's home.

Asha looked at the girl with amusement as Tia touched the bed and the walls. She watched with amusement when Tia discovered the bouncy bed and tried it out repeatedly, giggling with her hand covering her mouth, like the nuns had taught her to do.

Asha left Tia to amuse herself and made some fresh tea. Her mother would be returning from work soon. Tia slurped the hot liquid and gladly accepted the samosa that Asha offered. She was starving.

Asha's mother, Clara, returned in some time, patted Asha's head for the lovely tea and hugged Tia. After chatting for a while, Clara asked Tia about her education-related plans, inviting her to stay with them as long as she wanted. After a simple dinner of rice and curry, all of them turned in. Tia adjusted with Asha on her bed, curling up.

Dreams came quickly.

■

1980

Bhawanipur, Calcutta

THE GRADUATION CEREMONY for the final year students of the Arts program at the Bhawanipur Education Society College, Bhawanipur, Calcutta, happened without any ceremony.

Tia Kumari passed out in 1980 with distinction and a Bachelor of Arts degree. She didn't care too much for the ceremony, as much as getting the degree that pronounced her fit to mingle in the society and make a name for herself.

Getting employment was the tougher part. Nobody wanted to employ a fresher with no experience. Tia spent hours standing in serpentine queues waiting for that one chance to impress the recruiting managers in walk-in interviews. She had decided to work at a school. A local school was looking for an English teacher, and Tia fit the bill.

The employment exchange called soon enough. The appointment letter came the next day. The school wanted her to join at the earliest. It was located close to their house, and she could walk to work.

Asha had recently gotten married, and Clara had not been keeping well. When the call came from the school, Tia forced Clara to quit her job, promising to take care of her.

Tia joined the school as a primary teacher. Six months later, Clara breathed her last, leaving Tia shattered and alone. Asha, who had come down to be with her mother during her last days, tried to persuade Tia to shift with her to Bangalore. But Tia did not want to leave her job at the school. After Asha left, Tia continued living in the small house that Asha had written over to her name and worked at the school for a few months.

One fine day in March '81, while looking through the newspaper classifieds, her eyes fell on a well-designed ad. A local daily based out of Bhubaneswar was looking for writers. Tia decided to apply and sent a letter to the given address. She gave up when she didn't hear from them for a week. But after around ten days, she got a letter calling her for an interview in Bhubaneswar.

With a lot of nervousness, Tia made arrangements for her trip. She had never travelled by train, nor been to another city. She was excited yet nervous. But, whatever the case, she knew she had only herself to fall back on. She had no idea how long the interview would take, so she had bought a return ticket to Calcutta for the next day.

Everything went off smoothly. The interviewer was a kind lady who took to Tia immediately. She offered her the job on the spot. Tia was thrilled to bits at having nailed it and mentally thanked the Lord.

After returning to the railway station, she checked if there was a night train to Calcutta. Now that her work was done, she did not see a point in waiting till the next day. She enquired about advancing her ticket, but that was not allowed, *apparently*. She had to stay back in Bhubaneswar for a day. Sighing, Tia decided to roam around.

Since most of the day had gone by in the interview, she had to spend the night somewhere. She would somehow spend the next day roaming around the city until it was time to board her train, she decided. Spotting a food stall, she hopped towards it. A plate of poori aloo made its way to her stomach. That would suffice. She could just curl up with her bag in the station. It was so crowded that it had to be safe.

The night passed peacefully.

The next day, Tia got dressed in the railway station's rest room and went out to explore the city. She had almost nine hours to kill before catching her train back home at 7 p.m. She knew she didn't have a lot of time, so she decided to visit just two places – the Cuttack caves and the Nandankanan zoo. She could be back by 6 p.m. at the max.

Bhubaneswar was humid, hot, and musty. A weird layer of smoke hung over the city, making it hotter and more humid. Tia roamed around the zoo, watching in awe, moving from cage to cage, taking in the sights and sounds of the place.

After getting an egg roll from a street food cart, she got into a rickshaw to the Caves. It would take her a few hours to cover, she had heard. The rickshaw man kept telling her the best ways to see the caves. After thanking him profusely and tipping him, Tia made her way to the caves. The splendour took her by surprise. While she was walking around soaking in the stillness of the place, she noticed a man who was drawing something on a notepad. Curious, Tia went closer to take a look.

He was absorbed in his work and didn't notice her till she asked, out of curiosity, 'What are you drawing?'

He looked up at her, startled. His jawline was smooth and sharp, his eyes a sparkling dark brown. He had well-defined lips and a shock of wavy hair that kept distracting her from his serene face. With him being around six feet, Tia had to strain her neck to look up when he stood up suddenly.

'Ah… nothing… I'm trying to capture the beauty of this piece. Do you know what this is?' He asked, smoothly turning the conversation around.

Tia simply shook her head, 'I have no idea…,' she shrugged, adding, 'I haven't even read about it in school or college.'

'Let me help you, then. Let us get out of the way… I think we're holding up the others,' the man said, motioning towards a group of people looking on curiously. Tia turned and they moved to a corner.

'Here, these are some pamphlets about this place. You can keep them and read at leisure. Let me give you a quick tour of the place. Shall we?' The man offered a hand, which Tia refused when they reached a steep stair. She managed to get down by herself and noticed him watching her amusedly. The notepad had vanished into a satchel.

'Oh, by the way, my name is Shom. Shom Mahapatra… I live here in Bhubaneswar. What about you?' The man introduced himself, smiling.

'Tia… I am from Calcutta. I came to attend an interview here. Well… that's all…' She hesitated because there was nothing exciting about her life to share.

Should I tell him I grew up in an orphanage? Or that I work as a teacher?

'That's nice. Good to meet you, Tia from Calcutta. Let me show you around; I hope you don't mind. I just barged in.'

'Not at all. I am so happy to have some company. I was getting so overwhelmed. Thanks so much.' Tia could not believe that such a good-looking man was offering her a tour. He was having a weird effect on her senses. She was unable to breathe freely. Her eyes had frozen—they wouldn't blink. Her heart was beating faster, her hands were cold. She managed a stiff smile.

They spent the next few hours walking slowly through the caves. Tia drank in everything Shom told her, her fantastic memory registering every little detail. Hours flew by, and when they finished the tour, it was already closing time. They stood outside the exit, ravenous and tired.

Shom turned to Tia and asked, 'Would you like to grab a bite? I am starving actually,' Tia nodded enthusiastically, 'Oh let's eat, please. I have only a few hundred with me, so please choose a cheap place, if you don't mind.' She smiled sheepishly, looking away when Shom nodded and smiled.

His eyes are so kind. I like him so much.

They caught a rickshaw that dropped them at a small restaurant in the city. Tia got down and watched in awe. The restaurant looked very smart and grand. She began, 'I hope it is not very costly…'

Shom just cut her off with a smile and waved her in, holding the door open. The place was cool, and a pleasant aroma filled the air, making Tia's stomach grumble. 'This is so nice. I am starving.'

She sank into the soft sofa and smiled at Shom. After placing their orders, they settled down and discussed their tour in detail. Tia told Shom about her job interview and how the lady had offered her the job immediately. Shom's reaction took her by surprise.

'This is huge. We should celebrate!' Shom exclaimed, beckoned the waiter and whispered something in his ear. The waiter smiled warmly at Tia before rushing away.

Tia looked at Shom, surprised, 'What is all this? Let me at least join…'

Shom shook his head, 'No, no, I won't hear anything; we are celebrating this. Soon, you will move to my city, and we can meet often…' He cut his sentence short, seeing the look on Tia's crimson face.

They both burst out laughing at Shom's speed. Just then, the food arrived and grabbed their attention. For the next few minutes, they tucked into the delectable fare silently. Shom was the first to break the silence. 'Tia, er… I am feeling a bit odd for saying this…but do you know anybody in the city? Do you have any place to stay once you move here?'

'No, not really… I haven't thought much about it. I thought, maybe once I move here, I will look for a house or a hostel or something. I will check with my colleagues or the Manager. She seemed kind.'

'Yeah, you could do that. I wanted to tell you… Whatever be the case, if you face any difficulty, let me know! I will gladly help you out, okay?' Shom's eyes glistened with genuine care. Tia felt touched by the gesture. Maybe it was time to open up to the world. People were not all bad like how the nuns had described. *Shom is nice.*

The waiter appeared, carrying a tray with a small cake, and a small lit candle on top. Shom thanked the man and took the tray. 'Go ahead; it is for you… blow on it.' Shom watched as Tia closed her eyes and blew. *May this evening never end…*

Tia cut a small piece, put it on a plate, and handed it to Shom. He gently took the piece and fed it to her, smiling. She gulped it fast when his fingers brushed against her lips, making her jolt. She lowered her eyes and managed to assemble her errant thoughts. A strange feeling was overcoming her.

Shom kept chatting. When they were about to leave, the waiter came by and asked if they wanted something else. Shom patted him on the back and helped Tia out with her bag. While they were waiting for a rickshaw, she asked him, 'Why didn't he bring the bill? Are you a regular customer? The waiter seemed to know you well. How's that?'

Laughing, Shom pointed at something. Tia looked up and noticed the fancy board. It read: *Shom's.*

'So, the waiter better know me… I pay his salary.' Shom replied, laughed loudly, and winked at her.

Tia gasped audibly, feeling utterly foolish, slapping her forehead. This was Shom's restaurant! What an ass she had been!

Shom offered to drop her at the station, which she accepted since it was already 6 p.m. At the station, he ensured that she found her seat without issues. After settling her in, he stood outside the window, holding on to the grill. He pressed a card into her hand, and said, 'Call me before you board the train when you come here. I will come to receive you. Okay?' His eyes sparkled.

Tia could not look away. She wanted this moment to stand still. She didn't want to go back.

Why do I have to go back? If he asks me to stay, I will...

The train started moving. They said their goodbyes with heavy hearts and wet eyes.

■

The Hostage

MAY 10, 2000

Chirimiri Village
8:30 a.m.

ON KOENA'S KNOCK, the door of the hut opened, and a heavily pregnant Neeta stepped out, squinting in the morning sunlight. Koena drew in a sharp breath, seeing the distress stamped across the young woman's face. The little boy rushed ahead and wound his little arms around her, hiding his face in her saree. His doleful eyes searched Koena's face eagerly. Sagar bent down to pet the boy's silky hair, invoking a giggle from him.

'Come in.' Neeta said, allowing Koena and Sagar to step in. She held her head high, seeming to be valiantly braving the trauma.

'Neeta, I'm Koena, and this is my colleague, Sagar,' Koena introduced with folded hands. Neeta followed behind them and pulled out two *moras* for them to sit. She kept her eyes averted, pulling her thick saree around herself, purportedly shielding herself from any untowardness that might have been in store for her.

Koena looked around. The house was simple yet elegantly furnished. In one corner, on a small table, a colour photograph of her husband stood, covered by a flower garland. An incense stick that had probably kept the house smelling of life, had long gotten extinguished. A wooden bed stood in another corner.

Neeta seemed to be oblivious to many things around her, including Koena's empathetic stance, to the whole drama unfolding in that hut. Koena gently took the woman's hands and asked her if she was ready to speak to them. Neeta's almost imperceptible nod took Koena by surprise. She had been mentally prepared to make a hasty exit.

Speaking softly so as not to disturb the dead man's spirit hanging around, Koena managed to get a few valuable bytes from the distraught

Neeta. Sagar had chosen to engage the little boy and kept himself scarce till the interview got over.

When they were about to leave, a shrill scream from one of the nearby huts accompanied by a gunshot alarmed the four occupants of the tiny hut. Neeta looked up, her startled eyes scanning the premises and then the area outside her hut. Groaning under the weight of her unborn child, Neeta hobbled toward the door, with Koena at her heels.

A group of men with rifles slung across their backs and wearing army fatigues, were walking towards Neeta's hut. Koena's heart sank. *Terrorists? Naxals? Are they Shom's friends?*

A tall man wearing a thin cotton cloth around his face strode into the hut, his eyes—cold and determined. Koena moved in front of Neeta, with her arms around the pregnant woman protectively.

Neeta let out an anguished cry when she saw the man and rushed into his arms after slightly nudging Koena aside. Koena had to hold on to the wall to steady herself from the shock. *Was this woman crazy? She is mistaking this terrorist for someone else.*

Neeta's next words made Koena's head swim. '*Dada*! See what they did to our Nirmal!'

Neeta's sorrow seemed to suck the energy from everyone and everything in that hut. Koena felt a bit light-headed on seeing the unfolding scene.

The man gently hugged Neeta and wiped her tears, while one of his men picked up her son. 'Are you ready?' He asked, looking around and spotting her bag. He motioned one of his men to pick it up while leading Neeta out.

'Wait!' Koena's voice came out in a whisper, owing to the tension that had built up within. Four pairs of eyes turned to look at her, one of which scanned her coldly, daring her to stall the plan.

'Where are you taking Neeta? Can't you see her condition?' Koena's pulse had quickened, and her mind was furiously planning her next steps, throwing ideas into her conscious mind with alarming speed. She stood in front of the man, meeting his unblinking stare, and laid a gentle hand on Neeta, who was still sobbing on the man's chest. The man released Neeta, who quietly went out of the hut without a second glance at Koena, while the latter stared at her retreating back, stunned.

'Ma'am, would you please come with us?' The man had impeccable manners.

And Koena had heard that voice somewhere. Those eyes!

Have I met him somewhere?

He pointed towards the door, and Koena realised that following his orders was the best bet for her and Sagar. She turned to look for Sagar when she saw that he was already sitting in one of the jeeps parked outside, with a blindfold on his eyes and a gag in his mouth. Her pulse quickening, Koena stared at the men standing around the hut, waiting patiently for their orders. The man placed a hand softly on Koena's back, making her shiver.

I know that touch! Who is he?

Then everything became a blur when a blindfold made Koena's world go black, and a gag was placed – with surprising gentleness – in her mouth.

■

1940-1960
The Haldars

KESHAV HALDAR WAS born to a wealthy zamindar, Shashank Haldar, and his teacher wife, Uma. When Keshav was five, Rana was born. The Haldars hailed from Barali village near Bhubaneswar. The two children grew up in the lap of luxury, surrounded by unadulterated affection from their doting parents and the village folk.

Shashank was popular in the small village, where his wife taught at the local school. The Haldars had a sprawling bungalow in South Calcutta, which they used whenever they travelled to Calcutta. Once Keshav completed his schooling at the village, his father sent him off to live in Calcutta under the watchful eyes of a few trusted caretakers. By then, Rana had turned ten, so he also accompanied his elder brother. Around that time, Uma was carrying their third child. In a few months, a beautiful daughter was born to the Haldars. They named her Neeta. The two elder brothers doted on their little sister whenever they came home for vacations.

Life went on with the unbound joys of childhood, keeping the siblings busy. The Haldars decided to move to Calcutta so Neeta could also attend the same school like her brothers.

Around that time, an upheaval in the government made all the wealthy zamindars run for cover. Some of the landlords were rounded up on false pretexts and their assets frozen. Shashank Haldar was one of them. When the letter arrived that their properties would be taken over by the government, there was a huge uproar in the Haldar household. They had just a few days to hide their gold and precious jewellery worth crores. Shashank Haldar managed to sell some of his lands and stashed away the money in a safe house. His other landlord friends had been warning him, but Shashank had shrugged off the good advice, thinking this could never happen to him.

The next few days went in a frenzy.

■

NOVEMBER 1960

Calcutta

KESHAV HAD TURNED twenty and had just graduated from the grand Presidency college. He was planning to go to London to study Economics and Political Science. He would stay there with his maternal aunt.

The lofty plans never crossed the borders of the patriarch's mind.

One night, the whole family was forced out of their palatial Calcutta house. The government had frozen some of their assets. They could keep their home in Barali, the police said. The rest of it was 'ill-gotten wealth' and had to be frozen, they informed, smirking at the turn of events.

Shashank called several of his friends in a desperate bid to save at least some of his properties. Some of them promised to help; a few told him to grin and bear for a while. This will blow over, they promised. Hope you have something hidden away, they whispered. Take your family and shift to London, they advised.

Rana tightly clutched his father's arm and watched in horror and fury as their little sister was snatched rudely from their mother's arms and body searched, making her cry out in pain. The police searched all of them but did not find even an extra piece of jewellery or cash on their person. After putting a seal on the house, they left.

The family sat on the veranda, shivering in the cold, while Shashank ran around to make alternate arrangements. The next morning, one of Shashank's oldest friends came to fetch them.

The family temporarily shifted to the friend's house, and Shashank and his friend planned their next move. With all their bank accounts frozen and their houses attached, their life seemed to have come to a standstill. They had never known poverty, and this was not exciting at all. Everything was unreal.

They stayed at the friend's place for a month while Shashank managed to use his hidden money to realign their lifestyle. After much deliberation, the family decided to move to Barali. Some money greasing the palms of a police officer helped them move their stuff from their South Calcutta house to their Barali home. Rana was yet to finish school, and Neeta was just in the first standard. The Haldars had a bigger problem at hand.

What would they do for daily expenses?

Keshav decided to go to work.

■

MAY 9, 2000

Ashiana Apartments

6:00 a.m.

WHEN SHOM'S FLIGHT landed, the sky was still pale; an orange glow was spreading across the horizon, painting the spectrum in its hues. Shom had dozed off and was rudely woken up when the pilot announced that they were experiencing some turbulence. He thought of Koena, and how she seemed to have a mind of her own.

Never has that woman listened to me!

His cab was on time, and he reached home to a warm smell wafting from the kitchen. The cook had already arrived and was preparing breakfast when Shom let himself in and noticed her presence.

Thank God for small mercies!

'Saab, would you like some tea?' the cook peered out of the huge kitchen. Shom nodded and slumped on the sofa. His head was fuzzy. He was worried about Koena. She was supposed to reach soon.

Where is this, Rana? Should I check with him? Didn't he say that he would be in that area for some time?

As if on cue, the landline phone buzzed, catching him by surprise.

'*Dada*, is this a safe line?' Shom asked when Rana identified himself.

Rana had been changing his whereabouts often as the police were on the lookout after the deadly attack on the mines in Chirimiri. Not that Rana had anything to with it—they suspected him of being behind the blast. Rana didn't feel like proving otherwise, even though he had faced a personal loss due to the blast. *Nirmal*!

Shom made Rana promise that he would take care of Koena and Sagar, ensuring that no harm came to them. Rana had already chastised Shom about Koena's decision to travel to a veritable melting pot of trouble. Shom described to his brother the conditions under which Koena had left for the assignment and how he had had no say in it. Rana's promise to look out for Koena and Sagar warmed Shom's heart. At least his dear wife and that silly Sagar would not get into any trouble. Not that Koena was a stranger to getting into trouble – she often managed to do it all by herself.

■

MAY 9, 2000

New Delhi, CM's Office

4:30 p.m.

Swain was furious. As the rumours guessed in hushed tones, he did know about the planned bombing of his official bungalow. Overnight, he had packed his family and his painting collection–one of the rarest in the country–and had flown out to the Maldives in his private jet. The official memo about his travel was never sent out. The bomb dropped before that.

'Sir, please hear me out,' Swain's deputy CM, Sharma, pleaded.

'What do you want to say, Sharma *Ji*?' shrieked an angry Swain. He had been asked to throw a fit, making a huge hue and cry. He was doing exactly that. His bosses with deep connections and deeper perversions would be very happy. He salivated, envisioning the huge pay-out that awaited him. These corporates had unbelievably deep pockets, and he had no compunctions in dipping into the well now and then. Of course, he had to do their bidding, but what was a little action compared to the money they showered on him?

'You didn't know who the bomber was. We have no clues yet. The police are investigating… yada, yada, yada. Spare me the details. I want results, Sharma *Ji*, and now.' Swain barked at the man and stomped out, his white dhoti flying around him.

The phone call from the most powerful man in the country, simply called 'The Boss', had rattled him. Swain had been asked to present himself at a particular place. The Boss was not one to be trifled with. A rich daddy and a sharp brain had catapulted The Boss to the highest echelons of power. He hobnobbed with the richest and the deadliest. A kingmaker, he had the power to make or topple governments. Swain was almost shitting his pants. The mine blast had not gone too well, he knew. He had his answers ready. His pay-out was also pending…

Swain left his office and got into his car. The Boss never forgave mistakes…

A morose Sharma was dialling his minion Raju's number when he heard a terrifying noise, followed by ear-splitting screams. He rushed out of the office that Swain had just vacated. The scene unfolding in front of Sharma's eyes was horrific yet astounding—it was morbidly, grandly cinematic.

Sharma watched, awestruck. Swain's car had just flown up some twenty feet in the air, revolving all the while before descending and landing in slow-motion, leaving onlookers gaping. Women were screaming and rushing to get out of the way of the ball of fire that was once Swain's prized possession – a black Roll's Royce Phantom.

Sharma stood there, transfixed. He had never seen a blast in real life. This was pure evil. Though he had personally plotted to blow up Swain many times in his head, he didn't quite think of the actionable events. And he did not like the fact that a beautiful piece of machine like the Rolls should have met with this terrible fate. When the metal hit the ground, burning chunks landed all around, bouncing off the dusty ground, forcing people to hide behind the nearest wall or scale the closest tree, adding to the chaos and noise. In fact, nobody gathered there had seen a car being blown up, except perhaps in C-grade Bollywood movies. Sharma stood there, his mouth agape, taking in the chaos.

Suddenly, his rational mind poked him, and a little voice repeated, 'Your boss is dead; you are free!'

Sharma felt a bit ashamed of celebrating the disastrous death of his superior. He overcame it almost immediately and shrugged off the remaining guilt, rushing into the office. He had protocols to take care of. The State was without a CM, and something had to be done. His immediate worry was about the 15th August celebration invites that had to be sent out.

The place became a fortress in the blink of an eye. Police had swooped down almost immediately, cordoning off the entire area. The CM had been assassinated, and the newshounds picked up the scent. Soon, they arrived in hordes. This was breaking news and would grab the public's imagination for weeks. The assassination was a great opportunity for TRPs to skyrocket. The phones in the office kept ringing. People were scurrying around. Total confusion reigned.

Sharma spoke briefly over the phone. When he replaced the receiver in its hook, he was grinning. His dream of becoming the CM was coming true, even if it was just for a few days.

That the prestigious chair's previous occupant had just died a gory death, mattered not.

■

MAY 10, 2000

Somewhere in the Korba forests

10:30 a.m.

THE OLD WILLIS jeep trudged along the mud tracks. Despite the morning hour, it was semi-dark in the thick forest. Thin rays of light passed through the dense foliage and lit up the tracks. The group trudged along in silence, punctuated only by expletives from the driver when he encountered a rodent or a small animal in their path. The jeep was old, and Koena's bones rattled as it sped on rocky grounds and dusty roads alike. Somewhere along the way, Koena's blindfold had come undone.

Nobody bothered to put it back. She craned her neck to take a look at the elusive man's face. The cloth stayed in place. All Koena could see were the eyes.

Cold. Killer's eyes.

I have seen those eyes somewhere.

■

MAY 10, 2000

Somewhere in the Korba Forests
12:00 p.m.

WHEN THEY REACHED a clearing, the jeeps stopped. Rana jumped down and walked towards the hostages' jeep. He helped them get down and took off their gags. The two hostages blinked in the sunlight and coughed hard. Rana handed them water bottles, asking, 'Do you want to freshen up? We have a long way to go.' The black cloth stayed in place.

Surprised at the generosity, Koena nodded her head vigorously, and so did Sagar. They were hungry, too. Koena's curiosity knew no bounds. There was something eerily familiar about this Rana Haldar, and Koena wanted to know what it was. Gulping some water thirstily, she stared at the man who turned to a woman comrade and said, 'Rani, arrange for some food, please.'

'*Ji, dada*,' Rani said and hurried to unload a bag from the back of the jeep. 'Food' *apparently* referred to some bread and jam. Quickly, a few comrades got together and helped distribute the food. Everybody silently munched on their jam sandwiches. Koena and Sagar did not dare open their mouths to demand anything else. That the man had even thought of feeding them was a miracle! Koena noticed that the bread was fresh, and the jam perhaps locally made. The bottle had no label.

While they ate, Rana stood near a tree and checked the surroundings, puffing away at a cigarette and fiddling with a sophisticated device. Koena peered through her eyelashes and guessed that Rana was holding some sort of a communication device.

Thinking quickly, she got up, went up to Rana, and thanked him profusely. He simply nodded and covered his face with the cloth quickly before putting out the stub of the cigarette. Just then, the device tinkled, drawing his attention to it. He pressed a button and spoke into it softly. Koena just overheard a few words here and there, and her journalist's mind came alive. "There had been a blast…someone important had died…"

'What happened?' Koena mustered courage and enquired.

'Nothing important…the Delhi CM…that swine…Swain got killed. Good riddance of bad rubbish…' Rana muttered angrily. Koena stifled a shocked cry and managed to hide her reaction from Rana.

Stuffing the device in his back pocket, Rana moved to the jeep with long strides, dragging a mildly struggling Koena behind him. He then ordered his men to gag and blindfold the duo again. Koena and Sagar settled back for another rickety journey. This time, with their bellies full of food, the journey seemed less strenuous.

Suddenly, she felt the air becoming much cooler. Some of the comrades had fallen asleep. Koena's mind kept awake, trying to envision the scenery outside. She guessed that they were entering a deeper portion of the forests. She could even smell the sweet scent of the unpolluted greenery. If only they had not insisted on the blindfold! *The Delhi CM had been murdered! Who was behind it? The Naxals?* She wanted to have a discussion with Sagar, but it seemed improbable now…

■

MAY 10, 2000
Korba Forests
1:30 p.m.

WHEN THE WEARY group reached a settlement, the women escorted Koena and Sagar to a hut. The blindfolds and the gags came off. Koena coughed hard and requested for some water. A woman handed her a bottle and stared while Koena drank thirstily. A few comrades entered the room, grabbed their bags, and left after locking the door behind them. Koena walked towards the small window and looked out.

Sagar joined her, and they looked at each other, wondering about the turn of events. Their collective futures seemed bleak. Being taken hostage by a dreaded Naxalite was one thing; being forced to stay in a god-forsaken forest was another.

'What on Earth happened?' Sagar buckled first and blurted.

Shrugging, Koena looked at him, worry writ large on her unlined face. She placed a hand on Sagar's shoulders and said, 'Let us hope for the best, Sagar. I'm equally clueless at the turn of events. But I have this crazy feeling that something is amiss. Do you feel the same? By the way, did you hear about Swain?'

'I don't understand...what happened?' Sagar's voice trailed off. He looked petrified and clueless.

'Tch, tch... there is something we both missed... the whole thing, I mean, from the time we entered Neeta's hut and till now. Something is not what it seems. Also, this murder, I mean the death...' Koena's voice dropped to a whisper, afraid someone might overhear her.

'What?' Sagar looked at her face, searching for an answer.

'See, let us recount everything that happened, okay?' Koena moved away from the window and sat down on a plastic chair. Sagar followed suit, slumping into a chair and scowling.

'Sagar, the whole kidnapping seemed so easy and staged. You know what I mean?'

He looked unsure and shrugged.

'Think hard... focus.' Koena grabbed his arm and shook him hard.

Sagar was finding it difficult to put on his journalist's hat and see the issue for what it was. His eyes were still unfocused.

Sighing, Koena shrugged. 'I may be assuming... I am not sure.'

Maybe I am assuming things. Because of the shock, I might have lost my head. Let me leave it here. My gut still says there is something amiss.

Koena walked back to the window to stare outside. The women and men wore similar uniforms— olive green pantsuits with pockets of various sizes. They wore a belt for ammunition and had a rifle. A thin cloth hung around their necks. All of them had rifles. Some women had bombs hanging from their hip belts. They walked around with the weapons and ammunition easily, as if they were born to be Naxalites, or had trained with the best. Faces shining, they wore their hair combed back in tight buns or tighter plaits. The men wore their hair short, with a cloth wrapped around their faces and neck. Whenever they meet each other, they partly lifted their right hands, closed their fists, and said 'Lal Salaam'.

Clearly, they were enjoying this part of their lives. Despite her situation, Koena marvelled at their life. A strange thrill ran down her spine. She looked around. Her handbag was missing. Sighing, she stared outside. The brown earth extended till it rushed to meet the mountains, green and verdant. Wild. She could hear the gurgling of water. It was like being in a wild jungle resort. Some comrades were learning to read and write; some were doing martial arts training. Koena watched the organized yet deeply disturbing lives of the deadliest people in India, who had threatened successive governments.

Koena looked around the small hut. The walls were made of tin sheets held together with nuts and bolts. Koena observed that the hut was actually a compact work area, complete with a wooden work table! She also noticed a small kitchen and bathroom. And it was tidy. Sparsely furnished but neat.

Just as she was about to enter the kitchen to investigate, the door opened, and Rana walked in, followed closely by comrade Rani and a man who Koena had not seen till now. He was dressed in jeans and a T-shirt. Koena walked towards Rana and looked at Sagar, who had visibly shrunk when Rana entered.

'Koena, Sagar, this is Arun. He will take you home tomorrow.' Rana's words made Koena's heart sing.

We are not going to die, after all.

Her mind was filled with more thoughts than she could possibly handle.

Wait, I have heard that voice somewhere! How I wish he would take off that cloth from his face!

As if hearing her wish and acceding to it, Rana slowly peeled off the cloth covering his face. Koena's sharp intake of breath and the recognition that flashed on her face shocked Sagar. You!

'And… yeah, nice meeting you again! Our conversation from the other day... We will complete it… soon,' Rana winked, chuckling at Koena's stunned reaction.

'Chary!' Koena choked out, her thoughts in complete disarray.

'Just Rana... Original name. 100%' Rana smiled, lifting his hands in mock salute. He then left the hut, Arun trailing behind.

Koena stood rooted. Rana – the revered, feared Naxal leader – was Chary!

Why did Shom lie? He could have introduced Chary as Rana even that day! Why so much confusion? So, does this mean that Shom knows about this?

Now that she was reasonably sure that she was safe and would eventually reach home in one piece, she wanted to hang around and see what might turn up. She had not expected to bump into Chary, of all people. What had initially seemed like a life-threatening situation had quickly become an interesting social interaction masquerading as a hostage drama!

There is surely something brewing. I must find out.

Thoughts of her proposed family vacation, Shom's concern, or even their promise to Kit seemed kind of irrelevant to her at that moment. All she wanted to do was solve this mystery.

Meeting Rana in the forests seemed like an opportunity to pursue a thread that remained open in her mind space. She intended to close this chapter while she had a chance. Rana's presence there warranted her intense eagerness to stay. Infidelity was out of question—she loved Shom way too much for that. Her vague interest in this man was purely academic, to explore his mind and thoughts. She was a Seeker, and she had just trained her over-enthusiastic mind on her latest pursuit: Rana.

She had to know what made him tick. But even despite her repeated protests to herself, she realized the truth.

He makes me...want him. He is, after all, a Naxalite, a terrorist. I should stop swooning over him.

Stopping her scary train of thoughts, Koena repeated what Shreya had taught her: *I am married... I love Shom. I am fine... I am healed... I am good.*

Rana had accommodated Neeta and Koena in the same place. Most of the time, Neeta seemed to be in a chatty mood. She would sit with a cup of warm milk and chat with Koena. She shared stories about her relationship with Rana. One minute, Neeta had been expecting joys to fill her house, and now she was a fugitive, living on borrowed time. Some pieces of the puzzle started falling in place for Koena, who made a note of stuff that Neeta told her on a piece of paper.

- Rana and Neeta were siblings. Shom was their maternal cousin! *Whoa!* Rana had become a Naxalite when he vowed to take revenge for his parents' murder. Rana kept in touch with his siblings, looking out for them.
- Neeta's husband, Nirmal, was killed in the Chirimiri mine blast.
- Rana and Neeta had an older brother, Keshav/Keshto, who was killed by the coal mafia headed by Swain, the current CM of Delhi! And that could be the reason behind Swain's murder!
- The brothers had been constantly in touch with Neeta, who was then living with their aunt and her family in Calcutta. After completing her B.A., she fell in love with one of Rana's friends, Nirmal. She was hell-bent on marrying him. Keshav had refused to even hear of it. So had Rana. After several years of courtship, Neeta and Nirmal had eventually gotten married. Rana had agreed after a dejected Neeta had threatened to kill herself.
- Rana was not behind the blast and was instead on the lookout for the person responsible, as the blast had widowed his beloved sister.
- Shom knew about the 'kidnapping' (which was probably staged) and had requested Rana to take care of Koena.

After revealing his identity, Rana had become extra nice and regaled the small group (comprising Koena, Sagar, Neeta, and a few others) with stories about his escapades. His comrades seemed to enjoy these stories, whereas Koena and Sagar felt a bit out of place. Neeta seemed to be lapping it all up. She was so, obviously, in awe of her elder brother.

The next evening, Arun came over and whispered something in Rana's ears, making the latter pensive. Observing the sudden change in his mood, the others sobered up as well. Rana left soon after, followed by a few of his comrades and Arun.

Neeta and Koena sat back, chatting about how different yet similar their lives were...

A while later, Rana stormed in, looking angry, making Koena and Neeta look up. Sagar was slumped in a corner, his nose stuck in a comic book he had found lying around somewhere.

'Koena, we need to talk.' Rana said, beckoning to her.

She got up and followed him.

Will he ask me to kill someone? Or do something for him in return for my freedom? Should I ask him to call Shom?

A composed Rana and a slightly nervous Koena walked silently till they reached the edge of the clearing. The whole area was pitch dark—the only light was from the hurricane lamp hanging unobtrusively from the door of a hut, and all the huts looked similar to her. It was eerily silent, except for the sound of crickets and rustle of leaves.

Rana wasted no time and began, 'Picking you guys up was not a coincidence. There are things that you may not understand now, Koena. Shom spoke to me yesterday. We got intel about a probable strike, and I had to move you guys to keep you safe. I saw no other way of safeguarding you both until the local police took over. Initially, I had thought of dropping you at the edge of the forests so you can go back, but it looks like it is going to be very difficult. The whole media is going crazy about this kidnapping. So, I have a plan,' Rana paused.

'Sure, Rana... I understand,' Koena hesitated, her heart flipping in her chest, looking up at the tall and handsome face. She feared that it would somehow pop out.

I am good...I am healed...

Rana smiled, making Koena's heart beat harder. She gulped to keep herself from falling on him. She returned his smile, her dimples dancing and declaring the joy she was feeling at that moment.

'I will keep you posted on the developments. We might change our plans once we reach a safe house. Meanwhile, you guys take some rest. We have a long way to go tomorrow.' Rana said, leading her back to the hut, holding her elbow lightly. Koena felt touched by the gesture in more ways than she would have liked to accept.

The 'we' kept haunting Koena, as she allowed Rana to lead her to the hut.

It was time for bed. There were no soft mattresses or bed sheets, or pillows. The female comrades laid out thin plastic sheets on the floor of the hut. They took turns to guard the perimeter of the settlement.

The next day, they had to move to another location. Rani woke them up at around 3 a.m., saying, 'Get up, we have to start.'

'Where are we going?' asked Koena.

'How does it matter?' asked Rani, smiling at her. An unlikely friendship was forming between Rani and Koena. Koena nodded, understanding the frivolousness of her question.

This time, there was no jeep. Everybody walked. Actually, it made better sense as there were no roads, only thick foliage. Sagar was treating this like a trekking expedition. Koena was lost in her own world. She had thankfully worn good shoes and was quite enjoying the walk. But, walking for pleasure and walking when you are out in the wilderness are wildly different experiences. After walking for a few hours, Koena's feet threatened to disengage from her body. They had been walking without rest. The comrades however, marched ahead, showing no sign of fatigue.

Soon they arrived at the next camp, which was larger. It was on the outskirts of another village, where its people had cleared an area for the comrades. The entire village gave the group a hearty welcome. They had put up tents with plastic sheets that were waving gently in the wind. Blue and red ropes held the sheets together.

Koena turned to Rani, who was walking with her, 'Why do we keep moving? And what is happening here? Why are the streets decorated? What happened to Neeta? Why didn't she join us? I could not even say bye to her.' Koena's barrage of questions made Rani smile.

She placed a hand on Koena's shoulder and said, 'Take a breath, Koena. We keep moving because we do not want the police to track us. These villagers are our friends. They are welcoming us.

Neeta…she must have reached Nepal. She will be fine there. We are expecting to hear some good news very soon. I will let you know,' Rani smiled and replied, waving at some small kids.

'Oh, that's nice!' Koena remarked. She had painted a different picture of Naxals in her mind, fed by the media and the society in general. The villagers, belying the impression, seemed to be very happy to see the Naxal group.

Koena stared at Rana, who was leading the pack.

Are they generally bad, or are they good only to these villagers? They are probably like Robin Hood.

'You will see why we live the way we do, pretty soon,' Rani remarked with a faraway look in her eyes.

'Rani, why did Rana become a Naxalite?' Koena voiced her innermost thoughts.

The look of surprise on the younger woman's face was proof that Koena's question demanded a lengthy response, or maybe silence would be a better reaction. Rani did neither. She asked, 'Why would a man who had the world at his feet, leave all that behind and live like a fugitive, Koena?'

Her eyes spoke volumes. Koena's mind filled with imagery of all sorts as Rani recollected many disjointed stories about how Rana had been caught in the crossfire between the State police and some Naxalites.

Rani continued, 'I think it was when, many years back, Rana da heard about how some policemen had brutally raped some female comrades in their custody. The police were on a mission to curb the Naxal menace in the red corridor. The female comrades who were imprisoned, had undergone unmentionable, immeasurable torture at the hands of the policemen, leading to a violent retort from the head of their gang, Dev Sanyal. Rana had come in contact with Dev *babu* in London during a protest.

'Back home, Rana da helped Dev *babu* escape into Bangladesh using his connections. After things cooled off, Dev *babu* came out of hiding and contacted Rana da, who, by then, had become disillusioned with the system. He quit his job in London and moved to India. He helped Dev *babu* set up a better group and funded our modern weapons. That same year, Dev *babu* got killed in a shootout, and Rana da avenged his friend's death by burning down a police station after parading the policemen naked in the small town of Sharadapur. The entire village participated, quenching their lust for revenge.

'When investigating officers, flown especially from Delhi, came around asking questions; *apparently*, not a single villager could recollect anything about the incident. The burnt remains of the police station were the only testimony to the fact that such a building had even existed. The officers returned and closed the case. The incident was filed as an 'unfortunate accident'.

'Rana da celebrated their victory and vowed that he would never leave his group. The insult meted out to the twenty female comrades who had been paraded naked in front of the people, raped, and mutilated, had dug a deep scar in the psyche of their comrades. They had vowed to find and burn the policemen responsible. In such cases, the government often allowed the police to shoot at sight. The policemen, most often, termed these murders as 'encounters' and killed innocent people randomly.

'Rana da has seen many such horrors in his life, Koena. Right or wrong, he has become a leader of our group, and we are fighting a war... to retain our motherland, retain the forests, and ensure that our rivers are not polluted. We are up against the huge corporates. Rana da has given us all a new lease of life— a new purpose. Our group is one of the largest, and we have very modern methods of fighting this war. We are trying to save our Earth from the rampant digging and exploitation… that's all…' The fiery Rani became quiet.

Koena nodded, her head processing the information at a lightning-fast speed. *This was news!* She imagined a news headline:

'Rana Haldar, erstwhile zamindar and LSE graduate, turns to Naxalism: takes up arms and confronts the ugly underbelly of systemic rot and environmental exploitation.'

Sigh! What a waste of a wonderful life.

Rana was shouting out orders at some comrades. Koena squinted at him. At that precise moment, he turned and looked at her, catching her eye. A smile formed on his lips but faded as quickly as it took birth. Rana moved away, and Koena looked down. Rani had gotten busy catching up with some friends.

This time, Koena and Sagar were in the same hut, and the comrade left the door unlocked. This hut was larger, and characteristically neat and well kept. There was a small kitchen in a corner, a table and a chair, and a few mats rolled up neatly on a side. Apart from this, there was a small TV. Koena quickly updated Sagar, whose eyes nearly popped out of their sockets. He was about to say something when a comrade walked in, indicating that potable water and some food were available in the kitchen.

Always the hungry one—Sagar stood up and decided to check out the kitchen. He was surprised to find a small fridge in the kitchen. He exclaimed at the discovery: bottles of a local beverage. The fridge was like his link to the outer world—a link that satiated the need to feel connected to the world they had left behind. He wanted to return to civilization as soon as he could. This was certainly the weirdest, longest assignment he had worked on in terms of complexity and surprises.

'We are fighting capitalism, so obviously, you won't find Pepsi or Coke here. You will have to manage with this,' Rana's voice boomed from behind, making Sagar jump. Rana smiled. It was not everyday that he witnessed such a thing. An adult expressing joy at having discovered a fridge in the middle of nowhere. It was ironic!

Koena felt a faint sense of dislocation. A day in the forest had made her question many things she had earlier taken for granted in her life. Resignation to her fate seemed a more meaningful choice. Koena felt as if she had been there since eternity.

The comrades spent the day discussing their situation and the new information they had received. They had eaten the lunch sent in by the villagers. When night fell, a female comrade came in with dinner that the villagers had kindly sent.

While tucking into the yummy food, she observed the comrade who was very pretty. Silently, Koena took in the neatly braided hair, the smooth olive skin, and milky white teeth. Maybe in some other life, she could have been a highly paid model endorsing the very same consumerism-hungry goods that they were rallying against.

Koena felt oddly glad at this camaraderie in the middle of a Naxalite den. Food made her think of Shom. She wanted to talk to him so badly. Koena and Sagar quietly ate the food and settled down. Koena kept wondering about the various unanswered questions surrounding them. She had found a small piece of pencil and a notepad.

Idly doodling, she wondered, *Did Swain plan the blast? But why? Who was he doing this for? There is surely another guy or a group funding this whole drama. Who would gain from this blast? I must find out. Who killed Swain? Was it Rana or someone from his gang? Or Swain's corporate bosses?*

She looked at Sagar, who was fast asleep. Sighing, Koena also decided to catch a few winks. Just then, a sudden realization made her feel sad.

Tomorrow is my birthday! And I am stuck in the forests.

■

MAY 11, 2000
Unknown Naxal Camp
4:30 a.m.

IT WAS A beautiful morning. Dawn was creeping up silently on the tired souls resting on makeshift beds. Koena stretched and stood up, walking to the window. Remembering the date suddenly, she closed her eyes and wished herself a great birthday. Her lips murmured a small prayer. She badly wanted to see Shom.

A comrade entered the hut with cups of hot tea and some rolls of bun. Koena woke up Sagar, who looked like a zombie. After freshening up, they sipped their tea. Then, they went for a walk in the forests. Sagar gave her a side hug, a small wildflower and wished her a happy birthday. Smiling gleefully at the wish, Koena hugged the boy back.

'So, Koena, you got new family members, eh?' Sagar asked, clearly in a jovial mood. Maybe all the greenery was de-stressing him.

'Yeah… weird, no? When we got picked up, we were worried about our lives. Now, we are chilling in a forest, with a bunch of great people, new family members…' Koena laughed, looking wistfully at a distant hillock.

'It would have been good if Shom were here, I know…' Sagar seemed to pluck the words out of her head. Koena looked at him and simply nodded.

'So, Sagar, who do you think is behind the mine blast? And who do you think would have killed the CM? Rana?' Koena's voice trailed off while she struggled with a few stray thoughts.

The CM got killed when we were all together, and Rana was with us. Could it be Shom?

'I think we should not worry about who killed the CM. Rather, we should try to figure out why he was killed! Don't you think so?' Sagar's logical brain was working fast, piecing together facts. Koena simply nodded. *True!*

They reached a clearing and found a nice rock to settle on. It was warm yet cool. Sunrays fell on it sparsely, filtered from the thick trees.

'I also think somebody from Rana's gang has killed the CM. The same person who was behind the Delhi blast. Maybe they were not aware that the CM was not in station while they mistakenly destroyed the bungalow. They struck again, and this time hit their target. I feel it is personal… not political or money-driven. It could be for revenge…But we should find out the reason soon.'

'Yes, if we get the answer to the 'why,' we get our culprit.' Sagar seemed lost in thought. 'What do we know about the CM?'

'Hmm… He was a jerk! Apart from that?' Koena winked and laughed, and Sagar joined in.

Koena had recently spoken to one of her colleagues after her Delhi trip. The colleague had filled her in about the most notorious of men to have walked the Earth: A. K. Swain. She recollected the conversation with Sagar who took in all the data, processing it quickly.

A.K. Swain of the PDP party, the current CM of Delhi, is a complete asshole. He seems to have nine lives and has miraculously escaped multiple terrorist attacks. His resume reads like that of a Bollywood villain. Purely through his networking and extortion/blackmailing skills, he has moved up the ranks of the party. It is rumoured that Swain had killed around 250 tribal people in Bastar when he was a measly party worker. No FIR had been registered; no complaint was lodged, even. The deaths were attributed to a sudden landslide, and the media again had a field day describing the generosity of the local councillor – Swain's boss at the time – and how he had donated his money to the victims' kin.

A corporate biggie was eying the tribal land to build a swanky plant. Swain got the money and the tribals paid with their lives. Swain moved up the ranks, and the depth and number of crimes increased. When he was living in Kosa, he had murdered and looted with impunity. He headed the coal mafia there. Even now, the coal mafia was managed by his goons. They siphoned off and sold the coal from the mines in collusion with the managers.

Apart from being a murderer, he was also a serial rapist. Swain had an eye for pretty and young female workers of the mines. He usually targeted them or the maids working at the Babus' residences. Not a single woman lodged a complaint against him, fearing for her life. Swain and his meteoric rise in the party were the stuff of urban legends. Very conveniently, the local councillor, Swain's ex-boss, had been killed in an accident involving a truck. As was normal, the news died a natural death.

Swain lost no time holding the party together and moved up until he reached his goal: the CM's chair. With well-heeled friends at the right places, Swain squashed all rebellion in the bud. All his campaigns were heavily funded by the SK group when he was even touted as the candidate in the elections. Purely on the basis of money and muscle power, he won the election and was appointed the CM.

Koena and Sagar spoke aloud at the same time. 'This means Swain is behind the blast and that's why he was killed! Or maybe his boss SK lost trust in Swain and had him executed!'

They laughed.

Sagar continued, 'So, I feel strongly that SK finished him off. They surely have some guts. But how did they breach security? Did they have access to his movement and other details? Must have… otherwise, it is tough to plan this in detail….'

'Yea… I think so…' Koena's mind was again on Shom.

'Hmm… I know that SK was behind the mass murder of the tribal people. Of course, Swain was the guy who executed it. But would SK go to this extent? Maybe he wants to usurp the mines…or there is something that Swain hasn't completed for SK…'

Sagar was busy examining one of the leaves of a wild plant. Koena nodded at him when he looked for confirmation.

Koena's mind wandered off to Shom again.

Did he…? Shom is also Rana's gang member. In fact, he is family too. So, he could have surely helped Rana pull this off.

The more she thought about it, her assumption seemed more likely. She refrained from sharing it with Sagar, though.

'So, you are saying there's a high possibility that SK is behind the murder. For some motive and that he and Swain had something brewing… we must find out what SK was hoping to gain…or what if the mines blast and Swain's murder are connected. Maybe SK wanted to get his hands on these mines and had asked Swain to make it easy for him. When Nirmal got killed, Rana and his gang must have sworn revenge…'

Eyebrows drawn, Koena bit her lip, 'Hmm… I know. It must have been something huge, like the land he usurped in Bastar. Maybe, he was after the mines. Let's go back. We could ask Rana himself. What do you think?'

Sagar simply shrugged. They had made some progress on the mystery of Swain's murder.

They returned to the hut and found Rana and a few comrades standing outside, talking in hushed tones. Rana saw her and hurried towards her.

'Koena, we will drop you near the railway station tonight. Two of my men will guide you both to safety. In any case, I will tell you the final plan…'

Nodding at Rana, Koena and Sagar looked at each other. 'I want to ask you something…' Koena began, when someone called Rana away.

Sagar looked crestfallen. He had been enjoying this forced vacation. Just when their adventure was turning interesting, it was time to go home. Koena's heart was also not in it. She seriously considered asking Rana to allow them to stay back.

'Lal salaam.'

Koena heard the war cry first. Sagar and she turned to see what the commotion was all about. They stood still, their mouths agape, as they watched a whole contingent of comrades shouting 'Lal Salaam' and sweeping past.

Their leader, a diminutive woman of indeterminate age, stepped aside and ordered her troop to rest. The woman was wearing a red spotted bandana. The crowd dispersed while the woman entered Rana's hut. Koena stared at her from a distance till she vanished into the hut. The woman radiated power and energy, and she was strikingly beautiful—dark and stunning like Ma Durga.

There is something oddly familiar about that woman. Wonder where I have seen her?

'Rana! My brother!' The woman cried when she entered Rana's hut. Rana rushed to embrace her. 'Lokki *boudi*… How are you? You did some good cleaning…'

'Yes… much needed, na? How are you, *dada*?' She enquired, returning the embrace. She had not seen him in many years.

'I am good, see? I have become so prosperous!' Rana smiled, patting his non-existent paunch.

'Don't worry, we will get some good exercise and lose it,' Lokki remarked good-naturedly.

'Come, meet our special guests…' Rana winked and urged.

'I'm eager to spend some downtime… especially now that the pig has been roasted!' Lokki laughed and Rana joined in.

'Yes! That was a superb show. Bastard was just going to sell the mines to SK. You have surely derailed their plans for a few years. We will have to think of something if SK plots something else. By the way, you are in for a surprise…' Rana said, smiling softly.

'What surprise?' Lokki mouthed at him, narrowing her eyes.

'You will see... come.' Rana replied mischievously and escorted Lokki to Koena's hut.

When Rana introduced Lokki to Koena, the women looked at each other, simultaneously drawing in sharp breaths.

Rani walked in just then and exclaimed, '*Dada*, don't they look similar? If Koena didi were older, she would look exactly like Lokki di.'

Koena thought Rani had a point. *The eyes and the nose, especially…*

Lokki's face turned ashen, forgotten thoughts and emotions crowding her mind. Koena looked at the older woman with unabashed curiosity. Rana looked with amazement at both women standing before him, murmuring in awe, 'Now this is what I would call Mother Nature's wonder.'

Koena and Rani exchanged confused glances. Rana's words made no sense to them. But as though startled at the confirmation of her thoughts, Lokki looked at Rana and raised an eyebrow. He read her thoughts and motioned her to come outside. Lokki gave a quick glance at Koena and turned to leave before she could have a better look.

Outside the hut, Lokki demanded with pain and confusion warring inside her, suppressing the hope, '*Dada*, tell me… Do you know anything? About that girl… the woman? Who is she?'

'Lokki *boudi*, I have been waiting for this day…' Rana said softly, and smiling, he took Lokki's hands in his. 'See, I came to know of this when I went to meet my cousin, Shom. You would remember him. I have shown you his picture, too.'

Lokki nodded, recollecting the young man's enthusiasm for Rana's activism. She had heard of Rana's trip to Bhubaneswar earlier that month to tap some eager businessmen who wanted to fund the organization's objectives.

Rana explained. 'When I first met Koena, I was dumbstruck. Yes, like you, I could not, but wonder at the resemblance. I decided to find out. After some digging, I learned a few facts. Some pleasant, some downright terrifying. Well, when fate intervened again, and Koena and Sagar came here to cover the mine blast, I came to know of a terrible plan.

'Our dear friend Swain and his men had planned the blast. They had wanted to stop the government from interfering in their activities. By blasting the mine, they wanted to stop the modernisation of the mines and the eventual pay revision of the miners for a while. By then, as usual, they would have fit their guy in the ministry, who would have handled it.

'SK was behind it all. He was gunning for the land. He wanted the government to deem it unsafe and close the mines so he could usurp it. They had planned to make a spectacle of the murders of the journalists who had come to cover the blast. I kidnapped them so that no one could harm them.'

'That bastard, Swain… It was a relief to see him…his ugly face blow up into the air!' Lokki said, a smile spreading on her face.

'Yeah, but we lost Nirmal…' Rana said, both anger and sadness tinging his voice.

'Oh no, I am so sorry. How are Neeta and her son? Where are they?'

'Neeta and her kids are safe. Recently, she delivered her second baby…a girl. We named her Lakshmi, after you… I managed to ship her out. Now she is living with my aunt in Nepal,' Rana informed. They stood in silence for a few moments, each ruminating in their thoughts, anger coursing through their veins at the untimely death of Nirmal.

'Now… about Koena… From what I knew from Shom and now… Seeing her…' He paused, looking at Lokki's pained, eager face, unsure how to phrase his thoughts.

'*Dada*?' Lokki prodded.

She knew Rana had called her for a specific reason. She was beginning to have a solid guess, but she dared not get her hopes up.

'Lokki *boudi*, she is your daughter,' Rana said abruptly, with the air of someone deciding a straightforward answer was the safest.

Lokki drew a sharp breath and kept a hand on her chest to control her runaway emotions. Her heart knew that she was connected to Koena, but this was not something she had expected to hear.

'*Dada*, are you sure? And… What a day to hear this good news!… It… It is her birthday today!' Lokki said, her eyes beginning to fill up. She was feeling strangely emotional after decades.

She felt as if her heart would burst, trying to recollect the faint images (which were aided by her imagination over the years) of the helpless infant that her Pishi had taken away years ago and given to the Nun. She could not even recollect the infant's face clearly, never having seen her much.

'Yes, Lokki. I have made my enquiries. She is your daughter. And look at the way Mother Nature works. She has made Koena in your mould. Even if you refuse to acknowledge her, you cannot turn a blind eye to the fact that she is your spitting image…' Rana said.

It had taken Rana just a week to find out everything about Koena and her past, once he had seen her with Shom and wondered about her features. When his messenger visited the Orphanage where Koena grew up, it was easy to arm-twist the old, snooty nun to share information about a certain infant left in the care of the Church a few decades ago. The messenger got a photocopy of Koena's birth certificate too, along with some pictures of Tia as a baby and then as a grown-up girl.

Rana handed over the folder containing all this to Lokki. She burst out crying when she saw it. Her hands trembled so hard that the birth certificate slid out and fell. Rana picked it up. Lokki could not control herself and burst out crying. The sister who had carried Tia away had put the mother's name as 'Lokki' and place of birth as Kosa.

'*Dada*, my baby… Oh, God! After all these years, she has become such a beautiful woman. She is so pretty,' Lokki cried.

'You are also a grandmother. Koena has a son, Kirtibhushan. Go meet her, *boudi*,' Rana urged.

Lokki entered and stared at Koena, unable to utter a word. Rana followed, and beckoned Koena closer. He looked at Lokki and then turned to Koena, 'I need to tell you something, Koena.'

'Yes?' Koena asked, tilting her head, her thoughts elsewhere.

I must ask him about SK and Swain. I am sure SK is behind all this— That bastard.

'*Dada*, I… I want to…' said Lokki, her voice quivering. Koena stared at her, noticing her properly up close for the first time. Though she had noticed the striking similarities, Koena never paid much attention …but now…she wondered.

Who was this woman? And why did she look familiar?

'Sure, I will leave you two alone,' Rana said and stepped away, watching them from a distance.

Koena was staring incredulously at the older woman, registering the stark similarities in their features, and wondering how this woman could look exactly like her. Lokki, meanwhile, was trying to locate some trace of the helpless infant that she had glimpsed that day in 1960, desperately trying to match that imagery with the suave classy woman standing in front of her. Almost absently, Lokki walked up close to Koena. She gently touched Koena's cheek and gave out a choked cry when she felt Koena's skin.

Her baby! How pretty she was… With those dimples… Ah! What a lovely lady she had grown up into. Lokki thanked her stars for helping her old Pishi take the right decision. She shuddered to think of the life she might have given her daughter.

Koena was curious. Her heart was doing somersaults in her ribcage. She felt an electric current run through her body when Lokki touched her cheek. Her body knew that touch, strangely even seemed to recognize it.

What was happening? Who was this woman?

'Koena…' Lokki spelt out the name carefully, deliberately elongating the syllables, as if tasting the name. It sounded so sweet. *Her daughter— her little helpless baby—the baby with her dimples.*

Koena cleared her throat and managed to ask, 'Do you know me? Do you want to talk?'

'What? Aah, yes, yes! I… I wanted to… well, I… I am not good at all this, you know; where is Rana da?' Lokki looked around nervously. She could do with some help.

After all these years, after dreaming about her child for countless nights, now when she was standing face to face with her flesh and blood, Lokki didn't know what to say.

'Yes, please go on…' Koena urged kindly. She put a hand on Lokki's shoulder and gently helped her onto a *moda.* Rana re-entered and came and stood near Lokki. He put a firm hand on her shoulder. When she looked up, he gently nodded.

'Koena, Lokki is your birth mother.' Rana said, realizing that Lokki was finding it difficult to find her voice.

Koena was so shocked when she heard this that her feet buckled under her. She almost fell, but Rana held her up and carefully made her sit on the *moda*, too. Koena stared at Rana and Lokki incredulously before she managed, 'Mo... Mother? What… what are you saying? How can that be? It is not possible. I'm an orphan. I grew up in an orphanage, I remember those days…I…' She was hyperventilating.

'Koena… shh…' Rana urged, pulling up a *moda* to sit between mother and daughter. He looked into Koena's eyes, understanding the confusion that must be filling the woman's heart. He put a hand on Koena's shoulder, saying, 'Wait, I will show you something.'

'See this…' Rana said, showing her a photo. Koena looked at it, and then at Rana with a frown on her face, 'I don't remember taking such a photo. When was this?'

'Koena! That is not your photo. It is Lokki's… When she was around twenty-nine.' Rana clarified.

Stunned, Koena nodded, looking alternately at the softly sobbing Lokki and the aged picture.

In the picture, Lokki was standing near a wooden horse in what looked like a fair, happily smiling for the photographer. Koena ran a finger lovingly over the picture. Her heart was thudding, but no longer painful. Suddenly, all sounds ceased. She felt as if there were only the two of them at that moment. Koena pushed her *moda* back, sunk onto the floor and threw herself on Lokki, hugging her tightly. Tears flowed copiously.

Lokki, initially panicking at the emotional outburst, recovered and tightly hugged her long-lost daughter.

'Happy birthday, my dearest girl! Happy birthday. Oh! How many years I have waited to say this to you, to hold you, to kiss your forehead and bless you.' Lokki shed copious tears. The years of longing for her only child had broken the resilient woman. She let herself go, holding her child to her bosom. Koena's heart filled with sorrow and joy. She hugged her mother and bawled like a baby.

Fate had indeed played a terrible joke on them both. But had finally taken pity on them too. Koena had received such a beautiful birthday gift!

Rana left the room quietly, his eyes misty.

■

MAY 11, 2000

Unknown Naxal Camp

KOENA PACED UP and down, her brow knit in concentration. Mother and daughter had chatted for hours, with Koena filling up Lokki with details of her life in Bhubaneswar. Lokki listened with rapt attention, her eyes lighting up at the stories she was hearing about Koena's life. She felt so proud of her clever and pretty daughter. Whatever be the method of her conception, she was Lokki's gift from Nature.

At around 2:30 p.m., Lokki left to take some rest. They had talked a lot that day without resting.

Koena was unable to stomach the surprising developments. Years after she had even thought of her, she had met her birth mother and was now painfully aware of her birth details. Though her growing-up years were not very pleasant, Koena could vividly recall the faces of the kind nuns and the other people in the orphanage. She had always assumed she was one of those unwanted orphans. Learning the truth otherwise had not helped. Koena felt deeply disturbed by the story of her conception. She had felt Lokki's pain when her mother haltingly unveiled the story of that fateful day when she had been waylaid by Swain and had her life completely altered. Koena felt a volcano erupting inside her heart, knowing the helplessness of the frail girl whose life the tyrant had changed to quench his lust.

Lokki had also told her about how she had wanted to track down and kill the man, who was Koena's biological father, who had ruined Lokki's life, forcing her to pick up a gun.

The bastard, A K Swain, the recently-deceased Delhi CM was her mother's abuser,. and her father.

Even the word 'father' seemed like a bad abuse to Koena's mind. A father was someone who nurtured and cared, not a guy who trampled someone's life shamelessly. Koena's mind could not accept the vile excuse of a human as her father. He was simply a man who must be abhorred and detested. *And killed.*

A deep shudder ran through her. Had she just normalized the killing of a human? Did her mind just accept and worse, rejoice the killing of a man who was obviously a perpetrator? Earlier, she would have maybe said he deserved to be a jailbird, needing legal intervention.

Koena shook her head to clear it. She seemed to be slipping into an abyss. A quagmire of insensitivity and lawlessness. The enormity of her thoughts almost pushed her to the brink. She closed her eyes and tried to focus. The darkness within her had seemed to take on a different shape. *I am good…I am healed…*

Koena's heart twisted with hate, recollecting the man's face. If he were alive, she could not deny to herself that she would have definitely killed him, after hearing the earth-shattering truth.

She rubbed her forehead hard to get her brain to stop flooding her mind with useless memories. Her skin was hot to touch, and she wanted to walk or jog to control her rising anger. Obviously, she could not go for a run in the thick forest, so she did the next best thing. She started spot jogging. After a few minutes, Koena felt her heart pumping blood feverishly to her limbs and her nerves turning taut with tension. She kept jogging, remembering to breathe through her nose. When her mind eventually stopped its incessant chatter, she slowed down and stopped. There was no one around to witness Koena's distress. Sweat claimed her body's orifices, and she sighed with the satisfaction of having curbed the anger swelling in her chest.

Where is Sagar? Haven't seen him for quite some time. Should I go chat with Ma? Yeah, I guess I should.

Brooding over her plan of taking Lokki back with her, Koena stepped out of the hut, into the warm evening sun. She walked towards Rana's hut and noticed that the door was closed.

Koena looked at it, wondering, *Is somebody in there? Why have they closed the door?*

Hesitating, not wanting to disturb Rana or her mother, Koena turned to go back, when the door opened suddenly.

Rana stepped out. With him was a man Koena had not seen in days. All other thoughts forgotten, she jumped in glee and rushed into his arms.

Shom! My Shom! Even if he is a murderer, I am so happy to see him!

■

The Wife

MAY 13, 2000

Ashiana Apartments
8:00 p.m.

KOENA'S RETURN WAS quite uneventful after Shom came to fetch her. Rana had insisted that Sagar stay back in the forest. He would be dropped separately. Koena had worried about the boy till she got a call from Sagar a day after she reached home. Tim had suggested making a show on their stay in the forests. They had used Neeta's interview in a special broadcast, and it was a hit. Sagar got rare accolades from Tim.

Shom had flatly refused to let Koena go back to work and even asked her to resign from the network. A few heated arguments followed; rivers of tears could not change the firm decision that Shom had taken. Koena had to give in.

Her heart heavy, one fine day, a week after she felt somewhat mentally alert to resume work, Koena went to the office and handed in her resignation. The shock on Tim's face was palpable. It made Koena wince. She had expected to head the network one day. Her career was over before her dream came true.

Why am I exactly following whatever Shom is ordering me to do?

With a heavy head and a bleeding heart, she made it through the notice period. She could not fathom his intent behind making her quit her flourishing career. But she always did what Shom wanted. *I am mad about him. He is my life, my love.*

The fierce passion they shared had not dimmed even after years. How could she doubt his intent? He might have a better plan for their future. After thinking it over, Koena decided to accept the change gracefully. Maybe he wanted to do something different for both of them. She would have to wait, or maybe she could convince him to let her stay at the network. Yeah, she would try. Maybe all they needed was a calm and composed discussion after a while minus the tears and the melodrama that had ensued last time when she had suggested that.

Yes! She would do that tonight. Maybe offer some action in return for a discussion. Will he agree?

When Koena reached home around 7:30 p.m., things seemed normal. Shom was in the kitchen, and a heavenly aroma of smoked chicken and fluffy hot rotis filled the house.

She cleaned up and offered to chop up some vegetables for the mandatory salad. He smiled and handed over the cutting board, knife, and the vegetables. Koena quietly started cutting.

Chop, chop, chop.

Meanwhile, her mind wandered a bit.

In all these years, I never had a chance to suspect that my husband was anything, but a Chef and a restaurateur. He never said anything out of the ordinary, never ever. And, now, suddenly he was a Naxal sympathizer! And that too, cousin of Rana, who turned out to be her birth mother's brother-in-law. What a convoluted set of bonds!

Hey, wait. But Shom was not a Haldar. Maybe his mother married a Mahapatra…

'Shom, how are you a Mahapatra, while Rana is a Haldar? Didn't you say you guys were cousins?' Koena asked, keeping her eyes on the salad. The surname was not the most important question at this point. Having a meaningless conversation was the point. At some level, filling the scary space with some sound was also the point. To keep the thoughts flowing was her intention, filling the space with words and hear herself air out her thoughts. She had been wondering about relationship trivialities of late. Every nuance generated a question in her overtly fertile mind. It stayed till it burst out on the world.

Shom didn't turn; his back remained steady, like a concrete wall. Koena sighed softly. The wall could not be permeated. Not even with time. Koena felt as if her head would burst if she did not get some answers sooner. She prodded Shom with her elbow.

Eventually, he turned and smiled before replying. 'I was wondering why you hadn't asked me this yet… Sweety, I am related to Rana from my mother's side. My mother's maiden surname was Chatterjee. His mom and mine are sisters. My aunt, Rana da's Mom, married Shashank Haldar,' Shom continued, non-plussed at her incredulous expression.

'Oh!' It made total sense. And how they had started talking about unimportant things. But a small thought wriggled like a worm birthing.

'And now, my mum and I are related twice, if that makes sense. All of us are a big happy family…' Koena paused, completing the thought in her mind. *'…of Naxalites.*

'Yeah, shona, and we are all going to stay together. Rana da has plans.'

Does he? Koena's scepticism kicked in. *Of course, he would have plans. Doesn't he always have plans, big man that he is!*

She gulped down the sarcasm and diluted it further with a glass of ice-cold water. Suddenly, her eyebrows rose when a thought struck her. *Stay together? How's that possible? He is an outlaw… But neither of us are… wait a minute!*

'Are you suggesting that we all move to the jungles? Staying there for a while is fine… But moving there? Are you out of your mind?' Koena asked, her tone giving away her shock. Shom turned and gave her his famous warm smile, making her insides go gooey. She ignored the urge to kiss him and continued staring at him.

'Well, yea… That is exactly what Rana da suggested. He gave different reasons, though.' Shom looked pensive now, searching Koena's face for any hint of a violent protest or of a full-blown war.

'Shom… Are you out of your mind? We cannot shift to the jungles, leaving behind everything…' Koena's voice had an odd finality to it. Cold. Calm. Shom observed the twitching nerves near her temples and took in her determined expression.

His trained mind saw the impending fight from her stance. Silently, Shom watched her, wondering, *boy, she looks really tormented. Maybe this is not a good idea. Moving to the jungles actually doesn't seem like a plausible one anyway…*

Unaware of Shom's dilemma, Koena continued, 'Baby, I know the kind of complex situations we both are in; but think practically. We have a life here. We are respected members of society. We cannot just upend everything and go live in the jungles, especially with Kit… He will be sitting for his boards soon.'

Shom looked at her, silently turning over her words in his mind. *She did have a point.* Rana did not have a teenaged son whose future he had to worry about. Shom's imperceptible nod raised the amount of blood sloshing around in Koena's arteries. With the rise of the pressure of the blood, Koena's mind started forcing her to panic and she blurted, 'Shom, you must not accede to such crazy ideas.'

'Hmm… I have not made any decisions shona, just toying with the idea…obviously we have to discuss it further…' was all Shom managed to say, as he expertly flipped the near-perfect rotis.

'Come, let's eat.' Shom smiled, tugging at his wife's hand.

I will have to persuade her to move to a safer place, though. No longer here.

'No, you first promise that you won't make me do anything foolish,' Koena demanded.

'I won't make any hasty decisions, *shona*. Whatever we do, it will be our decision. Okay? Now, can we eat, please?' Shom had turned on his charm and his seductive smile.

Koena almost melted before reminding herself that she had to stand firm in this matter. Not completely satisfied with the way things had turned out, she decided to pursue this later. With better ammo. She had no power against his charms. She had often thought of him as a weapon of mass destruction, provided the opponents were all women.

Unexpectedly, the 'later' never materialised. At least not how Koena had imagined.

Shom had a question which caught her off-guard and stopped her meandering, 'Shona, do you remember how we met?'

His eyes had taken a dreamy look. Koena smiled, warmth spreading through her body and mind. 'Of course, I remember… We were so madly in love. I wonder if you had not come to meet me…' Koena left her sentence unfinished as Shom sprang up from the chair and pulled her into a deep kiss.

A while later, they lay side by side on a sheet spread in the balcony, watching the stars. Reminiscing about old times. How they had found and almost lost each other…

■

APRIL 1981

Bhubaneswar

IT HAD BEEN almost a month since Tia had joined her new job in Bhubaneswar. She had been shocked to realize that Shom had not kept his promise and had not met her. Her boss at the daily had helped her find accommodation. Tia's mind was not at all on her work. Nothing held her interest. All she could think of was Shom. She had tried calling him on the number printed on his card, but nobody answered. With a heavy heart, Tia kept trying it every alternate day.

The days when she would visit the PCO to make the call, she would dress up, in the hope that maybe Shom would attend the call and they could meet. She even visited his restaurant after work in the hope that she would bump into him. But nobody had seen or heard from him. After a while, Tia lost hope and decided to move on.

■

SEPTEMBER 1981

Bhubaneswar

OF LATE, TIA had made it a habit to visit the Lingaraj Temple and spend time there. It helped her soul. Growing up in a Christian Missionary orphanage, Tia never had a chance to experience Hindu culture this closely. She realized that she liked it and soaked up everything that came her way. Festivals, rituals, food, habits, folk tales and legends, the various deities, the works. Since the time she joined the daily, she had made many friends who invited her over to their homes and taught her new things.

One such friend was Aparna Chaudhary, a slim Punjabi woman from Delhi. Her parents had got divorced when she was young. And since then, she had been living in and out of hostels. Tia had put an ad for a roommate and Aparna answered it. One look at Aparna and Tia agreed to share the house with her. The women were poles apart. It took Aparna just a few months to make Tia dance to her tunes.

Aparna came from a very wealthy family. Her father was a famous film producer and had no time for the lonely girl. Her mother, an actress, didn't want to keep the girl as it would affect her chances at getting juicy roles. Hence Aparna was shunted from one hostel to another, each place worse than the last. Early on, Aparna discovered the ways to please men to get her work done. Be it her tuition teacher, her bodyguards, or even her father's middle-aged secretary, no man could escape her charms.

When she moved to Delhi at the behest of her then-boyfriend, she had decided to be by herself for a while, trying to earn a living. She had pulled some strings and landed herself a job at a hotel, at the reception. Tia was, of course, blissfully unaware of her roommate's background and manipulative nature. No amount of coaxing made her step out of her room.

'Tia *ji*! What do you see in those damn books? Don't you get bored?' Aparna had demanded once. Tia had simply smiled in response.

Tia mostly kept to herself, moping and thinking about Shom, imagining different scenarios of their meeting. She would occasionally distract herself by reading. During those turbulent years, Tia had read all the books she could find in the local libraries.

She had decided to get a degree in Journalism and enrolled in a distance ducation program at a local University. She would bury herself in her course books after returning from work. Aparna lost interest in her roommate until one night, when she returned late from a party, totally wasted. Tia helped her clean up. The next day, when Aparna woke up with a hangover, Tia nursed her back to health.

A few days later, taking pity on the lonely girl, Aparna asked if Tia would be interested in going out with her one evening.

'But I don't go out… Besides, I have a lot to study. My exams are coming…' Tia's reasons didn't cut ice with Aparna, who made Tia change into one of her own dresses and dragged her to a party at the hotel.

Although Tia had gone along unwillingly, not wanting to appear rude to her new friend, she had enjoyed herself a lot. Slowly, it became a regular affair. After returning from their day jobs, they would dress up and drop into multiple parties – some of them house parties, and some others, rave parties. They say there is always a first time for everything.

The first time Tia put her nose to a white line, she had no inkling about the quagmire she was walking into.

■

DECEMBER 1981

Bhubaneswar

IN JUST A few months, Tia was neck-deep in it all. Attending late-night booze parties that seemed never-ending, lying wasted in strange beds with stranger men, Tia had lost count of days and was just flowing along the torrents of life. Aparna had laughed away her concerns about police and the adverse effects on health, remarking, 'This is the high life, baby. This is how rich people live. You are rich now. See all the money you're making. There are so many unhappy people around you in this world. You give them some time and affection, and they give you money. That is all this is about. Isn't it? There is nothing wrong with this. Take it from me…I have been spreading love since I was ten. I found out that my Hindi teacher was so lonely, you know… poor man. I gave him a lot of love… In turn, he gave me great grades. Easy transaction, don't you think so?'

Aparna's laughter filled the tiny house, which both girls had decided to not vacate since it could attract unwanted attention. A quick snort was the panacea for all problems in the world.

That was when Tia started facing a new problem.

■

MARCH 1982

Bhubaneswar

IT WAS AROUND 1 a.m. when Tia untangled herself from the guy's arms. She was feeling weird. A strange sensation enveloped her. Stumbling, she got down from the stranger's bed and made her way to the washroom. 'Maybe I should get my ass home now.'

Seeing her face in the mirror, Tia cringed, muttering, 'Whoa! I look wasted, man.'

She rubbed some white powder on her gums and splashed cold water on her face to boot her system. It worked.

Softly, without waking the guy up, she dressed and let herself out of the flat. The man had already paid by cash, which she had tucked safely in her bag. She would just have to manage to get a cab. The streets were deserted at this hour. Only dogs were out, patrolling their territories, trying to make sense of their lives.

Tia waited for a taxi or a rickshaw. But at this time of night, not many vehicles plied. A car's headlight caught her full on when she decided to cross over to the other side of the road. Brakes squealed. A holler from the driver shook Tia.

'I need to get home, fast,' She murmured to nobody in particular. Walking slowly, in order to not harm her heels, Tia squinted when a car stopped near her, and a man, neatly dressed in formals got out.

Uh oh, not now! I am wasted.

She waved her hands to shoo away the potential customer since her hunger was satiated for the time being and kept walking towards the lake. She would surely get a rickshaw from there. This damn cocktail dress was irritating her. An impromptu shopping trip to Bangkok with Aparna and some other friends had made her poorer by a few thousands but had upped the wardrobe game by a few notches.

Tia turned when she heard footsteps behind her.

Why is this man following me? Must be very desperate to get laid...maybe he is like me...needs non-stop action...haha

With a smirk, Tia decided to make some more money... but it was not to be!

'Hi, Tia... Remember me?' The deep baritone sounded so familiar. It hit her core. Tia tried to shake herself out of the muddling dizziness. *Am I dreaming? Is that...?*

'Shom...?' She asked, her mind befuddled.

'Yes. It's me, Shom... You must be wondering... I am sorry! I know I vanished... But I have a reason. And I want another chance at... us... if...' He left the sentence hanging, as though unsure how to proceed.

Tia stared at the man as if he were an apparition. Stumped by the turn of events, Tia rubbed her head to clear it.

I am a mess! And this man had to appear today, of all days! Why? No no! I cant do this...I am too far gone...oh god!

Shom came closer, gently held her hand, and asked, 'Is there still a chance for me? Or is there someone...' He trailed off again, as if afraid to finish the thought.

'Uh… Can we talk some other time? I am not in a great state… I… am drunk, and I don't know what I'm saying…' Tia shrugged, looking defiant and apologetic.

Shom placed another hand on her shoulder, mainly to steady her, and also to get her full attention. He could see that her pupils were dilated. Some powder was still stuck to her nostrils. *God, this woman has ruined herself. Is she on drugs? Oh lord! I hope I did not do this to her!* Shom's heart broke into thousand pieces.

He continued, his voice shaky, 'It is okay. I just wanted to get back in touch. I went to your office, they said you quit long back. A kind lady gave me your house address. But you weren't there. Your roommate was around, and she gave me this address. I was about to leave when I saw you come out of the building. I could not recognize you at first. You… look… umm… different.' Shom's voice was unsure, as if he had expected something different. He was still holding her hand, his touch making her feel warm. *Is she a…or am I just over reacting? Why is she dressed like this?*

A thought permeated her drugged mind. *Of course, he expected to see his innocent Tia. I am not that person anymore.*

'Could you drop me home, please?' All Tia could think of was hitting her bed. She didn't care for anyone, any man or woman or cat. She wanted her bed.

Shom nodded and guided her gently towards his car. They rode to her place silently. He kept looking at her but she was zoned out.

He helped her up the stairs and bid goodbye at her door. Tia merely nodded and managed a small smile when Shom tried to hug her.

The last thought when Tia hit the bed was, '*How the hell did I end up like this?*'

Seeing Shom had sucked the buzz out of her. Everything in her life now seemed empty and vacuous. Seeing his earnest eyes and warm affection, she wanted to be sweet and clean. Pure.

She was none of these things. Not anymore.

Do I still love him?

■

MAY 30, 2000

Ashiana Apartments

8:00 a.m.

SHOM HAD MADE arrangements to move. His plan was elaborate but simple.

Kit would continue staying at the boarding school. Shom and Koena would stay with Rana and his group for some time.

Shom made some furtive calls and ensured that his restaurant would be taken care of while they were away. The initial plan was to stay with Rana for a while and then to move to the UK. The whole idea was to escape the scrutiny and start afresh.

When Shom conveyed the outline of the plan, Koena's ears perked up at the probability of moving to the UK. *Now, that sounded like a plan!* She would love to settle in London.

She knew that Shom had a property in London that he had inherited from his parents. But whether it was feasible and whether they would be under the police radar was not something she wanted to find out. She figured that Shom would have thought through all this, and she and Kit would just let him take the lead on this. She visualized how they could spend a few days in the forests… Then she could persuade Shom to pack up and leave for London. By then, Kit would wrap up his schooling. They would ensure he got admission into one of those fancy schools in London. Life would be just perfect.

And, anyway, there was nothing she could do about the whole SK-Swain episode. Those men were far too powerful for her to take on. Maybe Rana would find a way to deal with SK. But she had to focus on her own life and the small issues that she had to deal with, ironing them out. She could do that. Maybe, once they moved to London, she could ensure that Rana was kept at a distance. After all, Shom hadn't indulged any criminal activity.

Oh, I don't really know that. I hope he hasn't…

At least, that was Koena's version of the plan.

Shom's was *slightly* different.

■

JUNE 20, 2000

Ashiana Apartments
2:00 p.m.

IT HAD BEEN a month since they had started wrapping up their lives.

'Aren't we supposed to call the association?' Koena's voice was breaking. Her emotions were taking a toll on her mental health and her overall reasoning abilities. After that night of May 13th, Shom had become quieter, and Koena could feel something churning in his head. She could feel the change in her bones. The feeling was everywhere, like slick sticky sweat drops that clung to her body.

I am sure he is hiding something.

Doubtfully, Koena kept hovering around Shom, carefully studying his reactions and his behavioural patterns. But he was, as always, sweet, charming, and romantic. On her repeated insistence about the plans, Shom had briefly indulged and explained it briefly. He never let her into any of the details and remained firm in that decision.

I don't know anything even now. I must find out what he is planning.

Koena tried all the tricks in her arsenal. Everything. Nothing worked.

They had to move within a week, Shom declared. Seven days were all Koena had, to wrap up her life into small boxes. It felt like being in the path of an impending tsunami and being forewarned to pack whatever little you could. The gathering of essentials took very less time, owing to the meticulous regularity with which Shom conducted their financial and legal affairs. There was no worry about anything going amiss. Koena had served her notice and Tim had looked appropriately sad and shocked at the turn of events. Sagar had seemed truly heart-broken and had made her promise to keep in touch.

The one tiny thing Koena had to worry about was the preparation of the practised answers to be delivered verbatim to the various connections from their social life in Bhubaneswar.

The first one to receive the well-rehearsed script was their friend and neighbour. Koena delivered it as per Shom's expectations and felt confident when the man took it all in, without *apparently* doubting even a single point. The stubbornness with which Shom insisted that they give the same story to everybody they knew was beyond Koena.

Nowadays, many things went beyond her understanding. She was just drifting along, nodding to whatever Shom threw at her. She had no idea when she had agreed to Shom's version of the plan. Was it before or after they made love? Or was it during? Her mind was fuzzy, but the fact remained that she had agreed to tag along with him to the jungles. And surprisingly, Kit now seemed excited, almost treating this as an adventure trip.

Days went by in the blink of an eye. Kit had been pulled out of school mid-term. He had cribbed and whined about that initially, but he settled once he observed the grave faces of his parents and felt the heavy undercurrents in the house. He had trained himself to look at the exciting side of the unknown. Suddenly, they had been pulled apart by forces nobody could control. With a sinking heart, he had said bye to all his friends and packed his belongings. He refused to let go of his sports kit, though. Shom reluctantly agreed to the demand.

Bank accounts were closed, and lockers emptied. Their belongings shrunk minute by minute, vanishing into stowaway boxes. Some stuff went into cardboard boxes, to be given to charities; some sent off to a posh-looking information management provider's warehouse, to be retrieved later if they chose to return home. Else, they could also get the stuff shipped to whichever location they were at.

To Koena's tired mind, it seemed like an eternal wait – for stillness to descend again, a calmness to permeate their restless, nomadic lives. Would they ever have a chance at living a mundane, routine life? Or would they become fugitives of the law, forever running and hiding?

What would happen to Kit? How had there been no clue at all until even a few months ago? Had there been an entire world unravelling under her that she had been ignorant of? Had I missed the signs? Had Shom exhibited any signs at all? Was I too smug?

Another thought struck her. *Was Shom a man with a scary past and an uncertain future?*

She looked at Shom who was patiently going through some papers.

Am I doing the right thing? Have I taken the right decision?

Here she was, treating this as her fate. But she was an individual with her destiny, right? Couldn't she just walk away from all this and never look back?

Like I had done ages ago…

Koena adjusted her bottom on the soft sofa and stared at Shom from behind a magazine she was holding at face level. He looked so calm and serene. Almost monk-like. Damn this man. *The damn charmer.*

But, in the past few weeks, she had seen the 'other' Shom, the man who might have killed people. The man *who had trained* with the best killers and *hobnobbed with* the deadliest. The man who *scared her* nowadays. The man who *might be a lethal and sharp-witted criminal.*

The doorbell rang just then, loud enough to wake the dead. The couple jumped when they heard it, each pulled from their thought vortexes. Shom had just finished packing some important documents and was going through the discarded items to figure out if they would require any of them.

Koena dashed towards the door, announcing that she would check on the visitor. Meanwhile, Shom continued discarding the unwanted items.

A loud shriek from the living room jostled Shom into action. He dropped the files in his hands and ran to the living room.

The scene unfolding there shocked him. This was not part of the plan. His plan.

■

The Mother

JUNE 21, 2000

Road near the Airport
3:00 p.m.

A POLICE SIREN blared, piercing the late evening skies, throwing Koena into a tizzy. She hurriedly reached out to her son and pulled him behind the nearest car.

'Duck, quick,' Koena whispered fiercely. If her heart could have a separate existence outside of her body, it would have disassociated itself from her long back. A silent trail of perspiration traversed down her temple as she threw nervous glances at parked cars.

She and Kit were in a strange locality.

Koena adjusted the heavy backpack and held on to her son's arm, making Kit wince in pain. The boy somehow had the nerve to keep silent, bearing the inconvenience with silent courage and maturity. When the police jeep sped towards its destination, they got up and started walking.

'Ma! why are we walking like this? The police aren't looking for us... Or are they?' Kit's question threw her off guard, making her wince. He had a point. She looked at the boy who was dragging his suitcase slowly, head hung, brows knit. They had taken a cab from their house but had gotten down just before the approach road to the airport.

Once the siren faded into the late evening, they resumed walking towards the Bhubaneswar airport.

'Kit, I'm not sure if we are on their hit-list. I just... want us to be safe,' she said, hoping to assuage his fears. She herself was not convinced about her plan. She had explained to Kit about how she would go to drop him at school, come back, and try to get his father out on bail with the help of their lawyer. Kit didn't ask anything else. He agreed to go back to school as per his mother's plan. They kept walking, on the road to the airport, keeping their heads down.

'Ma, but if we are on their list, they are going to be looking for us at the airport too, right? Maybe with our mug shots...'

Koena nodded. Fresh worry lines dotted her forehead.

Kit is right! Why did I run? I should have stayed to ensure we were not on their radar. I did check. Nobody came for us, right. We are fine.

Her mind recounted the incident from the previous day, frame by frame, with painfully elaborate detailing.

■

JUNE 20, 2000
Ashiana Apartments
4:00 p.m.

IT HAD BEEN hours since the drama had ensued. Koena had immediately regretted her decision of calling the cops. But the deed was done. She had chosen this one-way street and could only move forward. She had given life to her assumption and informed the cops. Now seeing the scene unfold, she felt panic and remorse. Lifelong agony awaited her. Whatever happened thereafter, she had to live with this memory...

■

JUNE 20, 2000
Ashiana Apartments
2:00 p.m.

WHEN SHOM RAN into the living room, two burly policewomen were holding Koena by her shoulders. She was arguing with them.

Shom rushed to her aid when three more policemen arrived and held him back. Inspector Das who had questioned him earlier walked in and handed an arrest warrant to the struggling Shom, whose incredulous expression was painful to watch. Koena was whimpering in fear and confusion, and Kit had slumped on the sofa, watching the proceedings with terrified eyes, shock having paralyzed him.

Shom looked at the arrest warrant with mounting horror. His eyes bulged, a lone nerve throbbing on his temple. They were charging him with the murder of the CM, among several other charges of abetment of criminals and concealment of crucial details regarding national security.

'These are all baseless allegations. Someone is trying to frame me. I did not kill the CM, it was...' Shom began and clamped his mouth shut.

Koena looked at him, shocked.

Is this man crazy? Why is he not saying it? Should I tell them?

She had thought that on seeing the police Shom would buckle and have the nerve to safeguard his family first, revealing details about the Naxal attack on the CM. It was not to be. Shom stayed tight-lipped.

Just then, Inspector Das turned towards Koena and said, 'Thank you Madam for all your help...'

Koena noted the look of stunned disbelief, which quickly became revulsion and hatred, on Shom's face when he locked eyes with her. Her heart sank. *Damn!*

She watched, horrified, as the police handcuffed and led Shom away. He didn't turn to look at her even once. That was the moment Koena realized something – their marital life, as she knew it, was over.

Koena slumped on the cold floor once the burly policewoman released her, and cried her heart out. Kit came to sit next to her, laying his head on her shoulders, hugging her and crying along with her. Though a teenager, he still was a kid and had completely zoned out when he saw his happy family being torn apart.

'Ma, why did they arrest Dad? What did he do, Ma?' Kit shook her arm, demanding an answer.

Koena mutely shook her head, pulling her son into an embrace. They sat slumped near the open door, furiously hoping to undo the damage done to their life.

The sun traversed its pre-determined path, setting slowly in the horizon, shedding darkness on all creatures. Oblivious to everything around them, the mother-son sat enveloped in their sorrow. The silent living room was the sole witness to their trauma.

Koena was the first to recover. It had been several hours since Shom had been arrested and taken away.

Instead of looking at options to get him out, she had sat there, allowing herself to become weak. She kicked herself for her stupidity. This was not the time to be weak. She got up and made some tea. Kit declared that he was starving and was going to fix himself an omelette. Koena mutely watched her son potter around the kitchen.

The gene was strong, she noted, marvelling at the ease with which her teenager whipped up two happy looking omelettes and offered her one. She thankfully gulped it down along with the steaming ginger tea, realizing that she was famished.

With food in her stomach, she was able to think better. She noticed how Kit had tidied up the kitchen after cooking the meal. Her heart glowed with pride, and a small tinge of frustration crossed her mind.

He is so self-sufficient. He doesn't need me.

Koena's mind kept replaying the arrest scene, her heart berating her for tearing apart their beautiful family.

I must undo this damage. I shouldn't have done this. I will… do something.

Making up her mind, Koena thought about the various options. After she regained a modicum of alertness, she pulled out a notepad and began planning her next move. Their next move.

Before that, she wanted to check something with her son.

'Kit, do you think it is a good idea to skip a year of school? I want to know what you feel. Also, you should know that… I only turned Dad in… I misunderstood him, baby. I realise it was a stupid thing to do. I'm now going to try and undo the damage. I need your cooperation while I go about bringing Dad back, okay?'

Kit looked at her for a while, saying, 'Ma, I… Frankly, I don't know what to say. I am in the middle of my academic year. I have already lost a month or so of classes. I don't know how I will be able to catch up. I do want to go back to my school. I'm looking forward to my cricket selections and my academic year. I worked very hard this year and wanted to get into The League. And next year are my board exams. I can't mess this up. Can't you and Dad sort this out somehow?'

The innocence and clarity in her son's words shook Koena. In a moment of madness, she had nearly diluted years of his hard work. She had to ensure Kit's life ran smoothly. She could not pull him out of school or pause his education.

She nodded absent-mindedly, water pooling around her eyelids and stinging the delicate skin, making her cringe. No amount of gulping held it back. She hugged her only son and managed, 'you will go back, dear…I am sorry…'

He hugged her back tighter and planted a wet sloppy kiss on her cheek, thanking her profusely. 'Should I go and pack, Ma?'

Koena nodded, unsure as to how the school would react. They had asked for a long leave of absence for Kit, and not pulled him out. *Thankfully!*

'Kittu, you should know. I thought… I… didn't realize that… Oh, never mind. Kit, we need to leave… get up, let us pack.'

It had to be done some other day. Today was not a great day for confessions, Koena decided.

Kit nodded and went to his room to pack his things. Koena called up his school principal and explained the situation as succinctly as possible. The principal seemed to understand her predicament and agreed to take back Kit. Koena saw him nodding to her requests in her mind's eye. Almost as an afterthought, the portly principal also suggested that Kit should opt for some special classes so that he would not lose out on the lessons covered in the last month. Koena agreed, thanked him profusely, and disconnected.

She made a note in her pad.

1. Spoke to Kit's school principal. Kit goes back to school.

Now, she had to figure out her next move to get Shom out. Images from the arrest flooded her brain. Attempts at maintaining composure took her nowhere. She jotted down thoughts furiously as they appeared. Soon, the small page was filled with her meticulously neat writing.

1. Meet Shom in the station, get him a lawyer.
2. Withdraw money.
3. Rearrange stuff at home. Milk/Groceries/Veggies.
4. Call Rana ASAP.

She struck out the last one after pondering about it for some time. There was no point in calling Rana from an open line and drawing attention to herself. Just because she had squealed about her husband, the police would not ignore her. She might be on their radar, too, and her phone was probably being tapped. By doing this, she had invited unwarranted attention to herself and gotten Shom implicated.

Koena took a deep breath and called out to Kit. A decision must be taken immediately.

'Yes, Ma,' Kit appeared at the doorway, looking slightly lost. Apprehension about his current and future situations swam in his young eyes, making Koena feel terrible. She beckoned him closer, and he rushed to hug her tightly. Caressing his back and adjusting his head on her lap, Koena gently prodded, 'Do you think I did something wrong, Kittu?'

Kit burrowed his head in her lap, not meeting her questioning eyes. It was a while before he spoke. 'I know that you have a reason for doing it... turning Dad in... But Ma, I am not too bothered about the whys and the hows. I just want to be with you both. Maybe things would be okay soon. But I always know you have a reason, Ma. You would not have done it otherwise. You love us that much.' The overwhelming feeling in those words shocked her. The unconditional love from her son scared her.

Am I even worthy of such unabashed adulation? I have ruined our family, shattered it to pieces... Yet, this child of mine loves me unconditionally. I am blessed. Or am I?

A sudden thought struck Koena and she sat up, making up her mind about something. Kit looked at her quizzically. She stood up and located her purse inside her huge tote bag. She grabbed her house keys and turned to her son. Taking pity on the boy, she declared, 'I need to take care of a few things, Kit. I will be back. You lock the door and stay inside.'

Kit nodded and returned to his room to finish his packing.

Koena returned home, having accomplished a few crucial things. She had called and met the lawyer who promised to get a magistrate to let Shom out on bail as early as possible. She had withdrawn some money for their immediate expenses. She now had to drop Kit at school. She had also decided to inform Rana about the situation, as she had a feeling that he would be able to help her. He had given her a number to call in case of any emergency. *This was surely one.*

Next, she booked two tickets for the next morning. She would go drop Kit at school. *Just to be safe.*

The next day, on her way back home from the airport, Koena grabbed 2 cartons of beer and a few bottles of rum. She needed to arm herself adequately to sink into the hole – a deep dark hole that was beckoning her. Her hands shook when she opened a beer can. Immeasurably solid sorrow was enveloping her. She took a swig. It has been ages since she had allowed the darkness in.

Where had she gone wrong? Did she even deserve Shom? After everything he had done for her…

April 1982

Aparna and Tia's House

Bhubaneswar

Aparna had returned to Delhi after her boyfriend dumped her. She had left the very night Shom had asked her for Tia's whereabouts. Tia had allowed Shom to re-enter her life, but she never let her guard down. She didn't want to feel vulnerable ever again.

'Tia… just listen to me. Try it once. If it doesn't work, I promise I won't force you… ever… But just try it out,' Shom could get under her skin so easily. Tia realized this when she confessed to him about all her activities since they parted ways. Looking pensive, Shom had folded his hands and apologized, the melodrama tickling Tia enough to concede to his plan. Laughing, she muttered, 'Oh, my God! You are such a drama queen! Okay, what do you want me to say?'

'Just that, "Shom, I agree to let you help me!" Will you?' Shom sounded earnest, honest. Tia nodded.

The rehab costed a bomb, but Shom wouldn't hear anything about Tia footing the bill. Finally, she joined. One thing Tia never mentioned to Shom and he had no way of knowing…her mental state and the darkness that enveloped her sometimes… A few months later, after spending some traumatic and painful days struggling with withdrawal symptoms, Tia emerged as a new person. *Almost.*

Shom came to pick her up. And took her to his house.

Tia settled into a new routine, with Shom's constant care and unadulterated affection. She kept in touch with Asha occasionally, mostly over letters.

A few months later, she flew to London, to attend a course in Journalism. A year later, when Tia completed her journalism course, Shom proposed. Tia agreed to it almost immediately.

At the Registrar's Office, holding her hands, looking deep into her eyes, surrounded by some of their close friends, Shom asked, 'Tia, we are beginning a new life. I want you to have a new name and identity. Tell me if you like it – Koena.'

'I do…'

■

JUNE 21, 2000
Ashiana Apartments
11:00 p.m.

IT HAD BEEN such a strenuous day. The travel to and from Kit's school had killed Koena's back. Her mind had turned to glass, threatening to fall apart any second.

Koena stared at her reflection in the bedroom mirror. In the past eighteen years, they had had so many arguments. Shom had always shown so much patience. Sometimes, she had apologized. They had managed to move on.

Why did I do this? I must do something to undo this damage. But what do I do?

Koena turned and walked towards the fridge to get another beer. Some alcohol should do her good. It would clear her mind.

Tomorrow, I will go meet Shom and apologize. He will understand.

■

JUNE 22, 2000

Bhubaneswar Jail
10:00 a.m.

THE QUEUE WAS long. Koena patiently waited for her turn. She signed the register and went to meet Shom with her lawyer who had drawn out Shom's bail orders.

'Shom can get out. This case is based on pure hearsay. You will get rapped, but we can manage that, don't worry.' The lawyer had seemed hopeful.

As he predicted, Shom got out on bail but refused to even look at Koena. The lawyer promised to get the charges dropped against him and went his way. Koena went to the car and sat down, waiting for Shom. When he didn't come, she turned to check. He was nowhere to be seen. *Where is this man?*

Her Nokia phone rang just then. It was the lawyer. 'Yeah, hello?'

'Madam, Mr. Mahapatra is with me, I just wanted you to know that he is okay, and that he wants to stay with some friends.'

'Fine…' Koena's throat constricted. This was real!

He hates me.

■

The Woman

SEPTEMBER 4, 2000

Ashiana Apartments

5:00 p.m.

WERE IT NOT for Lokki, Koena might have found it difficult to reassemble the fragments of her shattered marital life. Life is funny that way— sometimes, all one needs is a person to row their broken boat out of choppy waters. Sometimes one also needs a strong will and a stronger intent to allow somebody else to help.

And right then, Koena had neither. Her brain was functioning, but her mind had frozen in a time warp. Unable to step out of the fuzziness that constantly surrounded her, Koena just disintegrated within. She had descended into one of the stupors that she often found herself in. Nowadays, when her phone rang incessantly like a hungry newborn craving for his mother, eager to be fed and cajoled, Koena ignored the first few rings. She had no time for the world. The dense gloom was comforting, like her mother's womb, gently cajoling her to cut off her connection with the external world.

The phone kept barging into her fast-closing gap of consciousness. People could die, for all she cared. Her heart had withered inside her rib cage, and she could only process the all-consuming guilt that had caused an implosion in her head. Fragile pieces had stuck to her skin, draining the blood out, slowly killing her.

The phone kept ringing again and again. Insistent. Shrill.

She huffed at nobody and crawled over from where she had slumped, a rum bottle in hand. To drown her selfishness, she reassured herself, for she had an ache that refused to go away. The rum helped her racing mind find a semblance of order, though it was just a fleeting momentary lapse. After the bottle's content mixed with her blood, her mind pulled back all the incidents into her conscious mind, with a vengeance.

The damn phone had to be gagged. It had no business announcing its presence like this when she wanted to become one with the thick air that seemed to hang around her like a bloody shroud. She reached out, nevertheless.

'Yes,' She snapped into it. A bit gruff for her liking but she heard herself loud and clear. *Damn!*

'Koena, it is me.' Rana always announced his presence as if he were a monarch.

He was calling to check if she had heard from Lokki yet. He was calling from an untraceable number, he said, pacifying her concerns about security and other irrelevant things that one tends to worry about in such conversations. He also gravely announced that Shom was doing well and that all charges would be dropped soon. He had pulled some connections, he said, and they should know something soon. He added hesitantly that Shom was still angry and in shock and that she should give it some time.

Koena's foggy brain registered a single piece of information.

Ma is coming.

A mother's embrace that might shut out the external chatter seemed comforting. And yet, the proximity of a long-lost mother and the probability of unsure emotions rising to the surface scared Koena. Rana informed that Lokki might take a couple of days to reach. Koena nodded, mumbled incoherently, and disconnected; her mind still fuzzy with the alcohol.

Koena's days went by in a daze. Kit kept calling her phone but could not reach her. Worried, he sent her many text messages. Koena lay on the living room floor, passed out. At some point, her body had stopped many of its digestive functions and focused fully on keeping the essential services running. Koena had given up trying to keep herself awake. She remained unconscious and asleep. Without food, without water, she lay on the floor, weeping her heart out and draining every last drop from the bottle. When her eyes closed, she let out a heartbroken sigh.

I just want to die. I have screwed up my life. Totally.

■

SEPTEMBER 6, 2000

Ashiana Apartments
9:00 a.m.

LOKKI REACHED IN two days.

The doorbell rang shrilly, announcing someone's arrival to the nearly inebriated Koena. It took several rings and loud knocks for Koena to register the insistent presence of a very composed Lokki. She dragged herself to the door and opened it a wee bit, uncertain of the hour and the condition she was in.

Lokki stood there, smiling, a small bag in her hand. Dressed in a plain cream shirt and black trousers, Lokki could pass off as any woman on the street, except that she was a master at subterfuge and handling weapons. She was also a trained assassin, with a hefty award on her head. She had chopped off her long hair and was now wearing a neat crew cut that made her look years younger. She held out her arms, and Koena collapsed into them. Dropping the bag on the floor, Lokki hugged her daughter tightly and allowed her to weep.

However much she tried, Koena could not shake off the melancholy that had descended into her pores, permeating her soul.

Lokki took charge.

She kept house for Koena, cooked healthy meals, and waited patiently for Koena to find her feet again. She also worked on Koena's mind, giving her the strength to deal with her ever-consuming guilt and sorrow. With gentle insistence, Lokki slowly pulled Koena out of the dark abyss. She called Rana and kept him up to date. She also kept calling Kit, who was super thrilled to hear from his grandmother.

Koena recovered slowly.

After a few weeks, Lokki and Koena settled into a domestic routine: cooking, cleaning, chatting, gossiping. Koena thrived under the tender loving care of her doting Mother. Lokki also taught Koena some basic martial arts moves, ensuring that she could tackle any opponent easily. Physical fitness and mental agility were integral for a warrior, she told her daughter.

Koena had initially agreed, just to please her mother. Once the fitness level increased and the brain fuzz reduced with the cessation of the steady supply of alcohol, Koena started participating with more enthusiasm. She had slowly started helping Lokki in cooking and cleaning. Normalcy still seemed a distant possibility, but Lokki was determined. Meanwhile, Shom had moved into a room in his restaurant, the lawyer had informed Lokki a few days back. As of now, the lawyer was the only link for discussion between the couple.

'What should I make for lunch, Ma?' Koena asked, nursing a hot cup of tea in her hands. Lokki was applying oil to her hair and massaging her head. Koena had also started cooking elaborate meals under Lokki's expert tutelage.

'Some chicken curry?' Lokki raised her eyebrow and Koena nodded.

Eventually, after a few days, Lokki indicated that she should make a move, but Koena had no intention of letting go of her mother. 'I can't stay alone, Ma. I have lost Shom. I don't want to lose you, too. Please, Ma. Please stay with me.'

Lokki ran a palm lovingly over her daughter's face. 'Koena, listen to me. I am not the regular serial-killing mom, you know that, right? I can *kill serially* if I want to, even with my bare hands. I am that type of Mom. And exactly because of this, I can't stay in one place for a very long time, *shona*. Please understand. It is a matter of time… the Police hounds will come sniffing around. And I don't want you to come under their radar because of me. By the way…your lawyer called…he asked me to tell you that all charges against Shom have been dropped. He is a free man.'

She tried to make her daughter see reason. Koena had regained most of her confidence and had been sober for a while now. However, the very thought of staying by herself pushed her into a whirlpool of anxiety again.

'No, Ma. I can't live without you now. Shom doesn't want to even talk to me. How many times have I called him now? Even the lawyer tried to make him speak with me. He hates me. I wish I had never done that… I am stupid. But I love him…' Koena's body shuddered, and she let go of her pent up sorrow.

Lokki shook Koena's shoulders and said, 'Listen to me carefully. I have to tell you something. It is very important. Get a grip on yourself.

Koena… listen.' The frail hands had the strength to shake Koena's fuzzy brain into wakefulness.

Koena looked at her mother, tears running down her cheeks.

Lokki continued, 'Koena, you know that the CM was your biological father, don't you?'

Koena nodded, her brain flushing her conscious mental space with images of the man. *That bastard!*

'Yes, ma… Unfortunately, he is not alive. Else, I would have killed him with my bare hands.' Koena let her frustration out, acting out her mental image, getting angrier at the memory of the man.

'That is why… this is exactly why… shona… I did it for you…and Shom knew,' Lokki said softly, waiting for it to sink in. Koena absorbed it and allowed the emotions to surface. Shock registered when she realized the ramifications of this confession. It was such a cruel thing. She had turned in her husband for a crime that her mother had committed.

Her most overpowering emotion was guilt – mostly at Shom's suffering. She had turned in the wrong person, hoping he would at least lead the police to the actual criminals. That had been her intent. She had done it despite knowing that the erstwhile CM was an evil villain, for she had still firmly believed in the course of law.

He had even kept his silence despite knowing the truth. To save HER mother!

But now, thinking from her mother's perspective, it looked more like justice. She had been wronged, and she had exacted her revenge. Koena thought of what Lokki had done – forgetting that she was her mother. Even as a woman, she felt that turning her hatred against the man and actually acting on it was not exactly wrong.

It seemed immoral in a way – to call it a crime, even.

The man did not deserve to live.

Mother had slain a monster— *a rakshas!*

■

The Person

OCTOBER 2, 2000

Ashiana Apartments

IT HAD BEEN a week since Lokki left. Koena had somehow managed to assemble the disparate pieces of her life and had decided to restart her life.

Shom was still not talking to her. After the case was closed, the lawyer had stopped contacting Koena altogether. So, she had completely lost touch with her husband. She had taken to stalking him at his restaurant. Years ago, where she had stood as a young girl, she stood now, as a repentant woman, a hurting wife.

Shom had noticed her but ignored her presence.

Kit had settled well into his routine and worried less about his mother now that he knew she was on the path to normalcy. He fervently hoped that his mother would get herself a job and pick up the pieces of her life and stop trying to get back with his Dad.

After desperately trying for two weeks to speak with Shom, Koena returned home, exhausted. She had to get a grip on herself. She was just humiliating herself.

That man!

Sighing, Koena just let go of all her anxieties and sank into the sofa. She had managed to bring back all the stuff they had stowed away. Her cook was back. That was some relief. After her mother left, Koena found it very difficult to manage her meals all alone. When the cook noticed Koena sitting on the sofa with her eyes closed, she made some hot coffee and offered it to Koena, who grabbed it, thanking her profusely. After she finished her coffee, the cook handed her a parcel. Koena looked at the cover, turning it over in her hands. Curious, she tore it and took out the documents. Her hands shook when it hit her, and she dropped the papers.

Shom had decided to officially end their relationship.

He's asking for a divorce. On the grounds of irretrievable breakdown of the marriage. What did that even mean?

She closed her eyes tightly. Massaging her temples with her fingers, she visualized Shom agreeing to divorce her.

How much he must hate her!

Stirrings of a different kind roused her from the abyss she was descending into. She groaned and wrapped her arms around her head, writhing. *No, no!*

She recollected what Shreya had taught her to do. Jumping up from the sofa and grabbing a notepad and a pen, she started sketching, forcing herself to draw steady lines and circles. Then the avalanche hit, like a wall of cement descending on her brain. She felt the impact. The intense emotional pain. Her body was on fire.

She kept scribbling, going round and round.

Her brain had turned to mush. She could not think clearly. Her hands kept going in circles. She shut her eyes tightly to dim the throb in her head – a result of the intense stress. It took her longer than usual, but she did it. The intensity of the avalanche reduced, and it abated. Koena reached out for her bag and took a tablet for the dull headache that had begun.

Migraine is one thing I can certainly control.

■

DECEMBER 2000

Ashiana Apartments

10:00 a.m.

KOENA NURSED A cup of coffee while typing on her laptop. She had resigned from the network for the second time after working for a couple of months.

After quitting, she had taken up a few freelance jobs to keep the bank balance up.

She had gone to the office only for a few weeks when she realized that whatever had happened in her life had changed her permanently. She could never be the same career woman anymore. Her priorities had changed. She tried hard to focus on her tasks. Her colleagues were caring and supportive. Sagar had quit immediately after she left, and nobody knew where the boy had gone. Koena got used to his absence slowly.

She stared at the cover sitting on her coffee table. She had not signed the papers yet. She had no intention to, either. Not just yet. She had called Kit the previous night to tell him about her decision. She wanted to convey it to Shom, personally. He deserved to know.

After wrapping up all her emails to the various people informing them that she was going to vanish for some time and that she would reach out if she returned. She also shared a forwarding address and a number to call in case of any emergency.

Wrapping up life is so much harder than building a life.

Thankfully, she had not unpacked a lot of the items they had initially packed.

A few days earlier, Shom's lawyer had called her out of the blue to tell her that Shom had asked her not to follow or stalk him. He had also informed her that he would continue to take care of Kit and that she should not worry about him. He sounded kind and apologetic. He added that Koena should sign and return the papers at the earliest.

'Okay.' Keona managed to say.

She had also given up on this expectation. Maybe it had to end like this.

After packing her things, she looked around. Just one more thing to do.

With a heavy heart, she took out the documents and signed them. She put it back in the cover, taped it shut, and left it on the table. The lawyer had specifically instructed her to do so.

Fine!

If only Shom had talked to me once… and let me explain…

■

Epilogue

MAY 11, 2001

Panchayat School, Chirimiri Village

10:30 a.m.

THE SOFT HUM of the computers enveloped the small tin-roofed room in a cozy maternal embrace. Young, swift fingers flew on the keyboards. Silent, focused eyes consumed knowledge as fast as they could.

Clackety clack… Clackety clack….

'Are you all ready for the test?' The teacher asked.

Twenty eager heads nodded.

'Alright, let's start. You have 1 hour to complete these 2 exercises.'

Leaving them to it, the teacher moved out of the classroom and looked up at the sky. A cool breeze had drifted in, lifting every piece of drabness and making it fresh.

It is going to rain. I should let the kids leave early. Maybe I will also leave and grab a chai with Ma.

Nowadays, her plans were short-term and very simple.

The bell sounded just then. Time was up. She collected the answer sheets and ensured that all the computers were switched off after saving each assignment.

Bidding goodbye to the kids, she wished them all a good holiday and extracted promises to keep in touch with her. After wrapping up her work at the school and after saying her byes to her friends, she made her way home. She was looking forward to a month's holiday.

■

MAY 11, 2001

Chirimiri Village
12:00 p.m.

BY THE TIME she reached home, it was pouring. She knocked, her drenched clothes clinging to her body. She ran her hands over her short crew cut, feeling the hair ends prick her fingers.

At least that was not an issue. The head would dry fast. The moist emotions in my heart won't. Ever. It's my destiny to mourn…and yearn. For my husband, my son.

Her Ma opened the door and shook her head, "tch tch".

'Koena, you are crazy! You didn't take the umbrella again. Why do you always get drenched like this?'

'Ma, I am trying to…you know! I told you.' Koena said, taking the towel her mother handed her and laughing.

Lokki glared at her daughter's refusal to care for herself and helped her get dry.

Koena rushed to take a quick hot shower and changed into dry clothes while Lokki made fresh ginger tea. When Koena came out of her room, Lokki handed her a cup of steaming tea.

Koena sipped her tea and looked out of the window, staring at the heavy downpour.

Lokki joined her with a cup. Koena side-hugged her Ma.

Lokki smiled at her daughter and whispered, 'Tea is best if had with people we love. You know that, don't you?'

'Yeah… And you are here with me, aren't you?' Koena countered, grinning, as Lokki raised a hand, asking her to pause.

Surprised, Koena looked at her mother, who went to get the door, grinning ear to ear. Koena craned her neck and shook her head in disbelief on seeing the visitor.

'Shom! How come…Ma! You knew?'

Lokki nodded and walked to her room, closing the door behind her.

It had been more than a year since Koena had last seen Shom. Here he was, standing at her doorstep, drenched to the bone. 'Shona! I know we faced a tough time…I am sorry, I didn't let you explain. Happy birthday shona….ummm..can we start afresh, please? Give me a second chance?' Shom smiled, arms outstretched, his adorable, sheepish grin in place.

Koena looked at him, taking in his drenched clothes and slopping wet hair! *Of course! What a lovely birthday present!*

She took a while to register the various changes that had happened in mere seconds, and finally nodded, rushing into his arms as tears streaked down her face. A few seconds later, Koena looked startled when another pair of hands encircled her. Kit! Laughing, they hugged each other tightly, promising to never let go again.

All I need is a cup of tea and Ma, and Shom, and Kit.

Now, life is perfect.

■

www.ingramcontent.com/pod-product-compliance
Lightning Source LLC
LaVergne TN
LVHW091303150826
845673LV00006B/1523

* 9 7 8 9 3 9 3 7 5 7 2 4 1 *